THE
FALLING
IN
Love
MONTAGE

THE
FALLING
IN

Love
MONTAGE

CIARA SMYTH

ANDERSEN PRESS

First published in Great Britain in 2020 by
Andersen Press Limited
20 Vauxhall Bridge Road
London SW1V 2SA
www.andersenpress.co.uk

2 4 6 8 10 9 7 5 3 1

British Library Cataloguing in Publication Data available.

ISBN 978 1 78344 966 8

Printed and bound in Great Britain
by Clays Ltd, Elcograf S.p.A.

For Steph,
Never gonna dance again.

1

I don't believe in love at first sight or soul mates or any of that guff you see in the movies. You know, where you meet someone in an impossibly coincidental way and you lock eyes and true, everlasting love ensues. I've read a bunch of think pieces about how the romantic comedy is making a comeback, but I think it's just a nineties hangover trying to crawl its way back into relevance. Like plastic chokers, glittery eyeshadow, and TV reboots.

I do believe in wanting to get the shift. You know, maul, snog, lob the gob, feek, meet, wear . . . or as the French say, kiss. That doesn't get its due as the beautiful phenomenon it is.

Wanting to shift the life out of someone was about as much as I could hope for if I went to the post-exam party, but it wasn't enough to get me out of my fluffy socks and sweatpants. I was exhausted. I'd spent two gruelling weeks sitting in a hall with no air-conditioning and the mandatory exam period heat wave making me so sweaty my thighs squelched every time I stood up. True to form, however, Dad found a way to make putting on clothes and running away to a party an appealing prospect.

"Saoirse," his voice rang out.

That's Seer-sha, by the way. I know Saoirse Ronan's been on an international tour of duty telling everyone it's Sur-sha and God knows she's a national treasure but it's Seer-sha. It's really messing things up for all of the other Seer-shas in the country. I don't know why the poor girl won't pronounce her own name the way I want.

I could hear the excitement in Dad's voice, but I needed another minute. My brain was so numb it wasn't sending any signals to the rest of my body. Everything I'd been storing in my head until a few hours ago was gone. This could be how it started. Or maybe this happened to everyone. What was the Franco-Prussian War about? Did I care any more? Could I remember how to spell Württemberg? Unlikely.

"Saoirse, come on," Dad called again, the foot-stomping tone evident.

I pasted a smile on my face and reminded myself that he was trying to be thoughtful for a change. I'd seen him put a bottle of champagne in the fridge when he got home from work a couple of hours ago.

In October, assuming I got the bundle of As I needed, I'd be moving across the sea to go to Oxford. Mum had studied there too. Dad was obsessed. He told everyone he met. Some people feigned interest; others, like the postman, stopped ringing our doorbell. Thanks to Dad, whenever we got a package we always had to go down to the depot.

I think he thought it would be something nice for Mum

and me to have in common, but good exam results were not the thing I was concerned about sharing with her.

When I applied, Hannah and I had broken up very recently, so putting the Irish Sea between us seemed like a good idea at the time. Fast forward to June, and the increasingly real prospect of leaving Mum behind was giving me second thoughts. Actually, I was having second thoughts about the whole university malarkey altogether. But I couldn't tell Dad that. He'd flip his lid.

"We don't have champagne flutes," he said when I walked into the kitchen. He frowned at the mugs on the mug tree.

"The banana one or the stripy one?"

Our kitchen was bright and cosy with a wonky spice rack on the wall and clutter on every surface, cookbooks with the pages stuck together with sauce, and crooked wooden cabinets that Granddad built because when we moved in here, we didn't have money for things like redoing the kitchen. Dad was no cook, though, so these days the spices were clumping together and there was dust collecting on the recipe books.

"The stripy one," I said.

"Right." He beamed and ran one hand through his hair, wavy and still black even though he was nearly forty-five. In the exact moment of noticing it, I realised he must dye it. "So, history today, wasn't it? Was it what you hoped for? Bernadette Devlin and Bismarck?"

"Yeah, I really don't want to dissect it. I'm fried."

"All right, all right. Let's toast instead. We have a lot to celebrate."

I squeezed the cork out of the bottle with a satisfying *pop!*

I had a lot to celebrate, technically. The last year of school had been hell topped off with the Leaving Cert, but it was over now and I would never have to go back there again. Dad, on the other hand, would not have realised my exams were over if the schedule hadn't been posted to the fridge for the last nine months. Ironically he was always the one with the scatty memory.

"Your exams are over," he announced, holding his mug aloft, "and you're going to Oxford—"

"We don't know that," I said quickly, my stomach churning.

"I'm certain of it. You'll have the time of your life." He hesitated then, and I could tell he was ramping up to something else. Suddenly, I knew what it was and my stomach did a giddy flip.

I'd been begging him to let Mum come home for months. He always had a million reasons why it didn't make sense, but for a second my heart expanded to allow hope in. It wouldn't be perfect, I knew that, but it would be better than now. I could see her all day. Not just a visit for an hour or two, which is not the same as living with someone. I could defer Oxford and make up for the time

4

we'd lost this year. Then I'd be ready to go and everyone would be happy.

"I have some exciting news. I know it's going to come as a shock. I wanted to tell you before but it's been so complicated and you've been so angry with me."

His words were not making sense. I mean yes, I'd been angry. Although I thought I'd hidden it remarkably well, seeing as I hadn't snuck into his room at night and set it on fire.

"I hope you'll be happy for me." The glass in his hand and his voice wavered.

Nothing good starts with *I hope you'll be happy for me.* The phrase is loaded with the unsaid ending *because you won't be happy for yourself.*

"Saoirse, honey, I asked Beth to marry me."

I dropped my mug on the table, champagne splashing out the top and forming a puddle. He set his down and held his hands up in surrender.

"Look, I know you haven't really got to know her yet, but you haven't given her a chance."

My mouth opened as though I was trying to respond, but my brain did not have the capacity to produce language. I closed my mouth and did the only mature thing possible. I ran upstairs to my room.

The small space between the door and the window wasn't long enough for pacing up and down to be satisfying but I did my best; smoke was practically coming out of my nose. I wondered if he'd follow me. When I started to feel dizzy, I stopped pacing and paused to see if I could hear his footsteps in the hall. After a few moments, I heard the TV coming to life, the sounds of a sportsketball game making their way through the ceiling.

How could he do this to me? To Mum? I conjured up everything I knew about Beth. She and my dad were having an affair. She worked at an advertising company. She was always trying to talk to me, and I had to come up with ever more creative ways to avoid these "friendly" chats. I hated Dad for being so weak, for betraying Mum like that, for hopping into bed with the first replacement he could find, like you could just swap one woman out for another if she didn't suit you any more. And the way he expected me to accept it was mind-blowing. But I never in all this time thought it was serious. I would have worried if she'd started coming around for dinner or worse, she'd been staying here overnight, but they always went out. When he didn't come home, I tried not to think about why and concentrated on being grateful for the peace and quiet.

On the edge of my bed, my finger hovered over Hannah's name in my contact list. I was so tempted to press call. Even after eight months, after everything that happened, I really wanted to talk to her. I wanted to call and let myself sink into her voice, the words soothing me no matter what absurdly well-reasoned, totally emotionless thing she actually said. But I was longing for something that didn't exist any more. That was the thing about breaking up. You think you're over it and then something happens and you feel the loss all over again. I put the phone down. There wasn't anyone else to tell.

Don't go feeling all sorry for me or anything, though. I hate that. It's the worst part of everyone knowing you have no friends. I really don't mind being alone, it's the pity I can't bear.

Once, about six weeks after the breakupocalypse, I was alone in our form classroom, eating a sandwich, when my ex-best friend, Izzy, walked into the room.

Now sandwiches are literally the stuff of life. You can't beat food stuck between bread by a thick layer of butter. But there is nothing that looks more forlorn and pathetic than sitting alone, eating a sandwich. It happens in films all the time. Whenever they want to show how sad and lonely a character is, they have them eat a sandwich at their desk or eat a sandwich on a park bench or eat a sandwich in front of the TV.

So there I am with my sad sandwich in one hand, listening to a podcast about grisly murders, minding my own damn business and graffitiing male genitals into the desk with a compass in my other hand. I find that teachers assume it is boys who graffiti such things onto desks. If you are a girl inclined to deface school property, may I suggest the classic penis and balls, as you will avoid suspicion due to stereotyping.

Izzy was swinging a locker key around her finger and humming show tunes loud enough to penetrate the description of dismemberment playing through my headphones. I used to love her penchant for bursting into song, but when you fall out with someone, you can grow to hate the same things you once loved. I didn't look at her but I could tell the moment when she noticed I was there. The air became thick, and I knew she wasn't sure whether to avoid me or not. We'd had this huge fight over Hannah, and I hadn't spoken to her in two weeks.

I pretended not to notice her even though I was counting the awkward, clunking seconds piling up. While her back was turned, I peeked. She was staring into her locker. Her shoulders sagged. I knew then that she was going to try to have a heart-to-heart with me. My options were to hastily try to wrap up my sandwich and get out of there or sit through the awkward attempt to reconnect. There was a small possibility that she'd start telling me off, but it was remote. Izzy was a gentle sort, not prone to confrontation. I was the *cross me once, cold shoulder forever* type.

I'm a real catch, did I mention that?

Izzy pulled a chair around and sat opposite me. I removed my earbuds and sighed pointedly.

"Yes?" I said, as if she were a teacher bothering me about missing homework, not one of my oldest friends.

"Saoirse, let's not do this. We're friends." Her face was open, vulnerable. She really wanted me to drop the defences and tell her how I felt. I admit I thought about it. Cutting someone out takes a lot of energy. The last couple of weeks had been the loneliest I'd ever had. Everyone I could talk to was gone, not just at school but at home too. Trying to manage my feelings by myself after years of always having Hannah or Izzy to talk to felt like I was trying to shepherd a clutter of feral cats into a pen. But I couldn't trust Izzy any more. It was just me and my cats and I would have to learn to be OK with that.

"We *were* friends, Izzy."

"So what, now we have to be enemies because we disagreed on one thing?" She put her hand over mine. "Nothing has changed between you and me."

I moved my hand away and crossed my arms.

"We're not enemies, Izzy," I said lightly, like it didn't bother me enough to get annoyed. "We're not anything. You kept something really important from me."

"It wasn't my place to tell you," she said. For the four hundredth time. I knew she really believed it too, but it was less than meaningless.

"I'm not mad," I lied. "I don't care any more."

You can't go around letting people know they hurt your feelings. It gives them too much power.

"So, what, you're going to spend the rest of the year alone? Sitting in an empty classroom playing on your phone?"

There it was. The pity.

I shrugged my best IDGAF shrug and put my earbuds

back in my ears even though she didn't seem to be finished talking. Her forehead creased and her bottom lip quivered. The kind of face a child might make if you chopped the head off their favourite toy.

I pressed the back button until I got to the place in the podcast where I'd stopped paying attention. Izzy waited a second. Keep fighting or give up? It was written all over her face. I pictured her finally getting annoyed with me and telling me to grow up, telling me that friendships don't end just like that.

But she didn't. Because they do.

I got annoyed with Izzy all over again just thinking about it. When Hannah and I broke up, I lost Izzy too, and it was all her fault. But in the intervening months I'd learned a neat trick for managing all those pesky feelings. I pretended it never happened and focused on something else.

Even if I didn't have any close friends left, it didn't mean I was a complete hermit who had to stay locked up in her room like an outcast. I scrolled through the messages on my phone and found the details of the after-party I hadn't planned on going to. The combination of cheap vodka shots and girls feeling post-exam relief who may or may not want to experiment was now my best option for avoiding staring at my bedroom wall all night, avoiding awkwardness with Dad, and avoiding being stuck in an endless loop of my own thoughts.

Since my breakup with Hannah, I've had a rule, you see. I point-blank refuse to get into a relationship. An important addendum to this rule, a part B if you will, is that I don't kiss lesbians or bi girls. I'm not saying they'd all fall in love with me or they're all looking for a relationship, but it puts the possibility out there. If I cross that line, I'm asking for trouble. But I have a perfectly good thing going. Every girl in my school who wants to see what it's like to kiss a girl knows (1) I'm super gay and (2) I won't try to date them afterwards. We kiss, we part ways, no one gets hurt. Win-win.

Hannah – when we were friends and before we were more than friends – used to complain about girls like that, the ones who wanted to use me to see what it was like, and to be honest there was a time when I would have agreed with her. Like when I was fourteen and Gracie Belle Corban said she only did it because she wanted to be able to tell Oliver Quinn that she'd kissed a girl. I cried to Hannah for a week about that. But now, well, I have different priorities. As long as we both get what we want, no strings, just good old-fashioned girl-on-girl kissing, then what's the problem? I still draw the line at girls who want to do it to make their boyfriends horny. But a girl who wants to satisfy her curiosity? I am all over that. Literally.

I snorted when I finally found the message. Of course, it was good old Oliver Quinn's party. It was always his party. He had an enormous house and the only reason he didn't go to some fancy private school is because there wasn't one anywhere near us. So if I ended up puking in his mother's rosebushes that wouldn't be so terrible. Not that I'm still bitter or anything.

The group text said to come any time after ten, which meant I'd be weirdly early, but if I didn't leave now there was a possibility that Dad would intercept me and force me to have a deep and meaningful about his new fiancée.

Just kidding.

We would avoid the topic until we both grew so resentful that we'd shout terrible things at each other across the living room.

That sweet father-daughter moment could wait. I pried my bedroom door open as quietly as possible and peered downstairs. The light from the living room flickered against the back wall of the hall. Open plan was a real bitch sometimes. The window it was then. I changed into something more suitable and laced my feet into black military boots. I felt kind of badass as I climbed out the window.

Dad would realise later of course and send me an annoyed text. He hated me sneaking out. As he figured it, he never actually stopped me from going anywhere, so the least I could do was tell him where I was going to be. But why confront today what you can argue about over breakfast tomorrow?

2

You know how the Great Wall of China is visible from space? Well, Oliver's house was audible from space. It was heaving with people and pulsed like a heart. I could practically see the sound waves. I needn't have worried about being early. By the looks of things, half the kids here had been day drinking since the exam finished at four. Why hadn't I thought of that?

The noise sucked me in like a black hole. Someone had hooked up their phone to enormous professional-grade speakers that stood outside the front door like odd, modern sentinels. The music was so loud I couldn't just hear it, I could feel it pounding inside my body, making my heart thump in rhythm with the beat. I liked it like that.

I let myself get pulled into the orbit of people congregating in the garden, slipping in between bodies, suffocating in a blanket of smoke, aftershave, and sweat. Being June in a heat wave, most people had opted for outdoors. It was still warm and bright at eight. Even so, once I'd got into the house, it was so crowded, navigating my way to the kitchen was like a special round of *The Crystal Maze* or the zombie apocalypse. I had my eye out for Izzy or Hannah so I could avoid them if I had to, but neither had replied to the group message that went out, so I wasn't expecting them. Hands grabbed me and people called my name, but I couldn't see who they were. I squeezed through arms and legs and a tangle of intertwined people who had decided foreplay was a spectator sport, and they were putting on a good show.

The kitchen heaved like a living organism. People slithered over one another, through gaps in cliques, to reach the fridge or the door. It looked strangely choreographed, and I felt out of place like a scientist observing it under a microscope instead of being part of it.

Luckily I'd been to many of Oliver's parties before and I knew where the solution would be. I skittered around two people who were basically dry humping against the kitchen island to reach the freezer and sure enough, several bottles of vodka were nestled among the luxury ice cream and ice cube trays. If you're wondering what kind of kid has free booze at their party, it's the really rich kind. I pulled a blue bottle from under a bag of frozen peas and used my sleeve to wipe off the frost on the neck. I took an empty bottle of Coke from my bag and started to fill it, clumsily spilling a little over the sides.

"Is that yours?" A girl had taken a stool at the kitchen island, and I hadn't noticed her watching me. She'd been obscured by the humpers before. She had messy brown hair to her shoulders and most of it was flipped onto one side, where it curved in a quiff over her head like she had the habit of running her hands through it. She was round and soft in her face and her body. I liked it. A gold lip ring drew my attention to her lips.

"Oliver owes me." I spoke far too quietly for the noise of the kitchen and gave her my crooked half smile that always worked. She leaned in over the counter to hear me better, and I could see a hint of bubblegum-pink lace peeking out of her top, which appeared to be an elaborate colourful scarf knotted like a halter top around her neck. I leaned forward too.

"Oh, does he?" The girl seemed unconvinced, but maybe a little amused. She was cute, even if she was an officer of the Vodka Crimes Unit.

"What's it to you?"

I watched her lips move as she replied. "This is my uncle's house. I'm staying for the summer."

I registered an English accent then. I couldn't place it but I knew it wasn't super posh and it wasn't Northern. That was all my English accent knowledge depleted.

"You're related to Oliver? How sad for you." I rubbed her shoulder sympathetically, casually, as if I wasn't noticing how soft her skin was. She locked eyes with me as I did.

"You'll need one of these," I said, and I poured us each a shot into (hopefully) clean plastic cups. I pressed one into her hand, letting my fingers linger for a second. I downed mine, the heat sliding down my throat and into my belly, but she set hers down and sipped from a can of Sprite.

"Living life on the wild side?" I remarked with a smirk.

"Is this the famous peer pressure I've heard so much about?" she said. She leaned back, breaking out of my orbit. Damn. "Are you the cool girl who's going to shove me in a locker because I don't drink?" She laughed to herself and hopped off the stool. My eyes followed her to the door, taking in the beachy waves in her hair, her bare shoulders, and tight jeans hugging curves that made me bite my lip, hard.

What a dick.

A quarter of my bottle of vodka and several dull conversations about exams later, I escaped upstairs. Technically there was a baby gate with a makeshift sign warning *not* to go up, but there was a really long queue for the toilet, so I used my initiative. After I left the ornate bathroom, I stood on the landing, drawn to the faint sound of a piano coming from one of the rooms.

Oliver was in the music room, no surprise there. I'd found him here before. He threw these parties and then he'd invariably get bored and leave. He looked tired as he tinkled on the piano, and a half empty drink sat on the lid sweating onto a coaster. He had a real glass, though there wasn't a single one to be found downstairs.

"So when are Mommy and Daddy getting back this time, sad little rich boy?" I said, sitting beside him on the piano bench. He barely looked at me, but I caught a hint of a smile.

"Tomorrow." He tucked a lock of ashy blond hair behind his ear.

"I think they're going to notice downstairs is kind of a bomb site," I said.

"I have a cleaner coming in the morning."

"Must be nice to have so much money you forget how to clean up after yourself," I sighed wistfully.

"Saoirse, it's nice to be rich enough that I'm not annoyed you stole a bottle of CÎROC Ten from me." He tapped the Coke bottle in my hand, which created an odd gap in the music. How he knew I'd filled it with his expensive vodka, I don't know. Let's call it an educated guess.

"Dude . . . this is vodka? It goes down like water."

"I bet."

"Besides," I said, stretching my arms overhead, "you owe me."

"Still?" His fingers fluttered over the keys impressively. Not that I'd ever tell him it was impressive, of course.

"Forever. You stole Gracie Belle Corban from me and I never really got over it. My cold, shrivelled heart still mourns for her."

"I'm sure. I hear there are plenty of girls since to take your mind off her."

Oliver acted like I was some kind of lesbian playboy with a harem of curious ladies lining up each night. His perception of my sex life couldn't have been more wrong. I hadn't done anything more than a sneaky shift since

Hannah and I split. OK, so the list of kissing partners was long, but so what?

I think the indiscriminate snogging started the rumour that I was getting it regularly, but in truth, a bit of over-the-bra action was as far as it ever went.

Oliver paused in his complicated sonata and then played the first confident notes of "Heart and Soul." After a moment I joined in, my fingers sloppy over the keys. I was tipsy and missed half the notes and Oliver laughed. We'd both gone to the same piano teacher at school when we were eight. "Heart and Soul" was about as much as I could remember. I'd quit after a few weeks. Oliver had been practising, obviously.

After our impromptu duet, we drank for a few silent minutes.

Oliver started playing again, and I took it as my cue to leave and continue my journey to the bathroom. When I reached the door, the music stopped abruptly, so I looked back. Oliver was frowning, fingers frozen, hovering above the keys.

"Her name was Gracie Belle Circarelli," he said.

"What? No, it wasn't." I shook my head emphatically, but after all the vodka it made me kind of dizzy.

"Yeah, it was. Her dad was this big Italian dude. They had an ice cream place on the promenade. Circarelli's."

"Huh . . . well, that doesn't even sound a bit like Corban, does it? First love can be so confusing."

*

Somehow the party lured me in again. The kitchen was greenhouse hot and smelled like sweat and hormones, so I rummaged in the back of the junk drawer and found the key to the French doors. They stayed locked at Oliver's parties since the time Loren Blake climbed a tree, jumped into the neighbours' garden, and got caught throwing up in their koi pond. Oliver's problem was that although he knew that I knew where the good vodka was, where he stashed the patio keys, and where the bodies were buried, he never remembered to do anything about it.

I slipped out through the smallest crack I could make in the door and locked it behind me. The garden would be no relief if everyone could get out there, after all.

The *thump thump thump* of the music followed me with the occasional squeal or scream, but it was like submerging yourself underwater – the detail didn't get through. I breathed in a lungful of night air and found myself following a stone trail that twisted and turned through flower beds of azaleas, past a Victorian gazebo that looked like something out of *The Sound of Music*, and down to the lilac bush at the end of the garden.

At one of the first parties Oliver ever threw, Hannah and I wandered away from everyone else. She took my hand and pulled me along to a carved stone love seat set into the overgrown lilac bush. If you shook the branches, petals landed in your hair. I was fuzzy from Bacardi Breezers that night and the garden seemed like the quietest, warmest place in the world. Hannah and I sat side by side, legs touching. I thought I could hear her heart beating in time with mine. She intertwined our fingers and hummed along, out of tune, to music playing in the house. I didn't even stop to think before I kissed her, as though thinking would break the moment.

That's how I kissed the only girl I ever loved to a corny eighties pop hit. When the sax solo kicked in, we broke apart laughing. For years afterwards all we had to do was hum a few bars and we would giggle. It became a refrain for our relationship. A code between us. Whenever I felt sad or stressed, she'd hum a few bars and I couldn't help but laugh and feel like everything would be OK. Because I had her.

Let me give you a word of advice. Never, ever have "your song" be something cheesy. Even if it's funny at the time. Even if nothing else makes any sense. I beg you, pick something epic, something soft and timeless and sweet. Because one day when you've had your heart broken, you will cry every time you hear that song. And nothing will make you feel more utterly ridiculous than being the girl who cries at "Careless Whisper".

I was about to sit down on the bench when I noticed, on the other side, a person lying on the ground, their torso underneath the bush, their legs and bum sticking out.

If I hadn't stared at that bum earlier, I would have assumed a drunk person had crawled under there and passed out. I stood for a second, wondering how to play this, then I heard her making strange kissing sounds and I burst out laughing before I could stop myself.

In a flash, the girl shimmied out from the bush and popped up onto her feet with surprising agility.

"So this is embarrassing," I said.

She planted one hand on her hip and looked at me, confused. "Why are you embarrassed?"

I stared.

"I mean for you?"

She frowned like she was trying hard to think of what she had to be embarrassed about.

"Don't know what you're talking about," she said, blowing a stray strand of hair out of her eyes, but I saw her try not to smile.

I reached out and picked a leaf that had nestled in the folds of fabric around her neck.

"You're right, totally normal to find a girl face-first in a bush at a party."

I saw her trying to work out if that was pun intended or not. Then she laughed and pulled on my hand, dragging me to the ground. Even in the confusion, as my face hurtled towards the grass, I hoped my palm wasn't sweaty.

She let go of my hand and I followed her lead, shimmying under the bush army-style. She pushed aside the branches near the ground, and we squeezed in as far as we could get. She looked at me and then peered into the tangle of branches and leaves. I followed her gaze but my eyes hadn't adjusted to the lack of light. Awkwardly, I manoeuvred my arm around to take my phone out of my pocket, brushing up against her as I did. When I shuffled back into place, I'd closed any gap between us and I could feel the length of her body up against mine.

I turned the lit screen into the darkness. A pair of green eyes flashed first and then I made out a kitten, curled up so far into the hedge it was almost on the other side, in the neighbours' garden.

I looked at the girl. She looked back at me again. There were only centimetres between my lips and hers.

"You lost your cat?" I said, trying to sound like I hadn't been thinking about the space between our lips. With my compromised sobriety, I didn't question that this girl would have brought a cat with her to Ireland for the summer.

This would come back to bite me in the ass, of course. Almost literally.

She was about to respond when, in the light from my phone, I noticed the strangest thing and I moved closer. Only slightly, but we were so close my nose bumped up against hers. She didn't move away. I think she held her breath.

She had a blue freckle, like a tiny spot of ink under her eye.

"You have a blue freckle."

"No one has ever noticed that," she said, the way you know everyone she's ever met had mentioned it.

I pursed my lips to hide a smile and I looked back at the kitten, suddenly aware that the vodka was making me dizzy. Probably the vodka.

"What's she called?" I asked.

"Why do you think it's a girl?" the girl asked.

"Dogs are boys, cats are girls," I said witheringly. "Everyone knows that."

She snorted.

"That's the silliest thing I've ever heard." She nudged me with her shoulder. Was that an excuse to touch me or was I reading into it too much?

"Well, you must not get out much," I said, nudging her back.

The kitten mewled.

"Aw, see, she's saying *rescue me, drunk girl, I'm so sad and lonely.*"

"How am I supposed to get her?" I'd done some ridiculous things when I was drunk, but I didn't believe I could fit my whole body that far under the hedge.

The girl looked at me with a pouty, sad face. I rolled my eyes as though that definitely wouldn't work on me. It was an eye roll of lies.

"Fine." I sighed. "I suppose I can try and get in next door somehow." I didn't think the neighbours would appreciate a drunk teenager on their doorstep in the middle of the night slurring about a kitten, though.

We crawled backwards out of the hedge. It took me a lot longer than it took her and my hair got tangled up on a branch. When I emerged, she was already upright, her hand extended to help me up.

I dusted myself off and walked along the wall, trailing my hand as though I thought I'd find a secret door into the garden, but I knew the only way I was getting in was by going over. I was really going to do this. Why was I doing this? I glanced over my shoulder. The girl was a few feet behind me, and I caught a flash of guilt before she grinned at me that made me wonder what she'd been looking at.

OK, so that was why.

Closing my eyes, I summoned any heretofore untapped athletic prowess. If I was sober this would be easier, I thought.

If I was sober I wouldn't be doing it.

When I opened my eyes, I didn't feel any different, but my head was swimming. I approached the tree next to the garden wall. The Loren Blake tree. The girl was still looking at me, I could feel it in the way my skin prickled. It was a good feeling. I resisted the urge to swing my hips or toss my hair. Then I spun on my heel.

"Turn around," I said, gesturing in a twirling motion with my finger. "I'm not climbing up there with you watching."

"Stage fright?" She smirked, but she covered her eyes and stuck her tongue out at me.

"Something like that," I muttered. More like if I had to pant and puff my way up this tree, I wasn't having a pretty girl watch me do it. It'd be like climbing up the rope in PE with Kristen Stewart at the bottom looking disappointed in you. I mean she'd look like that anyway, that's just her face, but you know what I mean.

I hooked my foot around a gnarled knot in the trunk and hoisted myself up. I looked down. I was a whole foot off the ground. I looked up. Only seven more to go. I quickly realised, thankfully, how a totally stocious girl with no athletic ability like Loren, had managed it. There were knobbly bits and ridges in all the right places. That didn't mean it was easy, mind you. My thighs burned and my hands stung from clinging so tight to branches. At one point I slipped and grazed my knee, letting out a string of expletives that impressed even me.

"You can do it!" the girl shouted out.

"Are you looking?" I shouted back.

"No, I promise." A pause. "But also we should probably clean that cut when you get down."

Great.

With one final push I didn't know I had in me, I reached level with the top of the wall and stepped gingerly from the base of the branch onto the relative safety of solid stone.

"I made it," I called out. I looked down at my leg.

My jeans were ripped and there was a trickling sensation trailing from my knee into my sock.

Then I realised the real problem was still before me. I had scaled a tree, risked life and limb, and there was nothing on the other side but an eight-foot drop.

"Shit."

She was cute. But she wasn't break-your-leg cute.

"What's wrong?"

I jumped slightly. The girl was right below me. She looked worried and ran her fingers through her hair, flipping it from one side to the other.

Was she?

"Don't scare me when I'm on a bloody tightrope," I grumbled. The world seemed to sway when I looked down. Or was that me swaying?

"Exaggerate much? The wall is two feet thick."

"Uh-huh, well, it's eight feet high and there's nothing on the other side except a pretty poky-looking rosebush, my friend, so I think your cat is going to have to chill over there for tonight."

Believe me when I say I wanted to play kitten hero for her and have her wrap her arms around me in gratitude, but a woozy feeling in my stomach said it was a terrible idea. The vodka hubris was wearing off in the fresh air. I couldn't do it.

"You can't leave her!"

"I really can."

Within a few seconds, the girl had scooted up the tree trunk like a monkey and was standing beside me.

"How did you do that?"

She grinned and shrugged.

"Why am I even up here?" I said indignantly. "Why didn't you do it yourself?"

"I don't know. I mean, you offered. I didn't think it would be that difficult and then when you were trying so hard I felt too bad to say anything."

I pressed my lips together and prayed for patience.

"I can see what you mean, though," she said thoughtfully. "That's quite the drop." She rubbed her chin.

"Right, so we should find another way. We could fashion some kind of cat-trapping device."

At that moment the kitten gave a loud meow of protest.

The girl shook her head and said matter-of-factly, "We're going to have to jump."

"You're kidding," I said.

She shook her head again.

"Hello? We'll break something." I put my hand on her arm to try to shake her out of this absurd determination to jump. She ignored me and stood, hands on hips like a superhero, surveying the distance.

Well, I wasn't going to be dragged down with her.

"How about this," I said. "You jump. And I'll go back down this way and just sort of hang out and wait for you there." I pointed at the relative safety of Oliver's garden.

Why on earth was I even doing this totally unnecessary thing for a girl I had just met? (I mean, you know why, obviously. She was hot, and I was weak and pathetic and the sensible part of my brain turned off and all I could think about was (1) what it might be like to kiss someone with a lip ring, (2) if she had any other piercings, and (3) whether she'd let me find out.)

"I really think it's only fair if we both jump," she said seriously, rubbing her chin again. She shook her left foot and then her right as though she was limbering up. I put my hand on her arm to get her attention, but she still didn't look at me. I wasn't jumping. Nope. No way.

If I could get her to look me in the eye I knew I could convince her this was a bad idea.

She locked eyes with me then, with a glint in her eye that made me wobble precariously.

"Fine," I said, admitting defeat.

She grabbed my hand and I felt a tingle up my arm.

"One," she said, and squeezed my hand tight. "Two."

"Maybe it isn't a good idea to do this holding h—"

"Three!"

The girl jumped. I hesitated. Of course, she was still holding my hand, so I was dragged right into the air.

I landed face-up in a rosebush, groaning. Somehow, magically, the girl was standing upright, a grey kitten in her arms, and peering down at me. She looked almost confused about how I'd ended up like this. When I look back on it, I'm sure I lost consciousness for a few seconds.

"I'm gonna be picking thorns out of my bum for a month," I groaned. Even as I lay there, I knew the alcohol was numbing most of the pain and I'd really feel it tomorrow.

The grey kitten meowed loudly and wriggled in the girl's arms.

"Well, at least you got your cat," I said, finally struggling to get up.

"About that . . ." she said, not quite meeting my eye. "It's not exactly my cat."

"What?!"

"So I saw her, in the garden, from the window," she said, and pointed at one of the windows of Oliver's house. "I thought she was lost. I came down to get her and she skittered under the bush."

I didn't know what to say to that but she continued anyway.

"I was afraid she'd be out here alone all night and scared. She looked so tiny." The girl lifted the kitten's paw and moved it so it looked like the kitten was waving at me.

"Don't be cross, drunk girl," the "kitten" said in a surprisingly gruff voice.

I sighed and dusted myself off a little. I was now bleeding, and covered in soil that smelled a little like the neighbours might use manure as a fertiliser. I figured my chances of kissing her in this state were rapidly dwindling.

"Well, she has a collar, so at least we can get her home, I suppose."

"Um . . . yeah. About that."

"I'm really starting to not like when you say that."

"So according to this collar, she lives . . . here." The girl spread her hands, indicating the very property we were currently trespassing in, and she bit her lip, waiting for my reaction.

"So basically by coming in here we have broken into the neighbours' garden and tried to steal their cat?"

"Yes." She nodded in agreement. "Basically."

I made her say goodbye to the kitten and she kissed it on top of its fluffy head. I couldn't bring myself to the same level of affection, but I patted the kitten on the head, and we stood side by side, watching it scamper off into the dark.

"Sorry you got hurt," she said, turning her body towards me, her face level with mine, eyes wide and cheeks flushed.

"It's not your fault."

"It is." She pushed a strand of hair back from my face. My breath caught.

"Yeah, I know."

She looked at me, and the moment seemed to close in around us, dark and enveloping like a blanket.

Then a bright spotlight shone between us. Patio lights from the house. Instinctively I pulled the girl into the shadows as the owner of the house stepped out into his back garden.

"Who's out there?" a sharp voice called out. "Marian, those bloody kids are at it again. Leave my fish alone."

We stealthed our way around the side of the house, trying not to laugh too loud.

When we got back to the party, we lingered around the bottom of the staircase.

"Do you think I should be a vet?" the girl asked, out of the blue. "I mean I love animals but there seems to be a lot of vet-finger-to-pet-butt action involved. But maybe I'd get used to that? Do you think I'd be good at it?"

"I don't know you," I said.

"Oh. Yeah."

I wanted to ask if she wanted to get a drink but we had already established that she didn't, and even though the outdoor excursion had kind of sobered me up, I didn't feel like getting drunk any more. I bit my lip, trying to figure out some way to ask if she wanted to go somewhere alone that wasn't too keen or embarrassing.

"Do you want to come up to my room?" the girl asked brightly, pointing upstairs. "We should really get you out of that filthy top."

For a second she had a mischievous twinkle in her eye, the same one I saw on top of the wall. I felt the wobble again even though I was on solid ground this time.

"I'll lend you a clean one," she added, as innocent as apple pie.

3

With her bedroom door closed, the noise of the party was faint and I couldn't help but marvel at the difference. I could hear my dad cough in his bedroom if I was in the kitchen, but in here, even the end of the world would be muffled by the thick walls and doors. There was a sports bag on the floor with clothes spilling out of it, and the bed was unmade with rumpled sheets. The curtains were drawn and the girl turned on a bedside lamp. Mood lighting. I was onto a winner.

She rummaged around in the bag on the floor, throwing a pair of shoes in the corner and setting a bag of penny bubble gums on the bed. She found a plain T-shirt and tossed it at me.

I hesitated, not confident about unleashing my nakedness at this early stage, but the girl turned around to give me some modesty and I changed as quickly as possible.

"Are you decent?" she asked.

"Just about."

"What about your cut?" She grabbed the gum before settling cross-legged on the bed.

"It's fine." It stung, but I didn't want to leave the room to clean up.

"Pink or blue?" She peered into the bag.

"What flavour are they?"

"Pink flavour or blue flavour."

"Of course. Pink, then."

I perched on the end of the bed beside her and unwrapped my gum. It came with a temporary tattoo of the Road Runner.

"Just what I always wanted. The Road Runner on my butt. The ultimate symbol of good taste."

The girl laughed. "It's your lucky day then."

I peeled the plastic off the transfer and stuck it to my shoulder. Getting my butt out at this early stage would have felt kind of forward. She dampened a cotton pad with water from a glass at her bedside and held it over the paper.

I know it doesn't sound like a scene from a romance novel, the kind with intense sweaty people on the cover, but when her fingers pressed against my skin, I felt wobbly again. It was like a current in my body had switched on. She leaned in close enough that I could count the freckles on her nose. Her eyes bored into mine, creamy brown ones framed by spidery black lashes.

She set the glass on the floor. There was barely space for light between us. Normally I am not shy about going in for a kiss, but for some reason, I was nervous. It felt different. Maybe I was imagining the tension, though it felt like you could almost see it in the air, like visible static between our bodies. I was almost sure this girl was a girl who was into other girls.

A little voice in my head reminded me that was against my rule. There was a whole addendum for it.

I thought about leaving.

"Your tattoo is really hot," she said.

"The Road Runner has that effect on girls." My words were nonchalant, but I was sure she'd be able to see my heart beating faster. She didn't reply. She bit her lip, her lip ring disappearing into her mouth. Vaguely in the background, I was aware of the thumping noise downstairs, but the room was a bubble getting smaller and smaller until it was just the two of us. She didn't move away. She ran her finger over my new tattoo and anything I might have said got caught in my throat.

"Are you going to kiss me?" she asked softly.

"I don't even know your name," I teased.

"Ruby."

I couldn't help but smile before I leaned in. I wondered if she could feel it in the kiss. Her lips were soft and parted already; her tongue tasted like bubble gum and Sprite. I could feel her lip ring, but it didn't get in the way like I thought it might. My body twisted towards hers; her hands found my waist on one side and my neck on the other. It wasn't like kissing those other girls. The ones who were tentative and giggling or the ones who went full force on my mouth but left their hands limp at their sides because my body didn't interest them. I forgot what it was like to be kissed by someone who might want more than a kiss. I knew then that Ruby was definitely not experimenting. I should have been scared. I should have left the room. I should never have gone upstairs with a girl who made me wobble.

I told myself I could have this, just for now, and it wouldn't hurt to let it go.

She pulled away, not so far that I couldn't still feel her breath on my lips. The question in her eyes was, *What more do you want?* I answered by pushing her back on the bed and kissing her again, not just with my mouth but my whole body, hands exploring the dips and curves, our bodies settling into a rhythm, a delicious friction until we were breathless.

We didn't "do it", if that's what you're thinking. Not that I didn't *want* to. I was a ball of energy ready to explode at the slightest touch (that's a euphemistic simile for the prudish at heart in case you were wondering). I don't know if she wanted more but neither of us tried to remove any clothing or put hands or mouths anywhere ... strategic (I'm trying not to be vulgar here, I hope you appreciate it). As much as I would have liked to do those things, I have a confession: I haven't done those things before. Everyone assumed Hannah and I had sex because we were together so long, but she wanted to wait and so we waited. We waited until she realised she didn't want to do anything with me at all.

Waking up the next morning with a groggy head, dry mouth, and bruised lips, but fully clothed, I was grateful we hadn't gone too far. The memory of her body on mine felt like a tangible imprint on my skin. But I felt guilty too. My rules were just for me, of course, but they were important and I had the feeling I might have done the wrong thing.

Nothing a fry-up and a shower wouldn't fix.

Ruby lay on her side, facing me, her hair sticking out in every direction and her lips as pink and tender-looking as mine felt. I didn't know whether to wake her before I left. What would I say? *I'm off now, thanks for the groping and inadvertent cat theft?* If I left without saying anything then I'd be a cliché who sneaks out of the room because they're too studly to cope.

The first option was uncomfortable, but the second one was downright pathetic, so I nudged her awkwardly until her eyes flickered open. I ignored how my heart sped up when she blinked a few times and fixed her brown eyes on me.

"I have to go now," I said, pointing at the door for no reason at all. She rubbed her eyes and yawned before answering.

"Last night was fun." A flirtatious note in her voice

made me want to get back into her bed and do it all over again.

Full awareness of my morning breath kept me strong.

"It was. Er . . . my name is Saoirse, by the way."

"I know."

"How?" I couldn't remember telling her my name and I really hoped that wasn't an effect of the vodka because social binge drinking was one thing but blackouts were another matter.

"I asked who the girl nicking the vodka from the freezer was."

She had asked about me. I tried to arrange my face to look like pretty girls asked about me all the time.

"By the way, it's my birthday next week. We're just having dinner here, but you should come."

Most people would be embarrassed to invite someone they'd only just met to their birthday party. It screamed desperate. And yet Ruby didn't look desperate or embarrassed. She looked like she was honouring me with an invite and yes or no would both be perfectly acceptable answers.

It took so long for me to say anything, she started to talk again.

"It's Friday at eight. I can't promise a wild night, but I can promise food. I think I heard my aunt talking about catering," she said, rolling her eyes.

It wasn't that I didn't want to see her ever again. But if I went to this dinner, would she think we were a *thing*?

Would going to the dinner mean that we *were* a thing? A thing was a precursor to a relationship. I'd already broken part of my rule by kissing her in the first place. I couldn't go on a big rule-breaking frenzy and start a summer fling like some kind of maverick, consequences be damned.

"Um, I'm not sure. I'll have to check that my dad doesn't have other plans for us. Is that OK?"

She shrugged. "Sure."

She didn't even seem to realise I was making an excuse. Or maybe she did and she just didn't care? I was confused. Did she like me or not? Did she want me to come or not? Why did I even care?

I tripped over her sports bag on my way to the door. Somewhere in all the confusion, I had lost my balance.

I was almost out the door when her phone rang and she sprang up.

"Mum? Is everything OK?" She sounded panicked. I paused, one hand on the filigreed brass doorknob.

"OK, no, I'm fine. It's just it's early there and I thought you were calling because something was wrong."

I couldn't conceivably hang around any longer without blatantly eavesdropping, so I turned the handle and stepped out of the room.

I stood on the landing of the Quinn house, getting my bearings. Why did she sound so worried on the phone? Why was her mum in a different time zone? And what about dinner? Should I have told her I wasn't going to go?

My brain was swimming with questions. It was my own fault. I should have stuck to kissing straight girls. When I kissed them there were no questions because I was careful. Be up front about what you're offering. Don't get involved with anyone who might expect something more than what you are willing to give. That was important. Sure, I'd never said I was going to date Ruby or anything, but maybe I'd given her the wrong idea.

And yet in spite of my guilt, I couldn't quite bring myself to feel the regret I was telling myself I should feel.

The house was quiet and my boots left grooves deep in the carpet on the stairs. I stepped over a body on the stairs and braced myself for sticky floors, empty bottles, beer cans strewn about, and the smell of a hundred sweaty, hormonal teenagers lingering in the air. But the sun that streamed through the windows shone on a pristine home you could use in an advert for cleaning sprays and furniture polish. Why did the magical cleaning pixies never come to my bedroom and sort out the pile of clothes under the bed?

I found said cleaning pixies in the kitchen, a team of brightly dressed women with rubber gloves, packing up supplies while Oliver handed over a wad of cash.

"Where did you come from?" Oliver smirked when he saw me.

"Oh, you know, around."

I took a crystal tumbler from a cupboard that had definitely been empty last night and poured myself a glass of water from the tap. Oliver opened the fridge and handed me a chilled plastic bottle, and put his hand out for my glass.

"Thanks, Oliver." I grinned earnestly and put the bottle in my bag while sipping from the glass.

"See, I think you were with Ruby," he said, tapping his fingers against the counter. "Which means you officially have to stop being pissed at me for stealing your girlfriend."

"Oliver, first off, gross, you don't own your cousin, and I especially hope that you don't have the same feelings for her that I had for sweet, beautiful Gracie Belle Corban."

"Circarelli."

"Whatever. Besides, I'm over it. I just don't like you."

"You don't like anyone."

"Well, sure, I'm not suggesting you're special or anything." I put the glass down with a deliberate bang that made Oliver wince.

"Why is she here anyway?" I tried to sound casual. I mean I was casual. What difference would the answer make to me? I was only making conversation.

Oliver gave me a withering look. "You two really didn't talk at all, did you? Ask her yourself."

I shrugged like I didn't care enough to ask. Which obviously I didn't. Because I didn't ask.

Shut up.

"You want breakfast?" Oliver took a pan from a copper rack overhead and set it on the stove.

"Oh, I'm having fried caviar and oysters for lunch, so I'll pass."

"Is that what you think rich people eat for breakfast?" His mouth twitched.

"Loren Blake is asleep on your stairs, by the way. You might want to check on that."

"I know. She drank her body weight in tequila last night, so I felt bad waking her." He sighed. "I suppose I could move her to the couch."

"You're a regular hostess with the mostess," I said on my way out the door.

Standing on the doorstep, I took my phone out to text Dad. There were two messages from last night.

Dad
Saoirse where are you?

Dad
Jesus Saoirse you could tell me
you're going out.

Saoirse
221 Holyden Park. Need lift. Bring
food.

To be fair to him, Dad didn't talk on the drive home. He handed me a bacon sandwich wrapped in tinfoil and let me eat in peace.

As soon as we parked in the driveway, he pulled on the handbrake and breathed in deeply through his nose, closing his eyes. A sure sign that he had *serious* things to discuss. I rolled my eyes and stared out the window, waiting for whatever it was he *needed* to tell me before my hangover had a chance to wear off.

"You're old enough to make your own decisions. I don't lock you in your room or stop you from going out. You don't need to sneak around. If I can respect you, then you can do the same for me."

"Did you spend all night coming up with that speech?"

"Jesus, Saoirse, you can be so damn difficult. You're not a child, you don't get to act like this any more." He took several more deep breaths, to let me know how patient and put-upon he was for having to deal with me. "I'm guessing you need to sleep it off, so go do that, but this evening we're having dinner and we're going to talk about it."

"About what?" I said brightly.

He ran his hands through his hair and when he spoke his voice didn't sound as firm.

"You know what I mean. The wedding. There are . . . other implications, OK? Things I need to talk to you about."

"So tell me now."

"Not like this. You're hungover. You smell like a brewery, and you need to get some sleep. "Oh, and . . ." He paused there and the silence was like the moment in a horror film before the guy in the mask jumps out and stabs you in the gut. "On Friday Beth is coming around for dinner. You *will* be there."

"Thanks for the invite, but I'm not interested."

"Get interested," he said. "You will be there. You're behaving like a stroppy thirteen-year-old. Your mother would be ashamed."

The words nearly winded me. I clenched my jaw so hard I thought my teeth would break.

"You know, Dad, I wouldn't worry about it. In a few years, I'll have forgotten your name and you and Beth can shove me in a home with Mum and get on with your lives."

He didn't say he would never do that. I wouldn't believe him if he did. He didn't say anything at all.

I got out of the car and marched inside, slamming the front door behind me. Up in my room, I dove under the covers. Though I was exhausted, it took me ages of tossing and turning to fall asleep. I didn't hear him come inside.

See, this is the thing I haven't really said yet. My mum didn't leave my dad. She didn't abandon me. She didn't shack up with a motorcycle gang member or a pen salesman. She has early-onset dementia. Last September Dad decided he couldn't look after her any more and she needed to go into full-time care. She is fifty-five and she sometimes can't remember how to wash herself. She forgot my name a long time ago. Do you think your mother can love you if she doesn't know who you are?

The other thing is that these types of dementia are often hereditary. There's no way to know for sure, but there's a good chance it will happen to me too. Sometimes I feel like I'm living with a timer over my head. So now you know why I don't care about going to some fancy university like Oxford. Why there's no point in getting into relationships with girls who might actually like me back.

I'm waiting for the day my brain catches fire. A spark that will slowly burn everything important to ash.

4

When I woke again it was still bright, but the light had that hazy late-afternoon quality, and when I checked my phone it was after five. For a moment all I felt was sleepy and thirsty, until I downed a litre of water that Dad must have left by my bed. Then I remembered a lot of things at once. The pain in my knee came first. Then my butt. Then Ruby and the memory of us on her bed. It felt like someone was tickling my stomach from the inside; flashes of sensation came back to me as if they were happening right then and there. Her brown eyes and her blue freckle, my hands on her waist. The taste of her lips. The sensation of her fingers trailing down my bare skin.

Should I be allowed to think of her that way when I had a nagging feeling I hadn't treated her right?

I shook my head. That was a mistake. It felt like a bunch of ball bearings were rattling around in there. I was overthinking it. Last night was fun, and I was being really full of myself if I thought for some reason that Ruby wanted to be my girlfriend because we kissed and she invited me to a dinner. We didn't even know each other.

When I got out of a long shower, where I definitely didn't think about what it would be like if Ruby was in there with me, thank you very much, how dare you imply such a thing. I could hear Dad clattering around the kitchen making dinner. I stood on the landing and sniffed the air like a curious dog. I did not like what I caught a whiff of. Nothing. It smelled like nothing. My father is not a terrible cook but he isn't a good one either. Everything he makes tastes like unseasoned Styrofoam.

My outfit from last night lay in a wrinkly heap on the floor and I threw it into the laundry, picking an almost identical ensemble for dinner. If all you own is black jeans and black tops then you never have to worry about what to wear. I didn't bother trying to tackle my hair. It's long and thick and takes years under a hair dryer to dry. Besides, although I pretend like I don't care about such things, in fact, my hair looks its most fabulous when I let it air dry. It's deep brown and goes halfway down my back. My mother used to trim the fringe when it got out of hand. She was really good at stuff like that. One Sunday a month she'd collar me. *Right, you, time to do your fringe, it's so long I don't know how you see out of it.* I'd protest but I'd always end up in the same place, on a chair in the kitchen with a towel around my neck. She'd snip the split ends and little clumps of my hair would fall into my lap.

I let my fringe grow out a long time ago. It's a small thing to lose, but I've been losing something small every day for years and years and they all added up to something really big.

*

Dad had his happy face on when I limped downstairs. I tried to muster up a smile, a gift courtesy of the vague guilt I felt for throwing Mum in his face, even though he did it to me first. I'm too good for this world.

"Thanks for dinner," I said, sticking my fork into a piece of unseasoned, grilled white fish. We ate in silence. I could tell he wasn't mad about earlier. He probably felt guilty about what he said too but neither of us are the type to actually apologise. We sweep it under the rug.

The rug had got awful lumpy.

There was a time when we were close, when things were easy. Dad is ten years younger than Mum and he was always the "fun parent." They used to argue about it. I overheard Mum complaining more than once that she always had to be the "bad guy." She'd roll her eyes at us when we'd hog the sofa and watch horror movies or when we'd play along, with life or death seriousness, to bad game shows. We had in-jokes and shared playlists. Now I think Mum might have felt left out of our silly club. She was always wound so tight and we made her stay in that role instead of inviting her to play. But even though I'm certain Dad believes I'm the one who pulled away from him, he's the one who put these huge boulders between us. I couldn't climb over them if I tried. And I didn't have the will to try.

When our plates were mostly empty, he shuffled in his seat and coughed.

"So." He cleared his throat. "So."

"So?"

"So I need to talk to you about things."

I pushed back my seat and took my plate to the kitchen. Dad followed but he hung back in the door frame.

"Look, I really don't want to hear about it." I leaned against the dishwasher, keeping a safe space between us so I wouldn't strangle him. I'd had such a good time last night – I didn't want Dad spoiling the delicious hangover of having kissed a beautiful girl with a conversation about how he'd found a great new wife to replace his old broken one. "I'm going to uni soon and I'll be living there. I won't be here anyway. Do whatever you want."

I was still unsure about going to Oxford, but in the pro-con list in my head, Dad marrying Beth was tipping the scales in favour of getting the hell off this island. Maybe when I'd gone he'd have a new daughter too. One without the faulty genes. Sometimes I thought about calling Izzy and asking her about Oxford. She has this incredible way of making everything seem simple. If I talked to her I knew she'd say the perfect thing and I would realise what I should do. She should be a therapist like my mum. I thought about it, but I never called.

"You'll be home on holidays," he pouted. "You need to get to know Beth. You can't pretend she doesn't exist."

"Oh, ye of little faith."

Dad ignored that.

"We want to have the wedding before you go away. We've set a date. The thirty-first of August. Lucky Oxford starts that bit later than most universities, so there's still plenty of time for us to get you sorted before you leave."

The silence was so complete I could hear the neighbours' cat meowing outside. It made me think of Ruby. I'd rather be climbing over another eight-foot wall than having this conversation.

"I know this is a lot of change," Dad said when he realised I wasn't going to respond. "You'll like Beth when you get to know her."

He actually said that with a straight face.

"Is she moving in here before the wedding?"

Before I move out was what I really meant. I didn't think I could bear seeing her replace all of Mum's things with hers. Watch her fill up Mum's side of the wardrobe. Sleep on her side of the bed.

Dad became very interested in chipping a bit of paint off the doorframe.

"That's the other thing I wanted to talk to you about." The strain was starting to show on his face, like a sweaty cop on the bomb squad who's unsure which wire leads to certain death. "We're going to have to move."

For a moment, I thought he meant him and Beth, and I had a glorious image of me swanning around this house by myself.

"We've looked at a few places but we don't want to decide on one without you."

"Are you serious?" I heard myself shout. "This is not fair." The words came out even though I knew they were childish. Even though nothing about this had ever been fair. I stormed past him into the living room. He turned to face me but stayed on the other side of the room.

"Saoirse—"

"This is my home and you're going to sell it so you can shack up with your new wife somewhere there are no memories of Mum. Is that what she wants or is that so you don't have to look at Mum's stuff and feel bad?"

Look, I realise this is the exact opposite of what I was thinking a second ago, but I'm a complicated person, OK? I have an endless capacity to be annoyed by anything Dad does. I didn't want Beth to move in here, and I didn't want Dad to move out with her either.

Dad hung back in the arch of the kitchen. When he spoke, his voice was tired and I almost felt sorry for him. But not quite.

"I don't know how you can think things like that. It's not like that. We have to move."

I waited for more information with an expression Dad refers to as my "Carrie" face. The one that looks like I'm about to set the room on fire and watch everything burn. (Word of advice – only watch *Carrie* with your friends. You think, sure, it's just another horror movie, but the real horror is watching the period scene with your dad.)

"We remortgaged the house when we split the assets. So your mum would take half to pay for her care and you and I would be financially protected. But it's been too expensive. I don't get as much freelance work as I used to and our savings are wiped out. With you moving out next year, it made sense to downsize."

I hate hearing this. He sounds like he's trying to convince me that this is an entirely practical decision, devoid of any emotional baggage, and I've heard that before.

I remembered hearing them talk about it before they told me they were getting a divorce. I know you're thinking *well, it's not an affair if they're divorced, Saoirse*, but it wasn't meant to be real. It's only for money reasons, they said. We aren't breaking up, they said. We love each other very much, they said.

I hid behind the kitchen door watching them through the crack. I listened behind doors a lot back then. They were talking money again. Some waffle about protecting the house as an asset. It was Mum's idea actually; her care cost money. She probably wasn't envisioning him shacking up with someone new.

"You're not going to one of those state places," Dad said, pounding his fist on the island. "We'll take care of you."

"God, Rob, please just kill me if it ever comes to that."

51

"Don't say that, love, it's not funny."

Mum got out of her seat and approached him. I could see her face as she put her hands on his shoulders and looked him dead in the eye.

"I'm not joking. I'd rather die than have you or Saoirse feeding me, cleaning me. I don't want her spending her life taking care of me."

"I'm sorry, but I'm too pretty for prison and I just don't think our thirteen-year-old daughter has the upper-body strength to strangle you," Dad said. I could hear a weak smile in his voice as he tried to lighten the mood.

She kissed him then, and I looked away. When I looked back she was burying her face in his neck, and I could tell she was crying.

I could never talk to my parents about what was happening then. About all the things I'd overheard or guessed or figured out. Mum tried to talk to me sometimes. She told me we could talk about anything. No feelings or thoughts were off-limits. I always told her I was fine. I didn't want to make her sad when I knew how sad she was already. The day I heard about the divorce, I ran down to Izzy's house and cried on her bedroom floor while Hannah rubbed circles on my back. Once I could breathe again, Izzy made us popcorn and gave us each a hairbrush and we sang along to *Mamma Mia!* When I went home, I could tell my mum I was OK and I could almost mean it.

*

The kitchen looked the same now as it did then: same island, same big clock on the wall that we forgot to put forward when the time changed, same broken tile by the dishwasher. It felt different, though. It didn't feel lived in, all chaos and cooking smells; it felt neglected, empty. And this time I was on the other side of the door for the hard conversations.

"I don't see why you have to marry her," I said, changing tack. I hated hearing all the stupid financial stuff. Like Mum's disease boiled down to how much it cost us. "Why do you have to keep changing everything?"

"Saoirse, I *love* Beth. I want to spend the rest of my life with her." He said it like he thought I'd finally understand. Like it would make everything clear.

Words didn't mean anything to him. Words like *love* or *marriage* or *we'll take care of you.*

"The rest of your life?" I shook my head. "Isn't that what you told Mum too?"

5

I sat in front of the mirror, grappling with an eyeliner pencil and grumbling to myself. I couldn't believe Dad was making me meet the woman he'd been cheating with for the last year.

OK, we can argue about the technicalities if you want. Yes, Dad is technically divorced, and he can't exactly have a normal marriage with Mum, but other people do it. Other people stick by their partner when stuff like this happens. I've seen it on TV, read articles about wives and husbands who spend the rest of their lives caring for their spouse even if they're in a coma or something. The bottom line is Dad is too selfish for that.

I wasn't putting make-up on to impress her or because it was an important event or anything. Because it wasn't. And it's not like I had anywhere else to be that night. I wasn't going to Ruby's birthday. I'd basically forgotten it was even the same night. I put the perfume and eyeliner on for myself, all right?

The last week had been awkward, to put it mildly. But Dad and I were used to that. It was a pattern we'd perfected. We'd have a blowout and we wouldn't talk for a couple of days. Then silence would turn to "Pass the salt," and by the end of the week, we'd be shouting answers at a game show together. It's not like in the movies where you storm out and never speak again or you have a huge meaningful conversation and work it all out. You just get on with it until it isn't so raw any more.

He really pulled out all the stops for dinner, as much as was possible for him anyway. He was in the living/dining room lighting candles on the table when I went downstairs.

"This is false advertising, you know," I told him, kneading my thumb into a scar on the palm of my hand. A nervous habit. Not that I was nervous about anything. "Is this woman marrying you because she thinks you do things like light candles and use napkins?" I lifted a Halloween-themed napkin with black cats on it from the table and turned it over in my hand. Dad laughed and it sounded grateful. I don't know why I was humouring him but it might have had something to do with the gnawing feeling in my stomach that had kept me up all night. I guess I felt bad about what I'd said. I mean, it was one hundred percent true, but the look on his face when I said it kept popping into my head.

It's hard to hate someone and love them at the same time.

The doorbell rang and Dad froze mid-fussing with a vase of flowers.

"Be nice," he said, eyes narrowing.

I gave him my biggest, fakest grin. "I'm always nice."

My face contorted into pursed lips when he wasn't looking. I'd thought about it a lot and I convinced myself that it didn't matter. I couldn't stop him getting married and what would be the point even if I could? It wouldn't make him love Mum again. This wasn't going to play out like some dementia version of *The Parent Trap*. Besides, it was only a matter of time before this marriage went tits up too. That didn't mean I liked it, but I only had to get through it for the summer.

So he was taking my home away from me – what did it matter? Everything good that had happened here was gone. Let's raze the house to the ground for all I care. Being forced to choose between staying in Ireland, trapped with him, or leaving Mum behind, made my chest tight. I didn't want to think about it. Maybe one of the two dozen CVs I'd put into shops around town before the exams could turn into a job and then I could stuff Oxford and get my own place. Mum could come live with me. Both problems solved. I made a mental note to chase up those CVs with a phone call.

Dad wove around me to the door and flung his arms wide.

"Come in, m'lady," he said, and I could hear the goofy smile even if I couldn't see it. Beth took a tentative step over the threshold. When they hugged, I caught her eye. She looked away and broke off the hug immediately.

"This looks incredible, Rob." She had medium brown skin, curly hair, and an English accent, but not like Ruby's. Ruby's accent was cute and her words sounded bubbly and joyful falling off her tongue. Beth sounded like she might read the news on the BBC. She shook her coat off, revealing an emerald-green sleeveless dress that showed off her tattoos. I knew she was the same age as Dad – some information about her had slipped through in spite of my best efforts – but (though it pained me to admit it) she looked effortlessly cool in a way Dad could never pull off. He always looked like he was trying too hard. Or maybe that was just because I knew firsthand how much time he spent doing his hair.

Dad took her coat and handbag and laid them gently on the back of an armchair. She looked at me. This was usually the moment where I'd make an excuse and leave the house.

"I'm so glad we're getting a chance to get to know each other," she said. "Your dad talks about you all the time."

"OK," I said flatly.

Dad shot me a look. He was standing halfway between us, still twisting a napkin in his hands. I shrugged at him. What was I supposed to say to that? *I'm familiar with your existence and I disapprove.* Seemed rude even for me.

"Saoirse, why don't you sit down. Beth, you can come help me in the kitchen."

I bristled. Why should she help? She didn't live here.

On the other hand, I didn't want to be handing her dinner – the urge to dump it in her lap would be too great.

I plonked myself at the table and scrolled through Twitter, pretending not to hear the giggling wafting out from the kitchen. When there was a crash and more giggling I instinctively glanced in that direction. I was punished with a glimpse of them full-on trading saliva. Gross.

I scanned the room for an overnight bag and thankfully didn't see one. Unless she carried a pair of clean knickers and a toothbrush in her purse.

Gross. Why did my mind go there?

I tried to get invested in a thread about a guy who met the president when he was high. Perhaps I also searched to see if Ruby had an account, but if she did, I couldn't find it.

When Dad and Beth finally emerged from the kitchen, Dad's cheeks pink and Beth's eyes twinkling, I rolled my eyes. The likelihood of me keeping dinner down was dwindling. *Enjoy it while it lasts. At least one of you is going to get seriously burned by this hasty decision.* My money was on Beth. Dad already had a track record of abandoning wives. It almost made me feel sorry for her. Run now, Beth! You better hope you don't get a cold or anything. Dad will be off riding the next girl because he had to heat up chicken soup for a week and it was so hard on him.

I decided against issuing that particular warning. She'd made her bed, after all. It wasn't my job to protect her from her own stupidity. Besides, maybe she'd dump Dad and he'd get a taste of his own medicine. A picture of Dad getting old alone, nudged its way into my head. I pushed it away. It was too confusing. Instead I shoved a bit of dry unseasoned chicken into my gob and focused on that.

Another thought occurred to me, though. If Dad was so keen on substituting my mother with a younger, healthier model, then I couldn't be sitting here all polite like she was a stranger. She'd already missed out on years of arguments and strops and sarcastic comments. I should make her feel more a part of the family.

"So should I call you new mummy or . . . ?" I chewed on the chicken with my mouth open.

Dad opened his mouth to tell me off, or maybe that was his jaw dropping.

"I'm only messing with you. Breaking the ice, you know." I gave them both my best innocent face. I think I wanted to start a row but to my surprise, Beth laughed.

At least she wasn't a total dry shite.

The next hour was a mixture of the sound of scraping forks against our plates and stilted conversation about as interesting as the plain boiled rice I was shovelling into my mouth. Beth asked how I got on in my exams and what I wanted to study at uni and I made up some suitable non-sarcastic answers. At one point Dad managed somehow to segue a comment about avocados into a conversation about the death penalty to get me talking. I don't know how he did it. That was his special skill.

"Right, but what if I was murdered. Would you not—"

"Dad, seriously, realistically, if anyone is going to murder you it'll be me. So no."

"But what if—"

"Oh God, make it stop," I wailed.

Once we'd all choked down dinner, Dad cleared the table and Beth settled on the sofa. She looked out of place. She didn't belong on our sofa.

I couldn't help but be reminded of the first time I'd met her. I'd been with Mum, maybe a week after she'd moved out at most, and when I came home Beth was there, looking guilty in the same spot on the couch. Dad had tried to act casual. "How was your mum?" he said, after Beth had jumped out of the seat like it was on fire and made some flimsy excuse to leave. "Did you do anything nice?"

"Who was that?" I said sharply, ignoring his attempt at diversion.

"Hmmm? Oh, Beth, an advertising client." He skittered out of the living room into the kitchen and I followed him. Dad was a web developer and worked with loads of advertising people. The client thing could have been true. She looked like the kind of person who worked in advertising. That's the best kind of lie, isn't it? The one that's technically true.

"Why was she here?" I took a seat at the small breakfast table and kept my voice purposefully steady. I wanted him to convince me. A sick feeling in my stomach had started churning the moment I saw her and I wanted it to go away. I really wanted to be wrong.

"She lives nearby. I said I'd meet her here to discuss some things so I could be home early for a change."

He started pulling pots and pans out of the cupboards. I watched him pretend to examine a package of dried pasta as though the nutritional information was suddenly important to him.

"So how was your mum?" he asked again.

I felt myself detach from the moment. The sick feeling in my stomach faded away.

"Did you sleep with her?" I felt like I was watching the scene unfold instead of participating in it. Like it was all happening in the mirror.

"What? Saoirse!"

I didn't reply, didn't lay out my case. I waited. I wanted to see what he was going to say. It was strange watching him, his face, his body language giving away every thought as clearly as if I could read his mind. I watched the shift from indignation to resignation.

Finally, he sat opposite me at the table and put his head in his hands, flattening his hair to his scalp, his forehead wrinkling so hard it would give him a headache later.

When he spoke, he spoke to the table.

"I didn't want you to find out this way. We met a few months ago and we got along. We've been on a few dates. I meant to tell you but I wanted to wait until I knew it was going to be something."

It helped that he sounded like a character from a TV show. That he was such a cliché, it made the whole thing feel less real.

"But Mum," I said. "You're cheating on her."

I remembered them telling me about the divorce, emphasising how it was only on paper. Was that always a lie?

"Saoirse, your mum's condition deteriorated a long time ago. She doesn't even know who I am."

"That bit is new," I objected.

"It's been at least a year, love."

A year is not that long.

"I wasn't looking for someone," he said as though that was a defence.

When I didn't say, *Oh, well, it's all right if she just fell in your lap then*, he continued. "Sometimes when I visit Liz she thinks I'm one of the staff. Twenty years we were together and when she looks at me like I'm a stranger it kills me. I know it isn't true and she can't help it but some days it feels like it all meant nothing to her."

That winded me. She looked at me that way too. Did that mean all the years she'd been my mum meant nothing? Did it stop counting the first time she called me Claire, her sister's name, or the tenth, or the two hundredth?

I could understand Dad feeling the way he did, but I could not understand him giving up and abandoning her for someone fresh.

"Is this why you put her in the home? So you could go off with someone else?"

He flinched.

"God. No. Of course not. You know that we weren't able to look after her here. It wasn't safe any more. She needs 24-7 care. You know that," he said, and locked eyes with me. "You agreed to that."

Disgust roiled in my stomach. He'd been pushing to get rid of her for ages before I finally gave in. I stood up, pushing the chair back against the tiles with a screech.

"I don't ever want to see that woman here again."

"Saoirse . . . ," he called after me limply. He wanted me to understand what it was like for him so I could feel sorry for him because he'd spent the last few years looking after my mother, the woman he married. The whole "in sickness and health" thing must have passed him by. He wanted me to understand why he needed to cheat on her. But in the end, his desire to avoid fighting about it was stronger.

I sought refuge at Hannah's house for three days. He tried calling but I ignored him. Eventually, her parents told me I had to go home, which was a bit rich considering the number of nights Hannah had spent at my house. The number of times she'd come around to my place to talk to my mum about her problems because her own parents always made her feel worse. I hadn't really noticed that I was going to her a lot more often than she was coming round to me.

Things thawed with Dad after a while, of course. I didn't know how to stay angry and I didn't know how to stop being angry and I wasn't sure which one I wanted more. The energy it takes to keep hating someone that much is hard to sustain. But I never really forgave him. We eased into a fragile peace, but it was never the same. Before Beth, I thought Dad and I were in it together. Even though I didn't always agree with what he thought was best, I thought at least it hurt him as much as it hurt me. After Beth I was alone.

"How about a film, then?" Dad stood, hands on hips, surveying us both and looking too pleased with himself. "We haven't watched *Gonjiam: Haunted Asylum* since it came out."

"I don't think so," I said coldly. "I don't like those mental hospital ones. They're offensive."

"Offensive how?" Dad rolled his eyes.

"How are they not offensive? People with mental illness are inherently scary?" I said, getting annoyed.

"Maybe it's a commentary on the mental health system causing iatrogenic harm to a traumatised population," Dad said, clearly pleased with his big words.

"And then they die and become scary ghosts?" Beth chimed in, sceptical.

We both looked at her for a moment.

"Exactly," I said. "Even if what you said was remotely accurate, how would making their spirits the villains be sensitive?"

"Well, what about—"

Then I realised I'd got sucked into another debate. Dad already knew I hated "asylum horror". Mum hated it too. She was a therapist, after all. She hated the idea of locking people away from the rest of the world just because they were struggling. She always said that wasn't compassion or care, it was fear. Was that what we'd done to her? If she'd been here, if she'd been well, she would have shut him down immediately. I wanted her here to say something smart and thoughtful that would make him get quiet and then nod and say *you're right, love*. She was so good at that. I wanted her here on my side. But it was just me.

I decided to pull the rip cord on this terrible evening.

"I don't have time for this. I have to go to someone's birthday thing," I said.

"Whose birthday?" Dad eyed me suspiciously. He checked his watch. "It's kind of late."

"All right, grandpa. It's Ruby's birthday thing."

"Who's Ruby?"

"A girl. A friend. She's new."

I thought for sure he'd put his foot down. Then I'd

have to sneak out and it would be a whole thing. We'd already played that game last week; I wasn't ready for another round. Instead, Dad got a twinkle in his eye.

"Ohhhh," he said slowly, "a new 'friend'. Ruby, eh?" He winked at me and I felt all my insides cringe.

"Dad, no—"

"Saoirse is a lesbian," Dad explained meaningfully to Beth, who to her credit didn't seem to know how to respond to this proclamation. If I was in a better mood I might have joked that genuflection would suffice.

"Dad, Ruby isn't—"

"Go on, Saoirse, get out of here. Go say hello to *Ruby* for me." He said her name in a way that made it sound like "Ruby and Saoirse sitting in a tree" would follow if I didn't scarper posthaste.

"That's totally the first thing I'll do. Tell her that my father who she's never met says hello. That's not weird at all."

"Ah now" – he grinned goofily – "I suppose your old dad will be the last thing on your mind when you see her. Young love and all that."

"Please stop." I shuddered.

Beth gave me a meek wave. Dad yelled after me that he still had some good points to make about the film *Gothika*. I slammed the door behind me.

Good thing I'd done my eyeliner after all.

6

My neighbourhood is nice. When I was little I thought it was "normal" – the kind of place most people lived. But I can see now that we have it really good compared to a lot of people. Things got a bit tighter after Mum went into full-time care, we paid extra to put her in the best home, but we were able to do that and I think that makes us really lucky.

Oliver's neighbourhood is many levels beyond that. The houses slowly got bigger and bigger until you couldn't see the houses any more because they were at the end of long driveways and stone walls. It isn't a manor or anything, but it is really big and has gardens (plural) and a pond and that sort of thing. I specifically knew that homes in this area cost a clean fortune because Hannah used to want to live in this really pretty grey-brick one with a legit turret. It was for sale last year so we looked up the estate agent's website and concluded that we would never be able to afford anything like it. We recalibrated and set our sights on living anywhere, as long as it was together.

Three months later she'd broken up with me so I don't know if she ever really meant it when we talked about the future together. That was one of the hardest things about breaking up. It's not a pair of bookends, the beginning and the end. It's the unravelling of the future. The flat we would never move into together, the cat we would never pick up from the shelter. It was all the times I wouldn't hear her go on and on about some boring film I couldn't sit through, or the way I wouldn't see her do that silly tap dance she does when she's trying on new shoes. It's all the things we used to do that we'd never do again and all the things we'd never do for the first time together.

As I put my finger up to the Quinns' doorbell, I realised I hadn't told anyone I was coming. I hadn't brought a gift or even a card. What was I doing here? Coming round here to see her again would give off some serious looking-for-a-relationship vibes and that was against the rules.

Or was I overthinking it? We could be friends, right? Ruby didn't have any friends here and neither did I. Who couldn't use a casual friend for the summer?

I stood for a minute, weighing up the options. If I wanted to be friends, maybe I should come back tomorrow. In daylight. Like a normal person. With a belated birthday card and an apology.

The front door opened.

Shit.

"You have to press it to make it do that sound, you know." Oliver stood in the doorway wearing a button-down shirt and actual khaki chinos.

"You look like the lost member of One Direction," I said.

"There will be a reunion and I'm ready for it," Oliver said. "How did you get through the security?"

"What security?"

"The big gate down the street to keep the riffraff out."

"You're rich, I'm not. Ha ha."

"Well, I wasn't expecting you, so I had to resort to something easy. I should have gone the slut-shaming route."

"A missed opportunity," I replied dryly. "How'd you know I was out here?"

"I was passing by and I saw you muttering to yourself." He pointed at the wall beside the door and I stepped over the threshold and saw there was a small security screen.

"I was not muttering."

"Yeah, you were. For ages. I was standing here laughing at you."

I peered around for signs of any other nonspecific Quinn family members. Off the hall a door was ajar and music and laughter wafted out.

"I'm going to assume Ruby invited you in some post-sex sapphic haze, but you're very late for dinner. Can I assume this is a booty call?"

"We didn't—" I started but didn't finish. I didn't have to answer to him. I felt a small thrill when he said her name, though. A friendship thrill. New friends are exciting.

"That must be a first for you," he said, smirking.

I rolled my eyes. Correcting him would only encourage him to think it was anyone's business but mine and the person I was *not* doing it with.

"And someday you'll have your first time too," I said, squeezing his shoulder.

I eyed the room the music was coming from. Light from a screen flickered against the visible sliver of opulent wallpaper. What if I walked in there and Ruby was annoyed with me and told me to leave? Or what if she didn't actually remember me? Maybe she kissed girls and invited them round all the time. She said it was a family thing but she could have met loads of people since last week. What if that room was full of hot lesbians?

Well, I mean, that didn't sound *terrible*, but still.

"You're right, though," I said, backing away, "I am very late and I shouldn't disturb your party."

"Oliver, is someone at the door?" a woman called.

I shook my head at him.

"Yes, Mum, we have a visitor."

I gave Oliver my most potent death glare. It didn't faze him. He dragged me into the room by the hand. It was lit by candles and expensive-looking lamps that cast eerie shadows on the wall, making the scene appear more sinister than it really was. It reminded me of the part of an Agatha Christie novel just before some rich person's body is found on a Persian rug. There were a few helium balloons with "18" on them that kind of took the edge off the atmosphere.

I wondered if Ruby hadn't finished school yet, or if she was just one of the youngest in her class like me.

Oliver's mum was sitting on one of a pair of Louis XVI–style couches, the kind that are fantastically uncomfortable but very chic. Did she know Jack Kennedy lost his virginity on one of those sofas? Judging by the fact that they hadn't set them both on fire, probably not. Oliver's dad was in the centre of the room, a microphone in his hand, paused, evidently mid-performance.

Ruby wasn't there.

"Mum, Dad, this is Saoirse," Oliver said.

"Nice to see you, Mr and Mrs Quinn," I said.

His dad bounded forward to shake my hand. I hated when parents did that. It was so awkward, but he had such a warm smile on his face when he told me to call them Harry and Jane that I couldn't hold it against him.

"Saoirse, welcome to the party. Do you have a signature song?" He indicated the TV screen, which was still playing the lyrics from what I recognised as a Sarah McLachlan song, though someone had muted the background music when I walked in.

"Er, no." I would not be singing. Not now, not ever.

"Don't put the poor girl on the spot." Jane shook her head. "Sit down, dear, I'll get you the list to look through."

I don't know what panicked me more, the list of song options or having to choose between the two sofas not knowing which one was the sex sofa. I tried to get Oliver's attention to silently ascertain the status of the couches but he gave me a blank look in return. As soon as I sat and no one was looking, Oliver made the universal hand gesture for hetero sex and pointed to the spot I was sitting in.

I shuddered involuntarily.

"Ruby, we have a guest," Jane said, and my head snapped up.

There she was, paused in the doorway, her eyes widened in surprise. I stood up automatically, as though she were a dignitary of some kind. She had a flute of something bubbly in her hand, nonalcoholic I assumed, and her messy hair was flipped onto one side, her lip ring glinting against the candlelight. She wore a denim pinafore covered in badges with pink tights and gold sparkly flats on her feet. I braced myself for the possibility that she would stare coldly at me and ask why I was there.

But she smiled.

I took her in, checking my body for signs of the wobble. For heartbeats skipped or stomach flipping. I was fine. She was just a girl. Just a girl I kissed that I could totally be friends with.

Then she crossed the room in a few steps and hugged me. The smell of fruity hair product wafted up my nose. Not that I smelled her hair, you understand. You don't do that to friends.

She whispered in my ear, "I'm really glad you came." Her breath tickled. She held my gaze for a moment as she pulled away, eyes twinkling. She gave me a long look up and down. Or maybe it just felt long. "I assume you're hiding a present somewhere?" she said, her lips quirking slightly.

The wobble returned.

The wobble was a liability.

Before I could say something clever or just apologise, Jane spoke.

"Did you get through to your mum?" she asked with a sympathetic wrinkle of her forehead.

Ruby shook her head. She seemed sad but shrugged it off. Perhaps realising that everyone was now looking at Ruby, Jane turned to me.

"Saoirse, how do you know my lovely niece already? She's only been in town ten minutes and she's made a friend."

Ruby and I sat at the same time. Close enough that I could smell her perfume. Close enough that when I let my hand rest beside me, her little finger tickled mine. In a friendly way, of course.

"Oh, well, Oliver introduced us. Sort of," I said meaningfully, reminding him I could rat him out about his party habit in return for not warning me about the sofa. There was panic in his eyes and I smiled smugly before continuing. "He is always getting people together, making connections and all that."

"You're in Oliver's class?"

I nodded.

"What are your plans, then, for next year? University? Or maybe taking a gap year like our Ruby?"

"Saoirse is Oxford bound, Mum," Oliver said before I could reply.

Ruby's head turned in my direction. But I didn't look directly at her. People have feelings about places like Oxford. They either think you're some kind of genius (I'm not) or that you're rich (I'm not) or that you think you're better than everyone else (definitely not).

"Oh, very good, dear. What are you going to study?"

I shrugged and swerved around the question. "I might not even get in. It's all conditional on getting enough points in the exams."

That was the thing I kept telling people, that I might not get in. Because you can't say *I don't want to go*. Although it answered the question of whether she was still at school, I then wondered why Ruby was taking a gap year. Probably going to travel the world or some other exciting bohemian thing only rich people do. Did she think I was boring for not doing something more fun?

She shifted slightly and let her knee fall against mine in way that felt deliberate. Not boring, then.

"What about your summer?" Harry rubbed his hands together. "Any exciting plans?"

"I suppose I'm looking for a job but I haven't heard anything yet."

"See, Oliver," Harry said, pointing at his son, who

looked around innocently, as though there might be another Oliver in the room. "You need to be looking for a summer job too."

"Father dearest, we've been through this . . . I'm busy."

Jane laughed. "I'll busy you. What do you think, Saoirse? Should Oliver have to get off his arse and actually do something?"

"What about a nice volunteer job? Give back to the community," I said with wide-eyed innocence.

Oliver looked stricken. Presumably, the only thing worse to him than working would be working for free.

Ruby had just taken a sip of her drink, so when she snorted with laughter at Oliver's expression she choked on it. I put my hand on her knee when I asked her if she was OK and then took it off quickly when I remembered the friend thing. I didn't want to give her the wrong idea.

"Oh, Saoirse, we haven't even got you a drink, what will you have?"

"I'm fine, really, thanks."

"Shush now, you'll need some Dutch courage if you're going to step up to the mike," Harry said, laughing.

"That's right, I said I'd get you the list of songs we have," Jane said, standing up. "Are you more of a pop girl or a rock star?"

"Uh . . ."

"Saoirse is obviously perfect for a power ballad." Oliver grinned, getting me back for my volunteer job comment.

I nudged Ruby with my knee and she caught my eye. I tried to send her panic signals but I didn't know if we were quite at the level of unspoken eyeball communication.

"Jane, I think Saoirse is maybe a little too shy to sing right now."

It was Oliver's turn to snort.

"Maybe later when you've seen the rest of us embarrass ourselves," Harry said, and held the mike out to Oliver. "Son, weren't you going to do 'Kiss from a Rose' next?"

I could barely contain my glee. I swivelled towards Oliver, expecting him to be embarrassed. He sauntered over to his dad and took the mike. He reached his arms overhead, and then stretched his legs on the arm of the sofa like he was warming up for a sprint.

"I have but one request." He directed this at me.

I assumed he was going to ask me not to breathe a word of it to anyone. I was wrong.

"Please save your applause for the end of the performance."

7

After three more renditions from Oliver in various genres, two more Sarah McLachlans from Harry, and one amusing duet from Ruby, and a very sozzled, slightly dramatic Jane, Ruby reminded me I'd left my top upstairs and why didn't I come upstairs and get it. Harry and Jane were too tipsy to question why or when I'd left articles of clothing in their house.

"Oliver's actually not bad," I said as I followed Ruby upstairs. "You know I wouldn't tell him that, but he can hold a tune. I won't be advising him to pack in his university plans or anything but . . ." I was rambling. I was nervous. Sitting beside her all night, even when I was watching Oliver belt out "A Whole New World" (both parts), I felt this hum of electricity, a static charge that kept building and building.

Her room was more lived-in than last time. The sports bag I'd tripped over was gone and there were books on the shelves. Ruby took a seat in a peacock-blue armchair that hadn't been there last week, folding her legs onto the seat.

"So where's my top?" I said.

"I have no idea. I threw it in the laundry and it disappeared." She grinned.

I perched on the edge of the bed beside her open laptop. It was frozen mid-scene from a film I didn't recognise.

"What are you watching?"

"*Four Weddings and a Funeral*," she said. "I'm at the bit where Hugh Grant is telling Andie MacDowell he loves her in the rain."

"Never heard of it."

She looked genuinely shocked. "It's a classic. It's my favourite. The romantic comedy to end all romantic comedies."

"I don't really watch those. They give people unrealistic expectations of love." If you were the kind of person who relied on romantic comedies to tell you what life was like, you were going to be very disappointed. Heartbreak isn't eating a tub of ice cream and then running into the new love of your life at the independent bookshop. If that was how Ruby saw relationships, she probably wouldn't understand my aversion to them.

"What films do you like?"

"If I had to pick a genre it would be horror."

"Doesn't that give you unrealistic expectations of how likely you are to be stabbed by a knife-wielding maniac?"

"Fair play," I laughed. "But it's the endings that bother me with rom-coms. You know, where they get together or get married or whatever and you're supposed to think it's happily ever after but you never see the sequel where the guy dumps her for her best friend or the girl gets sick of picking up skidmarked pants from the bedroom floor."

"That would be a terrible movie." Ruby's eyes twinkled. I think she thought my unbridled cynicism was funny. It made my cheeks warm.

"So you said you were staying the summer?" I said casually.

"Until September." She nodded. "My family are away, but they didn't want me staying alone all summer."

That was strange. If they didn't want her being alone, why didn't they just bring her with them? But their loss. I could keep her company for the summer. I was capable of spending a few weeks with a pretty girl and not needing to kiss her again. I wasn't some kind of sex pest.

"I'm glad you came tonight," she said, changing the subject. I watched her lips as she spoke. "You came late, but you came."

"I probably should have mentioned I was going to."

"But you didn't decide until the last minute." It wasn't a question. Her teeth toyed with her lip ring, twisting her bottom lip. She pushed her hair from one side of her head to the other with her fingers.

"Sort of."

"So what made you come?"

I thought we could hang out. I wanted to be friends.

"I wanted to kiss you again."

For some reason I let the truth out. Even though I hadn't admitted to myself until now that although we barely knew each other I felt like there was some kind of intangible connection, a grabbing, reaching, searching feeling that meant I hadn't so much chosen to come here as much as I found myself pulled in her direction.

Ruby leaned her elbow on the desk beside her chair and put her fist to her mouth like she was musing on something very serious.

"I'll keep that in mind," she said eventually.

I dipped my head to hide my amusement. I could endure a little teasing.

"So are you and Oliver really friends?" she asked.

"Oh God. No. Absolutely not. I think mortal enemies is a more accurate description."

"And why is that?"

"He stole my girlfriend in second year . . . and *technically* I dumped him before that, in sixth class. Broke his poor little rich boy heart. He was utterly devastated, I'm sure he'd tell you that. I think he stole my girlfriend as part of a long-game revenge plot. Poor fellow couldn't handle that once I accepted I was a lesbian I had way more game than him."

Ruby laughed.

I liked making her laugh.

"I don't think either of you have game."

I choked on my indignation, thumping my chest twice to get it all out.

"Excuse me. I bagged you *and* your cousin," I countered. "Sure, we were eleven, but we kissed with tongues and everything. Sort of."

"And yet you want to kiss me again, but you came to my birthday without even bringing a present?" Ruby pretended to fan herself like ladies of yore.

"I did too get you a present," I said, hopping off the bed. "Hold on a second."

With the paltry contents of an old pen pot and a sheet of paper ripped from a file pad on the desk, I got to work. After hastily scribbling for a couple of seconds, I beckoned her over to the window that looked out on the back garden. I thought I saw our cat creeping along the wall in the dark. My hand rested in the curve of her lower back, the left side of her body pressed against me. I handed her the sheet of paper.

I'd drawn a squiggly swirling border in blue marker, and with the black pen I'd written:

This hereby declares that "that star right there"
is named after Ruby Quinn.
Signed: Brian Cox, Owner of Stars.

Ruby giggled. "Which one is it?"

"That star right there." I pointed vaguely at the sky. "It says so on the certificate, Ruby."

"I'll treasure it forever." She wiped a fake tear away. Then she gave me a once-over, a look I can only describe as appraising.

"What is it?"

"Well, I don't know if you're going to like this," she

said, feigning a sort of theatrical sigh, "but you should know that is my favourite part of the romantic comedy."

"What do you mean?"

"You know, the grand gesture where the guy buys the girl a star because it's way more meaningful than, like, a necklace or a bunch of flowers."

"I'm no expert but I don't think this is the grand gesture," I said, and Ruby turned slightly so my hand was now resting on her waist. She was looking directly at me now and it was almost too close to bear.

"You gave me a star. How is that not a grand gesture?"

"The grand gesture comes after the fight, doesn't it? We haven't had the fight." I tried to sound relaxed though I felt like I might melt into a puddle.

"You're right, actually," Ruby admitted. "Like Hugh and Andie, or John Cusack holding up the stereo outside Ione Skye's bedroom window." Ruby poked me in the chest and narrowed her eyes. "How do you know that if you don't watch them? Are you sure you aren't a secret rom-com fan?"

"I don't need to be, that's my point; once you've seen one, you've seen them all. They meet in some quirky way like bumping into each other—"

"The meet cute."

"If you say so."

Ruby stuck her tongue out at me and pulled away. The tension that built up between us was like an elastic band pulled tight; the further away she got the more I thought I might snap. She got on the bed and lay back. I resisted the urge to follow her and I leaned against the wall, hoping I looked devastating in the stream of moonlight from the window.

"So meet cute, then they have a falling in love montage of picnics and dates and general merriment, but oh no, what's this contrived conflict? Big fight, hero realises he's a twat, then grand gesture and happily ever after. These guys wouldn't have to work so hard if they didn't act like twats in the first place, but I guess that would be anticlimactic."

"OK, that's the *formula*. All stories have formulas. It's the characters that make them special." Ruby looked thoughtful. "And there are hardly any gay romantic comedies, so our rules might not be the same. We could reinvent the genre."

"Oh, they're definitely not the same. If this was a lesbian film, unfortunately, one of us would have to kill ourselves at the end."

"Drastic."

"I don't make the rules. Do I wish there were lots of nice happy rom-coms with girls? Of course. We deserve as many glossy, high-budget films as anyone else. But there are, like, two and they kiss four times total across both films. Not even any . . ." I make interlocking gestures with my fingers.

"There's definitely never enough kissing," Ruby said, meeting my eyes. The way she said it made me want to leap across the room and kiss her but somehow my feet were glued to the spot. What was wrong with me?

"Right. I mean there's like two kisses in one film," I said, vaguely aware I was repeating myself.

Ruby nodded. She got off the bed.

"And you can't even really call them big budget. I just mean you actually recognise some of the actors in those ones."

Ruby walked towards me keeping her eyes on mine.

"I saw this lesbian movie once," I blathered on, "where a girl jumps off a building and it really looks like she turns into an eagle and . . ."

Ruby stopped walking when the toes of her glittery flats knocked against my scuffed military boots. The rest of my sentence got stuck in my throat.

"You talk a lot," she said.

I nodded.

She flipped her hair over to the opposite side. My stomach flipped over to its opposite side.

"I think we should kiss now. You got me the star, after all." She gestured at the night sky. "And I get the feeling you're nervous so maybe we should just do it."

I wasn't nervous. I mean, we'd kissed before. So why would I be nervous? I tried to say I wasn't nervous but nothing came out.

Shut up.

A moment of silence passed, the energy between us building. Her fingers found my arms and she traced a line from my elbow to the palm of my hand with her finger on both sides, holding my hands lightly when she reached them. Our fingers played gently. I could feel the rise and fall of her chest against mine. All the hairs on my arm stood up. A shiver ran from my throat to my stomach and further still. Our lips didn't touch yet, but the tip of her nose grazed my cheek and I could feel long eyelashes flutter against my cheek as she closed her eyes. For a second we breathed the air between us. Her hips moved, squeezing out the last bit of light between our bodies.

"I know some guys who'd pay good money to see this." Oliver leaned in the doorway, a smug grin across his face, as always. "But it's not really my thing, so close the door next time."

I was going to murder him.

"Oliver!" Ruby squealed. She buried her face in her hands.

"Go away, creeper." I started towards him and he jumped.

"Believe me, I have no desire to see my darling cousin lobbing the gob on my mortal enemy, but the door *was* open." He looked so genuinely affronted that I would think he'd spy on us that I believed him.

"It's fine, Oliver," Ruby said through gritted teeth; her face had reappeared but her cheeks were pink. She had retreated to her chair and had her knees pulled up to her chest.

"You left your phone on the couch." He threw it to me and I just about caught it. It must have fallen out of my pocket.

"You better not have messed with it."

"Would I?" he said, indignant. I made a mental note to check through my photos and messages later.

"Mum asked me to drive you home," he continued. "She said it was too late to let you walk home by yourself. I said you'd probably rather face a murderer in the bushes than spend ten minutes in the car with me but, for some reason, she thought I was joking."

I hesitated.

"I haven't been drinking," he added. "It interferes with the integrity of my instrument." He stroked his throat.

I could have called Dad to pick me up but at least this way I wouldn't run the chance of interrupting him mid-anything. And if it inconvenienced Oliver, so much the better. I looked behind me, Ruby's face was back to its normal colour. Was that disappointment I saw?

"Can you give me five?"

"Even I last longer than five minutes, Saoirse. There are pills for that."

I scanned the room for anything in grabbing distance but he ducked out too fast, and the pen pot hit the door instead of his head.

"You two are funny," Ruby said.

"He's like the annoying brother I never wanted and will have to poison with cyanide someday."

I wanted to go back to the kiss but I wasn't sure how to get the moment back.

"So what now?" Ruby said.

What was I supposed to say? I was the one who'd come back. I was the one who said I wanted to kiss her again but when it came to saying *Let's do this again* or *I'll call you*, it was like a stone dropped into my stomach, heavy and cold. It had been so easy to stick to my rule until now, and sure, I could throw it away, but I'd made it for a reason. I'd spent most of my life with Hannah, best friends and then girlfriends. When she told me she didn't want that any more I didn't know how to be without her. I had gone through the motions of my life with the constant refrain *She doesn't love you any more* and it made me feel like I didn't count as a whole person on my own. I'd barely gotten past that stage and I couldn't go back. And I couldn't say that to Ruby. It was pathetic.

But I could explain it a different way.

"So you know in the rom-com where there's always a person who doesn't want to be in a serious relationship?"

Ruby raised an eyebrow and it made me wish I could raise one eyebrow. Not that that's the thing to concentrate on here but it would be so cool.

"That's you, I take it," she said with the same expression

my French teacher would make when I told her I really did leave my homework on the kitchen table. I was a good student and yet somehow I always inspired nothing but scepticism. Can't imagine why.

"I want to be honest," I said (dishonestly keeping the real reason I didn't want to get in a relationship a secret).

"What's wrong with relationships? You want the stuff that goes with them."

"Some of it," I conceded. The kissing and groping stuff. With her. I wanted more of that with her than I had with anyone. Since Hannah. "The thing is, though, relationships are doomed to fail. No one stays together. Breakups are never mutual. One person gets blindsided and hurt and it's ugly and messy and . . . and besides, I'm leaving in a few months for uni and you're only here for the summer. So there's really no point."

I declined to mention the bit where I was seriously doubting my decision to move away. There was nothing to be gained from getting into all of that drama as well.

"Is that it?" Ruby said, incredulous. "Relationships end?"

"Pretty much." I braced myself for a lecture about how you have to give love a chance and true love is out there and you'll never find it if you don't put your heart on the line and a story about how her grandparents met when they were seven and they are still together now even though they're a hundred and sixty-eight.

"So what?" is what she said instead.

"Er . . . what?"

"I'm not trying to force you into anything you don't want to do. Trust me, I'm not in the habit of begging girls to go out with me. But I like you and there's another way of thinking about this."

I was interested but not convinced. I was also a bit miffed by this "trust me" business. I bet girls were all over her. I bet there were loads of hot girls in England just waiting outside her door. I forced myself to shut down that tangent and pay attention, Ruby was still talking.

"Like you said, I'm going back home in September. We already know exactly when it will end."

"OK . . . ," I said, my tone conveying that I did not get where she was going with this. She was proving my point. We were doomed from day one.

"Sooo," she said, impatiently explaining what she thought was obvious, "no blindsiding, no expectations of everlasting love. Our own experiment with a different type of lesbian story. The fun stuff. The kissing and the talking and the dating and no one dies at the end."

"Just the romantic montage," I said, finally understanding.

"Exactly. You don't have to take everything so seriously."

She had a point.

"You have a point," I said. Was it possible to have your cake and then not be sad when your cake leaves you and smashes your heart into a mushy pulp? "But how would it work?"

Ruby thought for a second. "We could try it out. One date, something classic from the movies. If we have a good time, we make a proper plan. If we don't or I fall hopelessly in love with you, I swear we can call it off."

She was making fun of me, but it did sound good. Did it count as breaking the golden rule of no relationships? *Technically*. But it was a loophole. Loopholes were fine. I hadn't factored in loopholes before.

All right, listen, I'm going to level with you, we both know I'm full of shit but just let me have this one, OK?

"What kind of classic are you thinking?" I asked. "I feel like people always go ice-skating in these films but we don't have an ice rink. And it's June."

"That's a 'Christmas film in New York' classic. We're doing summer by the beach. And that? Has to be a funfair."

"How convenient," I said. "We have a funfair here every summer." I hadn't been in a while. Honestly, getting whiplash and nausea gets old after a few years. With Ruby, it could be fun, though. It would be cool to get our grope on in the hall of mirrors.

"Of course you do." Ruby got out of her chair, stood in front of me, and tugged on the fabric of my top to pull me close. She kissed me softly. I rested my hands on her hips and just as I started to feel the urgent pull to hold her tighter, closer, she broke away.

"It's a romantic comedy," she said, finishing her sentence, leaving me wanting more. "In rom-coms people bust out coordinated dance routines, they run through airports without being stopped by security, and they come up with perfect speeches on the spur of the moment. Do you really think we'd have to *try* to find something as basic as a funfair?"

8

Saturday morning after Ruby's birthday, before I'd even got a chance to go see Mum, Dad begged me to go view a flat with him. You see, with the exams over, I had decided to switch up my schedule and visit Mum first thing. I had always gone after school during the week, but mornings are better for people with dementia. The doctors don't know why but in the evening they become more agitated. Part of me felt guilty that I was avoiding seeing that side of her, but I didn't dwell on it. It was better for her too, less upsetting. I also didn't like when my visits overlapped with Dad's and he always visited in the evening after work. There was something about being together as a family that felt like a lie. Especially when I knew about Beth and Mum didn't and couldn't understand. Now with the engagement, it was ten times worse. Every moment I let Dad pretend that "Dad and Beth" and all the changes they were making were normal, it was like I was complicit. I thought I should be engaged in some kind of nonstop protest but I wasn't. Sure, I grumbled and I made snide comments, but Mum deserved better than that.

The flat was smaller than our house of course, though that bit didn't bother me. It was out of the suburbs, closer to the promenade, near the tourist beaches. When I stood in my new bedroom, I could hear the noise of tourists, laughing, squealing, shouting, and it smelled like candyfloss. He asked me if I liked it and I grunted. There were other places, he assured me, but I could tell that this was the one he wanted. It was sleek and modern inside, black glass and chrome. So different from our cluttered, cosy home, which was thick rugs and knickknacks adorning every surface. I wondered if the crisp lines and monochrome were Dad's taste or Beth's. Maybe this was what they both liked. Maybe everything that made home, home, was Mum. I'd told him it was fine and his face lit up at my lukewarm tolerance. I felt sick to my stomach with guilt.

Coming straight from the viewing to see Mum felt like I was the husband who buys his wife flowers because he did something wrong. But I put it out of my head; I was getting good at that. I took a deep breath before knocking. I do it every time. It's the breath that says, *don't expect anything, don't let it get to you, don't get frustrated, don't get angry.* It's the shields-up breath.

When she didn't answer, I opened the door myself. She watching TV and a stream of sunshine lit up her face, making her skin glow. She was only fifty-five. When I walked through the halls of the Seaview Home building, I saw elderly people, wrinkled skin collecting in pools around their neck and elbows. Some could barely move; they had to be shifted by staff every few hours so they didn't get sores where their paper-thin skin broke. All of them had dementia of some kind – it was a specialist home – but none of them looked like my mother. She had always been beautiful and that hadn't changed. I topped up her roots every month so her auburn hair stayed glossy and grey-free, like she would want. It seemed to make her happy.

She looked up at me and smiled and I could breathe again. The good days were the days when she looked at me like that. When I could tell she was happy to see me walk into the room, even if she didn't know why.

"Hi, Mum," I said.

"Hello, hello." She ushered me inside, "Do you want a cup of tea?"

She asks everyone this when they come around. Her room is like a little self-contained flat. There's a bedroom/living room, a bathroom, and a "kitchen" with a sink. All the appliances are dementia friendly, like a shower that automatically turns off, or a sink with a pressure sensor that drains if it gets too full. One of the problems with having dementia when you're young is that you're still fit and able and can get into a lot of trouble that a less mobile person cannot.

"Why don't I make it and you can stay where you are," I said.

I had to ask one of the staff to bring us some tea. Mum's not allowed a kettle in her room but I don't like to embarrass her by saying so.

"Why don't you get us some biscuits, Mum?" I said when the girl came in with a tray. Mum pottered into the "kitchen" and took a melamine plate off the shelf.

Sometimes it strikes me how strange this all is. My smart, amazing mother couldn't even have a kettle any more. I followed her into the kitchen and threw my arms around her and hugged her tight. She hugged me back. Sometimes she doesn't. When I pulled away she was looking at me with that absent look. Mum was always so shrewd, so insightful. It was her job as a psychotherapist. When that sharp look in her eye is missing, she looks like someone else.

She stood in the kitchen dithering and I could tell I'd distracted her and she'd forgotten why she was there. It's funny; we've all had that moment where you go into a room and suddenly the whole reason you were there is wiped from your brain. You know it'll come back to you if you give it a second. I sometimes wondered if Mum felt that way, that whatever she'd forgotten, a task, a memory, someone's face, would come back to her in a second. Or if it's gone so far that she doesn't even know she's forgotten anything.

"Biscuits, Mum," I prompted.

"Do you want a cup of tea?" she asked.

"We've got tea. We need some biccies. Do you want me to get them?"

She shooed me away from the kitchen and arranged some chocolate digestives on a plate. She was getting clumsier all the time, as though her muscle memory was fading too, so I watched her carefully.

There was an Australian soap on the TV so I flicked through the channels until I found the news. Mum hated soaps. She was highbrow to the point of snobbish and Dad and I always teased her for it. She and Hannah used to talk about fancy-pants things all the time. They read the same boring books where nothing really happened with lots of wordy metaphors. They watched the same boring films where nothing really happened with lots of visual metaphors. Once they even went to a concert together. Vivaldi played by Vilde Frang. I only remembered the name because I thought it sounded funny and I still don't know if Vilde Frang is a person or a band. The same night, Dad and I had gone to an unauthorised musical version of *Jennifer's Body*. It was fucking amazing to be fair but I sometimes felt a pang of regret that I hadn't done the things Mum wanted to do even if I hated them. There'd been moments where I wondered if she would have preferred Hannah as a daughter. When we broke up, I was glad that Mum didn't really understand any more but I was angry with Hannah because it felt like she had abandoned Mum as well.

I could feel myself getting sucked into that black hole of ruminating on things I'd done wrong and honestly I could be here all day if I let that take over. As a great philosopher once said: shake it off.

"How are you, Mum?" I asked, trying to inject some lightness into my voice.

"I'm really good. Dad is picking me up soon."

Mum often thinks she's younger than she is. Sometimes she seems to think she's at work. She often thinks her parents are still alive – her adoptive parents, I mean. She doesn't remember finding out she was adopted. That didn't happen until she was in her late twenties. It felt like her memories unravelled up to a certain point. She could tell you stories from her childhood in vivid detail but she didn't remember that she had a daughter. Most of the time she thought she was in her early twenties, as near as we could tell. That person was Elizabeth O'Kane. She wouldn't even meet Rob Clarke for thirteen more years, let alone be my mother. It was like that part of her vanished. I tried to remember the last time she knew I was her daughter. But I hadn't known it was the last time then so it hadn't stuck out. Another memory gone, for both of us.

"That's lovely," I said. "What time is he coming?"

"Soon. I think. How are you? What would you like to talk about?'

How are you? What would you like to talk about? Mum's script. Phrases form on her lips, things she's said a thousand times before. I imagine her saying the same things to her clients. Sometimes when I arrive at her door she seems to think I'm one of them. Sometimes I go along with that too.

I spilled. I had so much swirling around my head, and it wasn't like I had anyone else to tell. I'd thought about calling Izzy. Not seriously thought about it, just felt annoyed with her that I couldn't tell her everything about Ruby and find out what she thought. If she hadn't messed up our friendship with her lies and betrayal, I could be dissecting it all with her right now. I didn't choose the dramatic loner life, it chose me.

Still, I had Mum, and it was easier to tell her things now that I would have never told her before. Every cloud and all that guff. I'd much rather she was well and trying to pry information about my life out of me like everyone else's mother, of course. It had taken me weeks to admit to her that Hannah and I had started seeing each other. I remember her sitting me down very seriously to ask if something was going on with us. When I told that we were going out now, she cried. Happy tears. She said she'd always hoped we'd finally see how perfect we were for each other and she said something silly about our future wedding. I had rolled my eyes and said we weren't getting married, for God's sake. I was pleased, really, but I was fourteen and I couldn't say that out loud.

"I met a girl." I blew on my tea to cool it down and Mum copied me. "I think she likes me."

Mum put her hand on mine and squeezed. "That's great," she said.

"The thing is, liking her is kind of the problem."

Mum looked like she was not quite following my train of thought. But who would? That statement was objectively nonsensical. Still, I don't like to let awareness of my own absurdity get in the way of expressing it. Mum frowned, like she was trying to concentrate. You don't lose your intelligence when you have dementia but it can be harder to express it in the way you're used to. At least that's what the doctor said. I continued anyway.

"She thinks that if we both know when it's ending, no one can get hurt." I ran my finger around the rim of the teacup, not really expecting a response. "That was the worst thing about Hannah dumping me, Mum. I never saw it coming. Do you think this could work or is it a terrible idea?"

I wasn't really expecting a response but Mum stroked my cheek with her hand.

"You have to do what makes you happy, Claire," she said. "You always look so sad."

Tears sprang into my eyes and I blinked fast. My aunt Claire isn't my mum's biological sister. No worries for her about inheriting the dementia. She doesn't visit much and I hate her for it, but in a way, I'm glad that Mum thinks I'm her. At least she doesn't know how many people have left her behind. She can't miss *me* – she doesn't know who I am. But she might miss Claire if she didn't come around.

This way at least I can make her happy.

9

So, the breakup. Obviously, you want to know. The way you want to gawk at any terrible accident to see where the blood and guts are spilling out of. After visiting Mum I couldn't stop thinking about it. I thought about it the whole walk home, so when I looked up and found myself back in my bedroom, I didn't really remember getting there. I do my best not to dwell on it any more. See, for months after it happened I played it over and over in my head so many times, like I was a camera operator looking down on the whole sorry cliché, cringing for the girl in the café who had no idea what was coming. Let's look at it again, shall we?

There I am, sitting across the table from Hannah. It's a cute café with gingham tablecloths and twee pictures on the wall that say things like *Baking: where the fondant stop*. All I'm thinking about his how pretty she is. I don't realise she's about to ruin my life. I'm noticing the adorable way her glasses sit on her round cheeks so that when she talks they kind of bounce up and down. I totally miss the tone of the conversation. I'm also really into the caramel cake I've just stuck a fork into.

"You're my favourite person, Saoirse. You're so generous and funny and sweet and I love those things about you, but . . ." Hannah says, and I smile. How did I miss it? This is the start of every breakup scene in history.

"I love you too." I stand up and lean across the table to kiss her. In a coffee shop. This is not something I would have done two years ago when I was a baby gay who thought everyone was looking at me.

She turns her head so my lips graze her cheek, leaving a smear of peppermint lip balm on her skin. That's when the word *but* travels to me from ten seconds ago and registers in my brain.

I sit back down. At least there's that – that the rest of the breakup doesn't happen with me in a half-hovering position, my butt sticking out in the air. My face freezes, blank, empty. But as the camera zooms in, you can see a hint of fear.

Our eyes meet. When you're with someone there's a secret kind of look that passes between you that you take for granted. Something in their eyes that tells you that they are home for you.

It wasn't there any more.

Later I'd wonder if it had been gone for weeks or months and I hadn't noticed.

"What's wrong?" I say.

I'd never been broken up with before but the scene was so familiar that I knew my lines. Do scenes like this happen so often in real life that they end up in the movies, or are the movies giving us a convenient script for inconvenient conversations?

"I'm sorry." Her chin trembles. "I don't want to be in a relationship with you any more."

The fact that she's close to crying freaks me out more than anything. You might think that's totally normal behaviour but Hannah is levelheaded and logical to the point of coming across kind of cold if you don't know her. She isn't often overcome by emotion. Or at least she doesn't express it the same way as most people.

If you look close now you will see a minute shift in my expression from blankness to utter devastation. It's all in the eyes. That's the moment when everything I'd planned went up in smoke. Back then I really, truly bought into the dream that we would be the one in a million first love that lasts forever.

"But why?"

This question makes me cringe. But at the time I had to ask. I loved her so much and I was so happy I couldn't understand what she meant. Even now when I think about it I have to shield myself from the answer.

"I love you. But I'm not in love with you."

It's such a cliché I didn't even really know what it meant. How was in love different from love?

"I want us to still be friends, but I understand it might take some time."

This was my big chance to play it cool and salvage some dignity.

"But I love you," I whined instead. "I think you're the best person I've literally ever met and I'm going to die if you leave me."

Don't say a word. I already know.

"Saoirse," she said, and she squeezed my hand on the table. It felt familiar and alien at the same time. "You'll be OK. I promise."

"Why now? What changed?"

This was a mistake. Hannah is unflinchingly honest. This is when I learned not to ask a question you might not really want the answer to.

"I don't know what changed. I've been thinking about it for a while. I was hoping that a time might come where things in your life would be calmer. I didn't want to hurt you when things were already so bad, but it's starting to feel like I'm lying to you and I don't want to do that."

The *things in my life* she's talking about are my mum having to go into a home, my dad having an affair, and the icing on the cake of shit: Surprise! You might end up with dementia too. A thought enters my mind, and once it does, it stays lodged there. This is exactly why she's breaking up with me. There is no future with me. If my dad had known my mum might end up like she has, I'm certain he would have bolted early too. It must mean she never really loved me, like Dad must never have really loved Mum. It's the end of the world. It's a pain I can physically feel.

Little old ladies at the next table lean conspicuously in our direction. Hannah stands and takes a tenner out of her purse, then puts it on the table. I am confused for a moment until I realise she is paying for the cake.

"You're my best friend," she says, looking at her feet. "I think we can still have that. If you want to."

I look at her. She's biting her lip. I don't know what to say. Whatever she says about wanting to be friends, it's still something she's willing to risk giving up to get out of our relationship.

She leaves the coffee shop. My eyes follow her involuntarily. I let my head fall into my hands, but my elbow slips and I accidentally flip the plate with the cake on it over the table, where it clatters against the floor, rattling the way a penny does when you spin it and it slowly stops. The cake slides across the café, leaving a long streak of caramel frosting on the tiles like a skidmark.

One of the little old ladies reaches out and pats me on the knee.

"It gets better, dear."

Later I found out Izzy had known for ages. Naturally, because life is just one humiliation after another, she didn't tell me that until I'd spent a month talking about it nonstop. Dissecting every tiny moment. Wondering out loud if there was some way Hannah would change her mind. Love didn't just disappear, did it? Mine didn't. It wasn't some light I could switch on and off. It was something that had grown inside me, its roots tangled around all the organs of my body. I needed it to live. For a long time, I hoped. Eventually, I stopped. Hoping, I mean. I didn't like to think about whether or not I could ever stop loving Hannah. I learned not to examine those feelings. Which is why I didn't ever want to see her again. I had to pretend she didn't exist. Izzy too. They were too inextricably linked.

People say you can't change the past, but it isn't true.

Dad had put Mum in a home. He promised he would never do that. He promised he would always take care of her. But he didn't, and that changed everything that had gone before, making old memories bitter instead of sweet. It was the same for me and Hannah. Everything we once had was tainted. It was all rotten.

Lying back on my bed, staring at the roof, unable to stop beating myself up for being so naive and stupid, I realised what I needed were new rules. I may have gently exploited the loophole in my relationship rule – oh, and the bit about not kissing actual lesbians or bi girls because it leads to loopholes, obviously – but that's why I needed a safety net. A way of protecting myself from getting my heart splattered again. If any of these things happened it would be time to pull the plug on this little experiment with Ruby. I took out my phone and made a note of the five horsemen of the apocalypse: the deal breakers, the harbingers of doom.

1. No acting like a sap. So if I catch myself gazing longingly and thinking things like *she's the most beautiful girl in the world*, I'm in trouble.
2. No we-ing. As in *we love this, we are cat people, we are going to live happily ever after.*
3. No daydreaming. Fantasies about a future we're not going to have is a major red flag.
4. Absolutely no serious conversations. That means conversations about Mum or not wanting to go to Oxford or my complicated feeeelings about things like Dad or the wedding.
5. No fighting and especially no making up. Fighting about stuff implies you have some kind of investment. Making up after a fight is protecting that investment.

I vowed to myself that I would not break any of these sacred edicts. No excuses, no exceptions.

I know, I know, I might as well be in a horror movie saying "I'll be right back".

10

The Ferris wheel on the promenade loomed overhead, and trilling bells merged with the pop songs playing on each ride. I shifted from one foot to the other, waiting on Ruby, wondering if I should buy us both tickets or if we were meant to split it. Hannah and I tended to just work off who had the best cash flow in the moment. How did dating work when you hadn't known the person practically your whole life? No one prepared me for this. I bought the tickets just so I could stop wondering about who was supposed to buy the tickets.

I spotted Ruby long before she saw me. She was wearing a pair of cropped colourful harem pants with a blue cropped tank top that had colourful embroidery around the neckline, and she'd paired this ensemble with tan ankle boots. An inch of squishy stomach peeked out and she looked cute and bohemian and I wanted to run up and kiss her. I didn't. I ducked out of sight before she could see me, to avoid the awkward walk where you see each other but you're too far apart to wave or say hello. I waited until she approached the kiosk, then snuck up and tapped her on the shoulder. She started but smiled when she saw me.

"Hi." She waved even though she was a foot away from me.

"Hi." I waved back. "Is this weird?"

"A little." She nodded. "But we'll get over it."

I snuck a glance at her a couple of times as we made our way through the throng at the entrance, which made me bump into the same middle-aged man twice. For the first time in my life, I had no idea what to say. We queued for drinks and I racked my brain for conversation starters but came up empty. I bought a half litre of Coke, because it was boiling out, and I gulped it down in one go. The heat wave hadn't abated, even though historically, it usually ended as soon as the exam season was over.

Sipping on Coke felt like a shield from having nothing to say. I'd never needed to make first-date conversation before. Hannah and I had been best friends for ten years before we went on a "date". Our friendship and our relationship were so blurry and melted together. Another reason why we could never have been friends after. How would us going to the cinema as friends have felt any different than going as girlfriends?

Then, like she was an evil spirit in a horror film, thinking about Hannah summoned her into existence. Her glossy black hair next to Izzy's blonde curls bobbing towards us, through a sea of people, like if Jaws was your ex-girlfriend.

I felt my heart thud against my chest. It was trying to

108

escape. I looked frantically around at where we could go that I wouldn't bump into her. To the left of us, a queue for candyfloss. Behind us was the exit and ahead was the ghost train – and to the right, the Ferris wheel.

Hannah was getting closer and even though there were a ton of people between us there was no way she wouldn't spot me. I swear there's something in your body that just changes when you know someone that well. They can't sneak up on you. Somehow out of the corner of your eye you'll see a familiar gesture, catch a word over the noise, and you'll know before you even see them that they're there.

I tapped Ruby's shoulder. "Ferris wheel?"

"Definitely," she said, and rubbed her hands together. "I've never actually been on one before."

Ferris wheels are interminably boring. Hannah would never go on one. She was terrified because you weren't strapped in by anything. She always said there was nothing to stop you from just opening the little door and walking right out. I never bothered to point out that, barring evil spirit possession, her body wasn't simply going to betray her by deciding to leave of its own accord. I actually would have preferred the ghost train, but it was riskier. Hannah and Izzy might go on it too, and getting stuck with them in the carriage behind us would be horrendous. In fact, a whole ex-girlfriend-themed ghost train sounded genuinely terrifying. You'd get in and instead of a mummy mannequin covered in toilet roll popping out, it's her and you look down and you're wearing a baggy old jumper with a stain on the front. You turn the corner and you find yourself being forced to scroll through her Instagram and there are replies from a girl with tattoos and she looks like the celebrity your ex fancies most. Right at the end, they play a video on a loop that's just screenshots of all the pathetic texts you sent when you were too heartbroken to have any dignity.

Of course, the question is why you'd pay money for that kind of trauma when life will serve it up to you free of charge.

"How have you never been on a Ferris wheel?" I asked, distracted and glancing over my shoulder. Not six feet away, Izzy and Hannah were queuing at the candyfloss stand. Definitely Izzy's choice; she was the one with a sweet tooth. If I turned back now there was no way they wouldn't see me. I whipped my head round again and pretended I'd heard everything Ruby had said.

"—didn't really go to places like funfairs and the beach when I was growing up."

I imagined they went on more exciting trips to Monaco or Aspen or wherever it was that rich people took their kids on holidays.

"Well, you're just going to have to slum it for today," I joked.

"That's not what I meant—"

"I'm only messing with you," I said, nudging her.

I felt the faint call of the half litre fizzy drink I'd

downed telling me I'd need to find a bathroom as soon as we got off this ride. I wrinkled my nose at the thought of a carnival bathroom in the middle of the baking afternoon. It could wait until the coast was clear.

We squeezed into one side of the cart beside each other and somehow, in spite of the fact that we'd previously achieved groping level two, I felt a silly thrill at having my leg touching hers. Our hands rested on our respective thighs but they grazed each other in a way that made me super aware of having arms. What had I done with them my whole life up to now? Were my arms weird when I was with Hannah too? I couldn't remember.

The Ferris wheel cranked along, letting other couples embark. Ruby breathed in the popcorn-scented air and smiled at me.

"This was a good idea. Definitely the kind of thing you'd find in a falling in love montage. We'll have to do the roller coaster too, and get our pictures. And possibly win each other a stuffed toy."

"The roller coaster here gives off the distinct aura of taking your life into your own hands, but I hear life-threatening circumstances bring people together, so why not?"

At the top of the wheel, the ride paused, and we looked out on the view. The sea stretched out for miles on one side and on the other, you could see the town fading into countryside. Ruby reached out and held my hand and I felt myself relax a little.

"Tell me something about yourself," I said. "How is it that you have the reflexes of a cat?"

She laughed and I felt a warm glow. I loved making her laugh. She had a pretty laugh and somehow it also had an English accent.

"I did gymnastics for years."

"But not any more?"

"Things got too busy at home. To be honest, Mum started to forget about my lessons because she had so much on and I didn't want to bother her. It was probably six months before she realised I hadn't been going. I told her I didn't want to go back anyway. I didn't want her to feel bad."

My heart ached for little Ruby. She must have been one of those kids whose parents were so high-powered and ambitious that they kind of forgot they even had a kid. It sort of made sense that they were off on holiday without her now. I opened my mouth to tell her that I knew what it was like to have a mum who couldn't always be there for you. Even if my mum would want to be if she could. Then with a jolt, I caught myself. How had I let my guard down so easily? I'd only just set new rules for myself and there I was about to break them immediately and invite doom right into my life. I would need to be a lot more careful than that. I could practically see her bleeding-heart reaction if I'd said what I'd been thinking. She'd feel so sorry for me. I felt sorry for her and I wasn't even the type to get on that way.

"The important thing is, can you still do a cartwheel?"

Ruby blinked, probably expecting a different response. I buried my guilt as she buried her surprise.

"Actually I can," she said, recovering quickly and grinning at me. "And a backflip. And if you're lucky I'll show you how I can put my legs—"

The Ferris wheel started again with a lurch, bringing us towards the ground, and near a toilet. Then a groan, a creak, and a screech of metal on metal. The wheel shuddered to a halt and a girl in the next cart screamed.

I mean, of course the Ferris wheel broke down. When you gamble on living the rom-com life, sometimes you're going to get to kiss the pretty girl and sometimes you're going to face abject humiliation for comic effect.

A terrible feeling took hold of my body and I clenched every muscle.

"Are we . . . stuck?" Ruby leaned over the edge of the cart, her head practically hanging off the side, and trailed off as panicked yelling reached our ears. One man screamed "I'm going to sue you!" and a child who was far, far too old for it started bawling loudly.

This was bad. Very, very bad. I looked around as if somehow the answer to my most pressing problem would appear out of thin air.

When Ruby's head reentered the cart, she was beaming.

"This is so perfect," she said, laughing, giddy with the thrill of it. Then she noticed my expression.

"Saoirse, what's wrong? We're totally safe."

I shook my foot furiously and rubbed my thumb into the scar on the palm of my hand.

"How long do you think it will take to get going?" I squeezed the words out.

"I don't know, but we're going to be OK. Are you afraid of heights or something?" she said, her forehead crinkled in concern.

I hesitated. Then I nodded.

"Yep. Super scared of heights. That's me. I get like two feet high in the air and I'm all, *Oh no I'm going to die.*"

I peered out the edge of the cart to see if anyone was doing anything about this disaster.

"Don't look down," Ruby said, rubbing the back of my neck in a way that was meant to be comforting but sent shivers through my body. It was a confusing mix of sensations.

"It's going to be fine," she said in a soothing voice, "I promise."

I nodded, unable to say anything. The terrible feeling got stronger.

She stopped rubbing abruptly.

"Why did you suggest the Ferris wheel if you're afraid of heights?"

"Um . . ."

"And the night we met you climbed an eight-foot wall."

"I was trying to impress you?" I said hopefully.

She raised an eyebrow and waited. Damnit, that was so cool.

"OK, fine," I burst out, "I'm not afraid of heights."

"Well, what is it, then?" she said, leaning back in her seat. I'd preferred it when she was being sympathetic.

I closed my eyes dramatically and paused before taking a deep breath.

"I'm afraid I'm going to wet myself. I drank half a litre of Coke and I am fucking dying to pee, all right?" I said it all as quickly as possible, as though somehow the embarrassment would be over quicker.

Ruby burst out laughing.

"Why are you laughing?" I demanded. "This is a real danger here!" My voice was getting more panicked and out of control now that my secret was out there. "Like if we were on a roller coaster and it stopped suddenly, sure, we could be flung to our death or be mangled or something, but that would be a tragic accident. What's going to happen to me? I'm going to wet myself and the girl I like is going to be right next to me. Not even in the same room. In the same two square feet. Oh God, what if my pee gets on you? What if when we finally get down, we open the door and a wave of pee just crashes out."

Ruby was doubled over with laughter at this point, but she made the effort to sit up straight, then wiped her eyes with her hand.

She took my hand in hers. "We are going to get through

this, I promise. You are not going to wet yourself. You're a fully grown human and you have control over your own bladder. It only seems so bad because you're focusing on it."

"How can I not focus on it? Trust me, my body is demanding I focus on it."

She bit her lip. A stray giggle escaped. "I'm sorry, I shouldn't laugh. This is all my fault really."

"How is it your fault?"

"I should have warned you."

"How could you know I'd drink my body weight in fizzy drinks and get trapped in a confined space?"

"Oh, come on," she said, like it was obvious. "In a rom-com, the couple always get trapped in a confined space. If they go into a supply closet, the door *will* lock from the outside. If they get on an elevator, the elevator *will* get stuck. And if they go on a Ferris wheel, it *will* break down. I can't blame you, you don't really know enough about these films."

"Well then yeah, you should have warned me. I'd have made an emergency backpack with snacks or something. A map, a first aid kit, and one of those enormous satellite phones for when our phones inevitably lose signal."

There was a surprising amount of overlap between cute rom-com disaster scenes and your average horror movie disaster. Of course in rom-coms there is only sexual tension; in horror there's a knife-wielding serial killer, so the tone is subtly different, you know?

"Ah, I get it now," Ruby said sagely. "You're the uptight one and I'm the carefree spirit who has to teach you how to loosen up, chill out, break the rules."

"Excuse me? I'm the one who scaled a wall and bought you a star. I'm obviously the carefree one," I said, although the bit about breaking the rules was a little close for comfort. I didn't have rules because I was uptight. I had them because I was afraid of what I might do without them. That's not being a control freak.

It's not.

"As the truly carefree one, I'm going to let you have that," Ruby said, with a wink that woke the wobble from its nap at a most inconvenient moment. I didn't know anyone could wink and not come off cheesy but she managed it. I wondered if I could do it. I'd have to practise in the mirror later.

"I'm just going to say it," Ruby said, while I was contemplating that the very act of practising winking did indeed make me the uptight one. "We agreed we were going to do one trial date and I think this is a resounding success."

I made a point of peering out of the cart to the earth, far far away, and back at Ruby.

"What you mean because we got stuck up here that's not a success? I told you, if you watched more rom-coms you would have seen it coming."

"I'm kidding," I said. "I actually am having a good time. You know, aside from the desperate need to pee while trapped in the air." Weirdly it was true. Somehow, I would have rather been stuck in a bathroom emergency with her than basically anywhere else without her.

Ruby scrunched her face up in a show of sympathy. "Let's distract you, then. If we're agreed on continuing with the montage, let's think of other things we can do."

"I'm relying on your expertise here," I said, opening a note file on my phone. "We've done the funfair. What else have you got?"

Ruby flipped her hair over, thinking.

"Frolicking?" she offered finally, her tongue absently toying with her lip ring.

I cleared my throat, thinking of how to respond to a word I'd never heard anyone use in real life.

"Frolicking?" I said. "You just made that up."

"No, I didn't. It's where the couple engage in scene of playful . . . frolicking."

I raised both eyebrows (because I can't do one at a time). "I'm gonna need an example. This sounds dubious."

"*10 Things I Hate About You*," she said immediately. "The scene at the paintball place."

"I haven't seen it." I shrugged.

Ruby's eyes bugged.

"I know you said you weren't into rom-coms, but that's just weird. OK – if I have to supply all the ideas, then you have to actually watch the films they come from. We'll add them to the list. Maybe you won't be so surprised next time

118

something obvious happens, like a Ferris wheel breaking down."

She looked giddy at the idea that I would have to sit and watch all her favourite movies, and I had to admit I wanted to see the smile on her face when I agreed.

"Oh all right then," I agreed.

She beamed. There it was.

"Oh, I know what's next. Meaningful eye contact."

"Frolicking and eye contact?" I shook my head but I typed it anyway.

"There is always *serious* meaningful eye contact in a montage. That's how you know there's sexual tension," she explained.

"I mean, you're not wrong, but it's not really a date. We can do that anytime."

"Exactly. We should do it now. Check it off nice and quick." She had a look on her face that I was beginning to classify as her "mischief" face. She had it when we jumped off the wall. She had it when she invited me up to her room. In fairness, it had brought me pretty good things so far.

"You want to have meaningful eye contact with me now?"

"Sure."

"Shouldn't it be, I dunno, more natural?"

"You're OK with a list of dates and a prearranged breakup but we can't schedule meaningful eye contact?"

"No, no, you're right." I held up my hands in surrender.

"Now remember, you're going to have to hold the eye contact for at least ten seconds," she said.

"This is silly. I can't keep a straight face and do this."

"You must. Now, we're chatting normally, looking around everywhere." Ruby glanced around. She waved casually to no one because we were two hundred feet in the air. "Casual glancing, just chatting, rhubarb, rhubarb," Ruby said, looking anywhere but directly at me.

"Hold on, rhubarb?" I interrupted.

"Yeah, that's what background actors say when they're supposed to be talking. Don't you know anything?"

I shrug. "Rhubarb rhubarb."

"Casual discussion, rhubarb, rhubarb. OK, now eye contact in

three

two

one."

Ruby locked eyes with me and I struggled not to crumple into giggles. Biting the inside of my cheek, I focused my eyes on hers and counted down the seconds.

10 This is so silly.

9   I'm going to laugh. I am going to laugh.

8   Bite your lip if you have to.

7   Focus on the eyes. Take a deep breath. That blue freckle is so cute.

6   Ruby's eyes are flecked with green. They're really more hazel than brown.
5   How come it's so quiet all of a sudden?
4   Is that my heart pounding in my ears?
3   It isn't funny any more.
2   This is too intense.
1   Don't look away.

Her eyes closed and mine did too. I felt her breath on my lips. Her lips touched mine, but barely. That's all it took to send signals firing to the rest of my body. I pressed my lips against hers more firmly and her lips parted, her tongue soft and breath sweet. One of her hands moved to my hips, the other hand moved to my face and cupped it. No one had ever done that before. There was something so gentle about it.

Then she pulled away and the rest of the world rushed back in like someone had turned up the sound and turned on the lights again. The wheel cranked to life with a crunching sound. We started our descent back to solid ground and I crossed my legs as I suddenly remembered how badly I needed the loo.

11

1. ~~Funfair date~~ (as seen in *Never Been Kissed*; *Love, Simon*). I was one date in and already two movies behind, so we agreed I would watch at least one film for each date. Ruby was convinced that once I got into it I'd watch them all of my own accord anyway. I remained sceptical.

   a ~~Meaningful eye contact.~~ I talked Ruby into making this an addendum to part one. It wasn't a date per se so it couldn't get its own category and by extension she couldn't add any more movies to the list.

2. **One person teaches the other a skill** (as seen in *Say Anything . . .* , *Imagine Me & You*). Slightly concerning as I don't have any discernible skills, but maybe Ruby was hiding a talent for tennis or pottery. One of those ones where she'd have to get up close and personal to guide me.

3. **Karaoke.** Where one or both people reveal their hidden singing talent or lack thereof (as seen in *My Best Friend's Wedding*, *500 Days of Summer*) I protested this one vehemently, pointing out we'd already done karaoke. Ruby insisted that I hadn't sung so it didn't count.

I privately decided I'd work on convincing her to replace this with something less horrifying.

4. **Frolicking** (as seen in all of them, apparently). I was still unconvinced by this but Ruby's insistence that it would be found in any rom-com gave me a sound argument for not adding any more specific movies to my watch list.

5. **Performing a synchronised dance routine** (as seen in *13 Going on 30, Easter Parade*). I was starting to feel as though I needed to be a West End star just to get through this summer with my dignity intact.

6. **Movie night** (as seen in *To All the Boys I've Loved Before, Notting Hill*). Obviously this should be replete with the tension of imminent kissing in the air.

7. **Passionate kissing in the rain** (as seen in *Four Weddings and a Funeral, Breakfast at Tiffany's*). OK, I was totally on board for this one.

8. **Date on a rowboat** (as seen in *The Proposal, 10 Things I Hate About You*). I did not fancy my chances rowing. My arms got tired when I was blow-drying my hair.

9. **Having one of those "No, you hang up" conversations on the phone** (as seen in *The Truth About Cats & Dogs, Pillow Talk*). She really had to dig into the vault for this one.

10. **The slow dance** (as seen in *The Gay Divorcee, When Harry Met Sally . . .*). Ruby explained that this was different from the dance routine, which was meant to

be fun and playful. The slow dance was romantic and passionate. They were both bloody dances as far as I was concerned but I let it slide nonetheless. Call me a hopeless romantic.

After the funfair date, I felt giddy and bouncing off the walls with energy. I went home and it hit me that there was no one to tell. Briefly, I wondered what it would be like to tell Izzy. We used to talk a lot about me and Hannah, especially when we first started going out. She never made it weird that we were all friends and suddenly the two of us had coupled off. Part of me wanted to call her and tell her. I knew that if I did, we could fall right back into our friendship. If I let that happen. But I couldn't.

I told myself I was only thinking of her because there was no one else. I certainly didn't want to tell Dad, and although I had told Mum, it isn't the same when she doesn't really get what it means. I wondered how she'd react if she was well and she knew I was with someone other than Hannah. But then, if she was well, maybe I would still be with Hannah.

I let myself splash around in those thoughts for approximately ten minutes and then I locked them in a box and put them away. I was afraid that if I let them out for too long, they'd take over.

Instead of wallowing, I bought *Never Been Kissed* on demand to start my rom-com journey. It's not like I was looking forward to watching this mindless fluff, you understand. It was research. Necessary research. And if the candy colours, glossy cinematography, and happy endings seemed kind of refreshing for a change, well, that could be my little secret. I texted Ruby to let her know what I was doing and she sent me back a GIF of a cat cheering. It had become apparent to me over the last few days that cat GIFs were her main form of text communication; she had one for every occasion.

I was arranging my pillows for optimal comfort when Dad rapped on the doorway. He came in without waiting for an invitation. Of course.

"What's going on here?" He frowned at the screen, which showed a candy-coloured Drew Barrymore.

"Um . . ."

"Are you watching a rom-com?" he said, incredulous.

"No. Maybe. So what if I am? I thought you were going out."

He was meeting Beth to pick gifts for the bridal party. Not entirely sure why you have to buy other people presents on your wedding day just because they held a ring or stood behind you in a dress but whatever. Come to think of it why do you have to buy the bride and groom a present either? It's already "the happiest day of your life" isn't it? Is that not enough?

"I am, but don't change the subject. I'm pretty sure you've described them as 'sexist schlock' before. I remember

125

because I'd never heard a person say the word *schlock* in real life."

"Whatever. Like horror isn't totally sexist? Oh, here, why don't I stab all these women with my phallic weapon while they run around in tank tops with their nipples showing."

"Please don't say nipples in front of your father." Dad shuddered.

"Yeah, I regretted it as soon as it was out."

"Let's move past it."

I waited for him to say whatever he'd come up to say. He fiddled with a necklace on my dresser instead of looking at me.

"You could come with us?" Dad said hopefully.

I plumped up a pillow and nestled it behind my head.

"I'm kind of swamped here."

"I really want you to get to know Beth better. You have to get involved somehow."

"Do I, though?" I mused.

I knew this wasn't the only reason he'd come up, though, to convince me to go and do wedding stuff. He had to know that was a lost cause. There was something else.

"I got an offer on the house," he said eventually. I felt the wind knocked out of me. The house had only been on the market two days. Only one person had been to see it that I knew of. We didn't even have one of those signs from the estate agent yet.

"We're not in any hurry. I put an offer on the flat and it was accepted, but it'll be a while yet before everything's sorted. We have until August."

My dad, who had decided to get engaged and set the wedding date less than three months away, absolutely had a warped sense of what was and was not a rush.

He waited, perhaps for me to say something that would let him off the hook so he didn't have to feel guilty.

"I hate this," I said.

He really didn't know me at all.

For a minute it looked like he was going to say he was sorry but instead, he tapped the dresser a couple of times, sighed, and left. Pathetic.

I sat on the bed and stewed for a few minutes, listening to Dad tramp down the stairs and out the front door. I hadn't lived in this house my whole life, but most of it, and I couldn't remember the parts from before. I'd known I'd have to leave sooner rather than later; I was the one who'd made those applications to a university in another country, without a second thought of staying home. Back then I'd thought this place would still be here when I needed it. Instead of moving on, it felt like everything behind me was being wiped out, as though I had conjured it into being and when I wasn't looking it all disappeared.

The doorbell rang and I groaned because I was the only one home to answer it. Whoever it was, they weren't invited.

Part of me hoped it would be Jehovah's Witnesses. I'd run off and join them. Give up this life and focus on . . . I had no idea what their craic was.

"Oh Jesus," I said when I opened the door. "What do you want?"

Oliver rolled his eyes and threw my top at me. I didn't quite catch it and I had to peel it off my face.

"It was in with our dry cleaning," he said. "Some people would say thank you."

"Some people would burn this just because you touched it," I said, but I threw it on the back of a chair instead.

"Are you going to invite me in or what?" he said, looking over my shoulder into the house. "I want to see how the less fortunate live."

"Everyone is 'the less fortunate' to you," I said, but I let him in.

He took in the cluttered, cosy living room I'd grown up in, with its knickknacks and colourful throws everywhere.

"So they live in chaos." He ran a finger along the back of the sofa and pretended to inspect it for dust. "How sad."

"Weak."

"Whatever. What are you up to anyway?" He looked around the room as though it would give him a clue.

"I *was* watching a film, and I'd like to get back to it," I said.

"I could watch a film," he said. "If you made me a cup of tea or something."

I thought about booting him out, but something about him coming around with my top in the middle of the day, in the middle of the summer holidays, made me feel like I'd be kicking a puppy. An obnoxious puppy who would pee on your bed and chew on your shoes. Or maybe refuse to chew on your shoes until you bought expensive designer ones.

I made us two cups of tea while Oliver inspected each of the cupboards until he found a packet of biscuits. I stared in disbelief.

"Are you forgetting how much vodka you've stolen from me?"

"Oh yeah." I had forgotten, actually. "Here, hold these a second," I said, giving him both cups of tea. He held one in each hand and the packet of biscuits in his teeth.

"Good boy." I patted him on the head and gestured for him to come upstairs. He tried to complain when he realised I was making fun of him but he had the packet of biscuits clenched between his teeth so all he could do was let out a muffled protest and follow me.

After setting the tea down on the windowsill, Oliver jumped backwards onto the bed and made himself all cosy in my pillow nook.

"What are we watching? I have to tell you I'm not interested in your sex tape."

With great effort, I pulled a pillow out from behind his back and hit him with it before settling on the bed myself.

"Tea, please, pervert." I held my hand out.

"I said I'm *not* interested and you think that's perverted? You sure think a lot of yourself."

"Do you ever give over?" I sighed. "We're watching *Never Been Kissed*."

"Ah, your biopic."

"I thought I was slutty? You can't have it both ways."

"Sure I can," he said, tearing into the biscuits. "I see an opportunity and I go for it." He stuffed a biscuit in his mouth and got crumbs all over my bed. Was this what being straight was like? A boy in your bedroom making a mess? Not for the first time, I thanked God I was a lesbian.

An hour and a half later we had completely demolished the biscuits and the premise of the film.

"Like, come on. Just because he knows now that she's not a student does not make it OK that he was into a student, right?" I said, incredulous.

"Probably not. I mean, he must have been going home at night, to his adult girlfriend, thinking, *I fancy my student.* That's not normal."

"Exactly, and then he has the cheek to be mad at her?"

"Let's not gloss past the fact that her adult brother is bucking a different student."

"Oh wait. Look. She's waiting for him now on the pitch. I wonder if he'll come and kiss her?" I said sarcastically, pretending to hide behind my hands.

"The suspense is killing me."

"I'd be so impressed with this film if he doesn't turn up at the end, she goes home, and a couple of weeks later she starts going out with a guy who doesn't get a hard-on looking at students in period costume."

The guy ran out onto the pitch and we both booed the screen loudly.

When it was over, Oliver sprawled out on my bed.

"That was terrible. Did Ruby tell you to watch it?"

"Why? What do you mean?" I said. Did he know? I'd die if Oliver knew about the falling in love montage. I'd never hear the end of it.

"She's really into these. I've seen her sing along to *My Best Friend's Wedding* at least twice already this summer and she's only been here a few weeks."

"She mentioned it. I thought I'd check it out."

"What's the craic with you two anyway?" he said, but so casually it sounded distinctly uncasual.

"Are you asking if my intentions are honourable?" I joked.

"I'm not expecting miracles," he said. "Just, you know, what's the craic?"

"I like her," I said lightly. But I felt my cheeks betray me by heating up. "It's not serious, though. It's fun. Summer fling. You know."

"Sure," he said, drawing the word out slowly, as though he was giving himself time to think of his next words.

"I think that's good. She's had a tough time. She needs something fun, I think."

I thought about the panicky sound of her voice when she got that call from her mum. The weird thing she'd said about her having to stop her gymnastics lessons. The fact that her family had abandoned her here to begin with.

"What do you mean she's had a tough time?"

Oliver narrowed his eyes. He opened his mouth to speak and then he closed it again.

"Ask her yourself; it's not a secret."

"If it's not a secret, then tell me."

"No. It's her business, not mine."

"*Now* you have ethics?"

"What's the big deal? I mean, I'm surprised you don't already know. Haven't you asked her why she's staying with us? Or do you two not talk a whole lot?" He waggled his eyebrows.

"Nope," I said. "It's all the nonstop scissoring. It really requires too much concentration to talk."

I was dying to know but talking about family stuff was one of the harbingers of doom. I mean, it would be fine if Oliver told me – that was like a loophole – but if I asked Ruby then I'd be breaking a sacred vow (no, that's not an exaggeration), and what if she started asking about *my* family?

"You wouldn't tell her about my stuff would you?"

I said. I'd never talked to Oliver about my mum but everyone at school knew anyway. It's a small town.

"Watch you don't trip over your own hypocrisy," he said. "But no. That's your business."

Maybe his ethics weren't so terrible.

"She likes you too, by the way. I can tell," Oliver added.

I looked back at the screen and bit the inside of my cheek so he wouldn't see me smile. The *films you might like* list on the screen looked a lot like Ruby's movie list for the montage.

"*The Proposal*?" I asked.

"I thought you'd never ask."

I pressed play and I decided to ignore the terrifying thought that crossed my mind: it was kind of nice having Oliver to talk to.

12

I quickly developed a routine. After my visit with Mum in the morning, I'd either watch montage movies or hang out with Ruby in the afternoon. We decided to do at least one official montage thing every week, but in between, we went for coffee, got ice cream on the pier, or walked along the strand, dipping our toes into the water. Ruby stopped to pet every dog we saw. It was kind of sweet. Every time Dad asked me to do something for the wedding, I shrugged super apologetically and said I had plans with Ruby. I wasn't going to pretend to have a vested interest in floral arrangements, the band vs DJ debate, or party favours (personalised mini bottles of artisanal gin – have you guessed my dad is a massive hipster yet?). Though I did helpfully suggest bottles of "fairy dust" for the children, which was a miniature corked bottle full of glitter.

They loved that.

They did not think ahead.

You see, there's an evil little imp that lives inside me that rubbed its hands together in glee, imagining Dad and Beth trying to siphon iridescent glitter into tiny jars. They'd be covered in the stuff for weeks.

It's the little things that make life worth living, you know?

I tried not to, but I couldn't help comparing being with Ruby to being with Hannah. Hannah knew everything about me and although that sounds good in theory, in practice it meant there was no getting away from the mundane, crappy parts of life. We talked so often about Mum and her diagnosis and how I felt about possibly ending up like her. No wonder we never had sex. It was better this way. Even if sometimes I wanted to tell Ruby something real, I wouldn't break my new rules; that would be like waving at the apocalypse and saying, sure, come on in, would you like some tea? Even the day Mum said my name. It was small and stupid because she'd forgotten again a few minutes later, but I had desperately wanted to tell someone who would know what it meant to me and there wasn't anyone left in my life who would understand. But it was better this way.

I said that already, didn't I?

Unfortunately, by the time we'd reached week three of me skipping out on everything wedding related, Dad started taking bookings for the Rob Clarke Guilt Trip Express and buying a ticket was not optional. So I agreed to the onerous task of cake tasting.

I mean, OK, there were worse things to have to do. I *had* managed to avoid looking at different types of table settings, after all, but it annoyed me that he was trying to make me be a part of this. Like he decided to "forget" the fact that I did not exactly give my blessing to this unholy union and if I ate enough vanilla butter icing then maybe I'd forget too. Still, because I'm basically a saint, I agreed to meet him in town. I was sick of looking at his "sad face" whenever I said I was too busy to do things like pick colours for organza chair covers.

The bakery was so painfully hipster I was embarrassed for Dad. He tried way too hard. The walls were subway tiled with botanical drawings as decor and everyone who worked there had a manky beard and a slouchy hat.

"What do you want to try?" Dad said, gazing up in wonder at the chalkboard menu.

"Is there an elderflower and cyanide sponge?" I asked.

"We have elderflower and gin," a beardy man in his twenties said, wiping his hands on his immaculate apron. I did not believe he did any actual baking.

"How fucked up can you get on this gin cake?"

The man frowned.

"Saoirse," Dad warned. "Ignore her. She's seventeen. Hormones or whatever." He smiled apologetically at the man. They shared a "kids these days" kind of laugh.

The shame hit me first. It prickled under my skin, roiled in my stomach. He'd put me in my place so he could buddy up to some guy he didn't even know.

Then came the rage. Me making a harmless joke was embarrassing him, but he wasn't mortified by his arse-kissing attempt to be bros with beardy douche?

Fuck that.

"My dad's marrying someone new after locking my mum up in an old people's home cos she got sick," I said brightly. "New mommy wants to get hammered on the cake so she doesn't have to wonder if he'd do the same thing to her."

Dad pulled me by the sleeve to a table while the man picked his jaw up off the floor.

"What is wrong with you, Saoirse?" Dad hissed.

"I have no impulse control?" I replied, like I really wanted to figure the answer to this question out with him. "No, wait, it's that I don't have any fucks to give? I'm all out of fucks, that's it."

Dad shook his head and looked at the roof. That was his "silent prayer for patience" look. Don't know who he was praying to; if he really wanted help, he should have been looking in the other direction. Only Satan could help him now.

In spite of his shame, he still managed to order a tasting menu of different cakes, including whiskey and ginger, Earl Grey and lavender, and strawberry and thyme. We didn't speak while we waited. I texted back and forth with Ruby, who was spending the day with Jane getting facials. Dad was also glued to his phone. Probably googling to see if he could grow a big enough beard in time for the wedding. When the cakes arrived, it was a different server. I was pretty sure the first guy was afraid of us now.

The cake bites sat between us for a second. Dad put his phone down. Reluctantly I followed suit.

"Do you really see it that way?" he said. He didn't look directly at me.

I shrugged. I waited for him to say that it wasn't like that. To say something that would make it all better. He didn't say anything.

I picked up the cake that looked most normal, a sponge with thick, creamy frosting. Dad took the one that looked more like a sticky loaf of bread with something drizzled all over it. We each took a bite.

I watched Dad's face contort like I was watching my own in a mirror. I snatched a napkin and spat the barely chewed-up bite of cake into it. Dad copied, but he glanced over his shoulder nervously first in case his heroes, the beardy men, were watching.

"Christ alive," I said. "What did yours taste of?"

"Grass?" Dad said, confused. "Yours?"

"Medicine." I looked at the little list of what we'd got. "I think I got aniseed and saffron."

"Do you think they're all this disgusting?" Dad asked, inspecting the platter with a wary expression.

"Yes."

We looked at each other. A silent understanding passed between us. His mouth said, "I can't eat another one of these," but his eyes said, *Your challenge, should you choose to accept it, is to try all of these cakes without boking your ring up.*

"That one," I said, pushing a grey-looking one with purple flowers on top towards him.

He responded by nudging one with green flecks towards me.

Challenge accepted.

13

Saoirse
Why are you in my phone as "Sex God"?

Sex God
Oh yeah. I forgot about that.

Saoirse
I'm changing it to something more appropriate

I added a GIF of a girl rolling her eyes hard.

Satan's Shrivelled Left Nut
Actual footage of the ecstatic sex
face of my many lovers.

I sent a GIF of a girl looking through a magnifying glass.

Saoirse
Actual footage of your date when you
take your clothes off.

Satan's Shrivelled Left Nut
Both can be true, sweet Saoirse. Lower
their expectations then blow their minds.

Saoirse

It's working! I want to blow my mind out right now having this conversation.

Satan's Shrivelled Left Nut

Why are you looking me up anyway?
Can't get enough of my great chat?

Saoirse

I'm watching Love Actually in July. I needed to confess my sins to someone. Have you seen it?

Satan's Shrivelled Left Nut

Of course. Everyone's seen it.

Saoirse

I'm sorry but can we talk about how they keep saying the tea girl has big thighs? I mean 1. big thighs are awesome, 2. inaccurate anyway, 3. why would you need to comment on that? Is Hugh Grant supposed to be dead on because he doesn't mind thighs?

Satan's Shrivelled Left Nut

That counted as woke in 2003.
We've come so far and yet fallen so low at the same time.

Saoirse

Depressing.

Satan's Shrivelled Left Nut
You haven't seen the worst of it yet.

Saoirse
Oh, you have to be talking about the guy with the signs? What is this dude's craic? Imagine turning up to your best mate's house and miming to his wife that you love her on a bunch of handwritten cards. So inappropriate.

Satan's Shrivelled Left Nut
Aye, he could have bust out a bit of calligraphy.

Saoirse
And she kissed him! Cos he's not a creep he's just a sad nice guy, right. Fuck sake.

Satan's Shrivelled Left Nut
Have you got to the bit where Emma Thompson cries?

Saoirse
No?

Saoirse
I just got there.

Satan's Shrivelled Left Nut
You cried, didn't you?

Saoirse
No.

Satan's Shrivelled Left Nut
Come on.

Saoirse
Fine, maybe I welled up a bit.

Satan's Shrivelled Left Nut
You bawled your eyes out.

Saoirse
Shut up.

14

"Dad, come on."

"I don't know. You're a terrible driver." He clutched the keys to his chest.

"Why did you get me insured on your car if I wasn't going to be allowed to drive it?"

"In case of an emergency."

"This is an emergency. I already bought tickets and the Lamborghini is in the shop."

"I don't know if you fully understand the term *emergency*."

"I don't like this any more than you do but needs must." I wrestled the keys from his death grip and dangled them. "I will not drive into a tree or off the pier. No one will die. It's going to be fine."

"I'm not really afraid you're going to *die*. We live in a thirty-kilometre-an-hour zone. I'm more worried you'll rear-end someone and my insurance premium will go through the roof."

"Your concern is touching," I grumbled, but he didn't stop me.

"Don't forget to put your lights on, it's dark," Dad called after me. He really did think I was stupid.

I stalled the car six times on the way to Oliver's but by the time I got there I'd kind of got the hang of it. Ruby was waiting at the gates for me, dressed in a pair of stripy socks and embroidered dungarees with a crop top underneath. I could see a clear six inches of skin in the gap. I didn't know I could be attracted to the side of someone's waist until I met Ruby. I had a black tank top on with black jeans. The ones I hardly ever wore because they were so perfect and they didn't sell them any more so I was afraid to wear them out. We looked like Wednesday Addams and Pippi Longstocking on a date.

I felt silly for thinking it, but part of me was embarrassed picking her up in my dad's car. I didn't know anyone my age, except Oliver, who owned a car because this was not an American TV show, but I felt stupid anyway. It didn't help that the car was old, beige, and had a ding in it from the time I reversed into the corner of the house because I didn't fully get how to use wing mirrors. It's not like I think I have to be rich or that Ruby would think anything of it, but somehow it still feels weird knowing that the person you're with has tons more money than you do.

Ruby kissed me on the cheek when she got into the car and then she looked a bit embarrassed. We were in an uncomfortable phase. We'd had the intense groping stuff early on but somehow things had taken a step backwards since we decided to actually go out on dates. I absolutely wanted to jump on her (with her consent) and smush all our body parts together, but it was easy to feel sexy when we didn't really know each other. Now that we were having actual conversations, including one about me wetting myself, it was like she knew I wasn't a sexy, mysterious stranger – I was an awkward weirdo with commitment issues.

"Are you ready for number six – movie night?" I said the title of the date as though it was the voiceover in a film preview.

"Yep. Not at all terrified," Ruby added.

We decided to skip down to number six when I saw *Scream* was playing at a pop-up drive-in. The list didn't have to be completed in any particular order and this was too perfect to miss. Besides, we agreed I could pick a horror for our film date. I was watching all of her beloved rom-coms and I wanted to share one of my favourites with her.

I may have declined to mention that the following week they were playing *Casablanca*. I'd had to watch it with Hannah and thought it was the most boring film I'd ever seen.

As we drove, Ruby seemed kind of distracted. She kept getting texts and even though I knew it was probably her mum, I felt a flash of curiosity. I didn't really know anything about Ruby's life back home and I was kind of afraid to ask. An innocent question about her friends would naturally lead to questions about mine. Which led to Izzy and Hannah. Which led to pain and feelings and doom. Like the mature human being I am, I tried instead to surreptitiously see who was messaging her. I didn't get a good look.

"Sorry," she said, noticing me glancing over. "I'll put this away in a second, I swear."

"No worries," I replied, like I hadn't even noticed.

Ding. Another message. I craned my neck to see if I could catch a name.

"STOP!" she yelled.

I slammed on the brakes.

A screech.

A horn.

A loud "FUCK YOU."

I stopped only an inch from the car in front of me. I hadn't noticed them braking or the light turning red. My heart was beating so hard I could practically hear it in my ears.

"Are you OK?" I said breathlessly.

Ruby laughed in a relieved sort of way. "I'm fine. We were going fifteen miles an hour. But maybe keep your eyes on the road. It's just my mum."

I blushed, absolutely mortified.

"I wasn't—"

"Don't even try and pretend."

"Sorry," I said, pulling away as the light turned again.

I wanted to ask why her mum was simultaneously so needy and yet didn't call Ruby on her birthday. They seemed to talk a *lot*, but she'd gone on holidays without her daughter. It was bizarre.

Ruby squeezed my thigh and I nearly jumped out of my skin.

"Seeing as we didn't die, I'll forgive you. But creeping on me is not cute."

She didn't really sound mad, which I didn't deserve; I was acting pretty creepy, after all.

"Oh, sure, unless I'm Hugh Grant," I said, name-dropping to show I'd been doing my homework.

She grinned. "*Four Weddings* Hugh or *Notting Hill* Hugh?"

"*Notting Hill*," I said, "I watched it last night. I swear I thought when he turned up on the set, he was going full *Fatal Attraction*. He's got serious stalker vibes."

"No! Don't. They're meant to be together."

"I thought I was meant to be with Chloë Grace Moretz from age thirteen until sixteen, but I didn't follow her to her work."

Ruby laughed, and a little fire glowed inside me.

"But I love the speech," I said.

"I'm just a girl? How come?"

"It's always Hugh or the other White Male Lead who gives the speech, but in *Notting Hill*, the girl gets to do the big speech."

"Hugh has a speech too. Sort of. He has his moment. At the press conference?"

"Yeah, but no one remembers that bit."

We arrived more or less intact and stopped debating the merits of one Hugh versus another Hugh long enough to find a spot and figure out how we were meant to tune into the sound.

The car park filled up quickly and there were a bunch of food vans around the perimeter, so we stocked up on supplies, as though the end of the world might come, and waited for the film to start.

"This is so cool," Ruby said as we tried to arrange drinks, a bucket of popcorn, and an array of sweets you'd normally only see at Willy Wonka's factory, in a three-door Fiat.

"Is it?"

"Yeaaah," she said emphatically. "You'd never be able to do this where I live. The neighbourhood is too built up; no one would use parking spaces for something fun. And look how cosy this is."

She held my hand and squeezed.

The way she crackled with enthusiasm for the little things was contagious.

"It is cosy," I agreed. "Are you warm enough, though?" It had been boiling all day and so neither of us had anything warm with us. A nip had begun to creep in when the sun set.

"I'm a bit cold," she said, so I turned the engine on and let the heat blast.

"It's starting," I said, and turned the radio up. Somehow I actually had managed to tune it in correctly. I felt proud of myself for navigating this primitive technology.

"And you've really never seen *Scream*?" I asked, wrapping a strawberry lace around my finger before popping the perfect coil in my mouth.

"It was made before I was born."

"So were nearly all the films on your list for the montage."

"Yeah, but love stories are timeless. Look" – she pointed at the screen – "that person is calling on a landline. If they had mobiles, this movie wouldn't even make sense."

"Not true." I shook my head. "The burgeoning technology of mobile phones actually plays a key part in this film and as such it's basically a historical artifact. You need to treat it with the reverence it deserves."

Ruby laughed. "My apologies."

"Besides, I believe you're the one who put having an actual phone call on our list, are you not?" I pointed out.

"As an homage to *classics* like *Pillow Talk* and *Sleepless in Seattle*."

"This is a classic too. You're going to love it. It's basically the horror movie version of the falling in love montage. It plays with all the tropes of horror movies."

"I don't know any of the tropes of horror movies."

"You do. They seep into the collective unconscious somehow. Same way I knew the grand gesture comes after the big fight, remember?"

Ruby raised an eyebrow. "You should really be a lawyer or something. You just keep talking until you win."

I put my hand to my heart and gasped, "I feel so attacked right now."

"Do you think I should be a lawyer?" she asked.

I took a long look at her. "No way. You're far too good. You keep cat treats in your pocket in case you see a stray. That's not lawyer material."

Ruby blushed and I felt a warm rush, realising that maybe I had been able to make her feel the way she made me feel.

Throughout the film, I kept looking at Ruby out of the corner of my eye. Her eyes were fixed on the screen. We chatted at first – Ruby did not appreciate all the stabbing – but after a while, the conversation died off, except for a few comments here and there. *I don't normally say this sort of thing, but Monica's hair is horrendous. Wait till you see this bit, it's wild! Aww, no, I liked the sassy friend.*

There was an elephant in the room. Or in the car. I mean, the whole point of coming here was to smush our faces together. We weren't supposed to actually watch the film, right? But I wasn't sure how to cross over into smush land smoothly. I eyed the space between us, assessing it for

151

pitfalls. I was really far too close to the steering wheel to actually manoeuvre even if I wanted to try to kiss her.

Maybe if I let the seat back a bit.

"Ooof." I hadn't realised we'd been parked on a slight slope and when I released the seat it slid back dramatically. Subtle.

"I was just, too close to the . . ." I trailed off, gesturing at the steering wheel.

Ruby smiled that uncomfortable smile, you know the one, where your lips are pressed together and you sort of nod to go along with it.

I wasn't even paying attention to the film any more and it didn't look as though Ruby was either. The fizzing tension in the air was too loud. Every part of my body was on high alert; every slight brush of her arm against mine seemed to charge the air around us. Was she doing that on purpose? Was it just me? How did you transition from having a conversation to kissing? I tried to think back to any other time I'd kissed someone but I drew a blank. It can't always have been this difficult. I'd have remembered.

"I like your top," Ruby said lightly. She reached over and fingered the hem of my very plain black tank top. Her hand grazed an inch of bare skin where my T-shirt had ridden up and it sent electric shocks through my system.

"Fuck it," I declared, and I launched myself on her like I was diving into a pool for the first time. You just had to go for it and drown if you were going to drown. I didn't drown. I kissed her and she kissed me back and I felt myself sink into it. After a few breathless moments, I pulled away slightly.

"Thank God," she breathed, "I didn't know how to start."

I laughed and kissed her again and her giggle escaped into the space between our lips, like if kisses had champagne bubbles.

"You know what would really kick this up a gear?" she whispered. With a flourish, she pulled on the handle that released the back of her seat and she flew back with a thud. I couldn't help laughing, trying to disentangle myself from my seat and climb over the handbrake. I propped myself up over her, head to head, toe to toe, and it stopped being funny. I kissed her gently this time, soft like a question, and she answered by pulling me close. I leaned into her, pressing against her, wanting to feel more of her body against mine than just our lips. My hands found the curves of her hips and her breasts.

When my heart was beating so fast I thought it might break free of my chest and fly away, when our legs intertwined, finding a delicious friction that charged my whole body, when all I could think of was pulling off her top and finding skin to touch and kiss, Ruby broke away, her hand on my chest forcing air between us.

"Do you think the people next to us can see us?" she asked.

I glanced out the window. Just like in the movies, they were steamed up, but I could still see the film was nearly over. Neve Campbell had just thrown a TV on the bad guy's head.

"Not exactly."

"Do you think they know we're . . . ?"

"Yes, definitely."

"Maybe we should go back to your house," she said. I felt something lodge in my throat. Did she mean . . . ? (In case you're wondering, by the ellipsis, I mean sex, but you knew that, right?)

"Uh, sure. Yes." Had Dad gone out to Beth's? He'd said he might but he didn't have the car, of course. What if she had gone to our house? Why hadn't I emancipated myself at sixteen and got my own place and decorated it like a romantic boudoir? Past me had absolutely no foresight.

Deciding I'd risk it and see what happened, I disentangled myself from Ruby and clambered back into my seat, adjusting it to its normal position. I turned the key to start the engine. Click click click. I turned it again. Click click click.

I looked at Ruby. She frowned.

Click click click.

"What does that mean?" Ruby asked.

"I've driven three times since I got my licence. I have no idea. Google it."

154

A couple of seconds later she told me the battery was dead. The car, not her phone. I checked the dash and realised I hadn't turned the lights off. Dad was going to kill me. Although that would come later. Right now I had no idea what to do.

"What do we do?" I asked, getting panicked.

Ruby googled again.

"Do you have a battery charger?"

"No?" I didn't even know they made those for cars.

"Jump leads?"

"Uh, I don't think so?" But I got out of the car and looked in the boot. There was an old sports bottle and a damp-looking Stephen King novel.

People were starting to pull out of the car park. I knocked on the window of the car next door and a woman in her thirties rolled down the window.

"Do you by any chance have jump leads?" I asked.

"Sorry, love." She rolled her window back up.

I opened the driver's side door of Dad's car again and leaned in. "Anything else?"

"What about them?" Ruby pointed to the car on the other side of us. It was one of those cars that had been lowered to the ground, and it had rims that probably cost more than my dad's whole car. I tried to sneak a glance at who was inside. A bunch of boys, maybe the same age as us, maybe a little older. Definitely too high to drive.

"Um . . . I don't really want to ask them." I said,

imagining what they might say to two girls stranded at night in a rapidly emptying car park.

I got back in the car and locked the door. This was the part of the horror movie where we got murdered by a "helpful" passerby. It was bad enough that our groping session had been hit by rom-com-style farce. I didn't want to tempt fate with horror. The consequences were a bit more gruesome than a bruised ego. Then again, if it really was a horror movie, the murderer was already in the back seat. I glanced back there. Just an empty pick-and-mix bag.

"I guess you're going to have to call your parents?" Ruby said, biting on her lip ring. "Do you think they'll be angry?"

I realised then that Ruby had no idea my parents weren't happily married and normal. Why would she? I hadn't told her anything.

"I'd really rather not call Dad. He'd never let me hear the end of it."

"What about your mum?" Ruby said. "When I broke the TV by doing a backflip in the living room, Mum covered for me and said my little brother did it because he was too little for anyone to be annoyed with him."

Dimly I took stock of the fact that Ruby had a little brother. I hadn't realised. Was he on holiday with her parents too? What was wrong with them? There was something really weird about their family. Although right now the more pressing issue was Ruby had hit on my number-one thing I didn't want to talk about.

"Mum can't help," I said firmly.

My mind went blank when I tried to think of a good reason why. I didn't want to make up some elaborate lie I'd have to keep track of so I hoped she'd drop it at that.

"Why?" Ruby asked. "Are you being sexist? She's a grown woman. I'm sure she's had a dead battery before."

"Trust me, she'd be no good in this situation." I felt my irritation grow. It was like she knew what she was doing. She couldn't, though, right? Oliver said he wouldn't mention it.

"Well, maybe she can tell us what to—"

"Jesus Christ, Ruby, give it a rest," I snapped. "She can't help."

Ruby blinked. Her eyebrows furrowed and her lips parted slightly. Guilt washed over me immediately.

"I'm sorry," I said quickly. "I shouldn't have snapped, I'm just stressed about the car. Dad will kill me."

He wouldn't. He'd be annoying about it but he wouldn't really get too worked up.

"We better figure out what to do, then," she said, but her tone was cool and she didn't look at me.

Shit. Shit shit shit.

I dialled a contact on my phone. It was the only person I could think of who might be able to help. That said a lot about my total lack of friends, but that was something to worry about another day.

*

157

Oliver drove up in his stupid fancy Jeep twenty minutes later. Twenty long minutes where the air around us cooled down literally and figuratively. Ruby spent most of it on her phone. After the first ten minutes, I couldn't take it any more so I got out of the car and sat on the hood. What was I supposed to do? I'd apologised. It wasn't that bad, was it? I'd been a bit snappish but I hadn't run over a cat or anything. I realised I'd been stupid. If Ruby had known about my mum, she would have just come out with it; that's what she was like. I was paranoid.

"Ladies." Oliver jumped out of his Jeep and tipped an imaginary hat. "I hear there are damsels in distress?"

"Oh, bugger off." I knew I'd have to listen to his nonsense if I called, but honestly, the boy never let up.

"I'm here to rescue you like the manly man I am." He used a voice that was at least an octave lower than his normal voice and swung a set of jump leads seductively.

"Why are you doing a man voice? You are, in fact, a man." I rolled my eyes.

Oliver shrugged. Ruby got out of the car and our eyes met. I tried to apologise again with a smile.

"Any idea how to jump-start the car?" She directed her conversation at Oliver only.

"Obviously not, but that's what YouTube is for."

Ruby's smile was full of gratitude and relief. It made her a little less scary. I'd talk to her on the way home,

I decided. Once the stress of being stranded had passed, she might be in better form.

Between the three of us, we managed to figure it out. I nearly wept with joy when the engine started making proper engine noises again.

"Want a lift home?" Oliver nodded at Ruby.

She hesitated. I tried to communicate via telepathy that I was really sorry for being a dick and that I wanted her to come with me. Going back to my place was obviously off the table. I didn't want it to happen like this anyway ("it" is sex, you know that by now, right? I don't have to keep saying it?). If it was going to happen, it should be on a perfect day.

"Saoirse's going to drive me home," Ruby said.

Apparently, I *did* have the power of psychic thought transmission. Would I use it for good or evil?

It was only when I dropped her off with a good-night kiss (and a good-night hand on the boob – high five!) that a terrible thought occurred to me.

Did that count as a fight? And if it counted as a fight, did we make up? Had I invited one of the harbingers of doom?

No. Surely not. It wasn't a fight. It was so tiny. It was barely even an *f*. A fight would be like a big disagreement about something important. A screaming match. Horrible words exchanged and tears shed. That's obviously what I'd meant when I said fight. Everyone has little tiffs. That's normal, even for a montage. It's all part of the antagonistic nature of the chemistry.

It didn't count.

Shut up.

15

Five days later I began the process of boxing up the entire house to get ready for the move. I knew Dad would be lax about getting everything together. He always underestimated how long things took, resulting in him being late for basically everything. It made me mad that while I was the one who didn't want to move, I was still doing all the work.

I thought maybe it would be sad, packing away the last ten years or so. I had visions of myself wistfully examining knickknacks and crying a single tear of reminiscence. Actually, it was so painfully boring that I didn't have the energy for that kind of carry-on. I cut myself several times when I overenthusiastically used the tape gun to seal the boxes and lost control, the momentum swinging the sharp end into my knee. Which meant I yet again had a life-threatening knee injury. The worst part was thinking about maybe doing it all over again for Oxford. I couldn't quite picture being there and yet I couldn't picture being with Dad and Beth in the new flat either. I felt in limbo, unable to settle even in my own mind, so I played music incredibly loud while I worked to try to drown out my inner voice.

Packing up the whole house was eating into my falling in love montage time and that was unforgivable. Ruby and I had taken a walk on the beach the morning after the drive-in and I was confident we had moved past the non-fight, but I hadn't seen her since. She'd gone with Oliver's family to visit their grandparents for a couple of days and when she wasn't out of town, between visiting Mum, packing, and filling in ten more job applications, there hadn't been time. We'd texted but it wasn't the same and it was making me antsy.

And yet here I was again, in Dad's room of all places, folding his shirts into a box.

"Saoirse, if you bleed on that carpet I'm going to have to get it cleaned again before we move out." Dad loomed over me, which, given that he was only about five foot ten, was quite the feat. He was dressed in his day-off outfit. A long-sleeved, fitted shirt, tweed waistcoat, jeans from the children's section rolled up at the hem to show off his lace-up brogues with no socks. Honestly.

"Your concern for my well-being is touching, Father." I hoisted myself up and leaned against the bed. "How can I help you today? Would you like Dobby to press your underpants or shine your shoes?"

"Less cheek would be a great start and then after that if you could let Beth in when the door rings. Make sure you listen out for her over your death music."

"By death music, you mean Scandinavian folk singers?"

"Yes, I saw a news report that Norwegian girls with acoustic guitars lead kids to witchcraft and heroin."

"Can't you let her in?" I whined.

"I have to go down to the home. I was supposed to take your mum out later for—" He cut himself off. "Anyway, she's having a bad day. Was she OK this morning?"

Your mum. Like she had nothing to do with him.

"She seemed fine this morning."

A bad day meant she was distressed, crying, shouting, possibly violent.

"I tried ringing Beth to cancel but she didn't answer," Dad said on his way out. "I bet she left her phone at home. Tell her I'm sorry and I'll call her later. Oh, and if you can do that pants thing too that would be great."

"I can't promise I won't sacrifice her to the Goat King if the music tells me so," I said, half joking. I was inclined to be a little kinder knowing he was going to make sure Mum was OK. Especially as I hadn't offered to go with him.

"I understand that. What kind of unreasonable tyrant do you take me for?"

I was loading books into boxes when the doorbell rang. Technically, in some mature part of my brain, I knew I had no right to be mad at Beth, but I wasn't going to let that part win. I wasn't some kind of quitter. I trudged to the door. Beth stood in front of me, a big grin on her face that slid off, comically, when she saw it was me. She replaced it as quickly as she could.

"Saoirse. How lovely to see you again," she said.

"I'm sure. Look, Dad had to go . . . out." I didn't know whether I was supposed to tell her where he really was. Obviously she knew about Mum but it felt weird to bring her up.

"Should I wait? Did he say if he'd be back soon?"

"I honestly don't know."

He would likely be at least an hour or two, but who was I to make wild predictions?

"I'll wait for a bit then," she said. "If you don't mind."

"Knock yourself out," I said, and I turned to leave. Beth was sitting primly on the edge of the sofa like she was waiting in a doctor's office for bad news.

Sighing heavily, I made myself turn back. "Do you want a cup of tea or something?"

Her face brightened. "That would be lovely, thank you."

I brought her back her tea and I sat in the armchair next to the sofa to be polite. I realised I was also perching on the end of the seat. Maybe that's just how you sit when you're planning to bolt any second.

"So . . ." I searched for any topic of conversation except the wedding. "What are you doing today, then?"

"Dress shopping for the wedding." Beth smiled.

This was my first lesson that when there's a wedding

being planned, there is no such thing as conversations not about the wedding.

"Wait, *with* Dad?"

Beth nodded. Steam from the mug rose in front of her face and fogged up her glasses.

"Isn't that kind of against the rules?"

Beth shrugged, looking uncomfortable. "I don't really have anyone else to go with me. My mother passed away when I was little. I don't have any sisters. I don't really have very many girlfriends here."

It's a pet peeve of mine that straight women call their friends "girlfriends." They are not your girlfriends. If you are not getting up close and personal with the lady garden then there are words for that: friends, mates, buddies, pals, etc., etc. Leave us our word, OK?

But I didn't say anything. I vaguely remembered Dad saying Beth moved to Ireland a couple of years ago to open a branch of her business in Dublin and yet she still didn't have any proper friends. Having had no friends for a while now, I thought it could be kind of hard on someone. If they were the needy type like Beth obviously was. So I didn't suggest she take Mum's friends too, even though it was the first thing that occurred to me. I actually felt kind of sorry for her.

One-nil for maturity.

She waved her hand, insisting it didn't matter. She wanted Dad to be there for the dress shopping anyway.

I didn't know what was more pitiful, that she had no mates or that she only had Dad to make up for it.

Then something happened that I can't quite explain, even now. The pity I was feeling for her somehow morphed into the words:

"What if I go with you?"

As soon as they left my mouth I wanted to snatch them back and I prayed she'd say, *Oh, I couldn't ask you to do that* and I would nod and run upstairs before I got myself into any more trouble.

"Really?" Her whole body perked out of a slump, and her eyes shone.

"Well, I'm sure you don't actually want me there—"

"No, no, I do. That would be brilliant. You know, they give you free champagne and everything," she said, like it was a bribe.

I checked my pretend watch. "Well, it's about time for my three p.m. drink so that works out well. What time is the appointment?"

"In half an hour."

"I'll get dressed," I said, pasting on a smile and trying my hardest not to shudder visibly with regret.

Half an hour. How had Dad thought he would be able to get in and out of the home in time to make that? Classic scatterbrain. They'd have missed this appointment if I hadn't agreed to go, or she would have ended up going alone.

This was like my good deed for the year, maybe even the decade. That remained to be seen.

We were greeted at the door to Pronuptuous by a woman with a mess of grey curls bound up in a colourful headscarf, some completely indecipherable age between sixty and a hundred.

"Come on in, girls, come on in," she ushered us in, in delighted tones. I had been expecting someone younger, snooty and disdainful, because my only experience of wedding dress shops was from TV and films. Everything else was fairly spot on, though. She led us into a huge dressing room with so many reflective surfaces I felt like I was in a hall of mirrors. Why would anyone want to see every inch of themselves at once? Some things are better left unseen if you ask me. The old lady pushed a glass of something bubbly into my hand and I obliged, taking a sip. There was a plate of chocolate truffles wrapped in gold paper too. Oh well, it would be rude not to partake.

"OK now, dear, tell me what is it you're looking for? A-line, flared, trumpet, ball gown, tea length, princess, mermaid, sheath, sweep train, court train, panel train, watteau train, chapel train, cathedral train, no train at all—" The woman took a breath.

"Uh . . ." Beth blinked several times.

"Cathedral veil, chapel veil, waltz veil, mantilla, double-tier veil, square neckline, scoop, V-neck, sweetheart, Grecian, bateau, sheer, off the shoulder, Queen Anne, halter, strapless, basque waist, dropped waist—"

"Stop." Beth held a hand up. "Words have lost all meaning now."

The woman chuckled. "One of those," she said, without judgement.

"One of what?" Beth asked.

"The ones who don't know what they want. There's two ends of the spectrum, dear. The brides who know exactly what they want down to the number of sequins on the bodice, and the ones who have no clue. Worry not, Barbara knows what you want before you do."

I stuffed one of the chocolates in my gob and shrugged at Beth. I guessed this was Barbara.

"OK, let me see you." Barbara made the universal gesture for "give me a twirl" and Beth turned slowly and uncertainly on the spot.

"Well, you have a cracking figure, dear, but no tits whatsoever."

Beth's eyes widened in disbelief and I burst out laughing, dribbling chocolate mush on my chin.

"It's nothing to laugh about," Barbara said, shaking her head at me. "It is what it is. We must be honest with ourselves." She turned again to Beth. "Do you want the chicken fillets then or are you happy enough as you are?"

"As I am," Beth said, bewildered, "I suppose."

"No supposing here. You have to be certain. I have

168

plenty of dresses for a flat chest but if you're going to stuff your bra with those jelly tits then you need to tell me now."

"No, no. No . . . jelly," Beth said.

I got the feeling she was a little bit scared of Barbara. I thought Barbara was incredible and I wanted her to be my grandmother. I sat on the little tufted couch at the side of the room to watch it all unfold, the plate of truffles in my lap.

"How do you want to feel on the big day?" Barbara hooked a tape measure around Beth's hips.

"Happy?"

"Well, I would hope so, but that's not what I mean. Are you wanting to feel like a fluffy pretty princess or a sensual seductive woman? Or are you thinking more of the refined older bride look? Virgin, whore, or crone? Those are your only options, dear." Barbara looked shrewdly at me. "And never a truer word spoken," she added with her lips pursed.

"Preach, Barbara." I held my hands up to her inviolable wisdom. I briefly considered getting my phone out to record this and send it to Ruby, but I had a sneaking suspicion Barbara would happily snatch it from my hands and flush it down the loo or something.

"Um, sexy, I guess?" Beth half glanced at me, embarrassed. I tried to block off the part of my brain that connected Beth looking sexy from anything to do with my dad and popped another truffle in my mouth, letting it melt on my tongue.

"Good choice. I don't like to judge, you know, but at your age, the princess look is a little bit sad. And you're not old enough for the wedding skirt suit quite yet."

There were some very strict age and gender roles in the world of getting clothes to wear to your own wedding.

"You hold tight there, have another glass of champagne, and I'll be back in a couple of minutes with some options."

Beth sat beside me and gulped down some champagne.

"This is kind of intense," she whispered.

"I think if you make the wrong choice Barbara will put you in the stocks and pelt you with truffles," I whispered back.

"Why are we whispering?" Beth asked, still whispering.

"Because she'll tell us off for talking in class."

Barbara returned with a single dress in a plastic cover.

"With your skin tone, dear, you could wear whatever colour you like, but I thought a brilliant white would be pretty." She unzipped the plastic and held a bit of the fabric up to Beth's face. Sure enough, it popped, making her glow. Barbara nodded, satisfied.

Beth took the dress uncertainly and shuffled into the changing booth, giving me a bewildered look behind Barbara's back.

"Not you, though." Barbara rounded on me. "Whenever you come to me, it's ivory or a champagne gold for you. That pasty pink skin of yours won't take anything else." She pointed at me like my pasty pink skin offended her.

"Cheers," I said, "but I won't be getting married."

"Why not?" She twisted her face, personally offended by my rejection of marriage. "Sure the lesbians can get married now."

"How do you know I'm a lesbian?"

I shouldn't have been surprised. This was Barb. She was wise and also psychic apparently.

"Oh, wisht. You think you can work in the business of love this long and not get some of that gaydar? I've known some brides in my day who shouldn't have been marrying grooms, that's for sure. You still get the odd one here and there who doesn't know it yet, poor dears. I try and give them a hint, you know, subtle, *would you not like a nice pantsuit, dear.* That sort of thing."

"Truly you are doing God's work, Barb."

Barbara nodded sagely and tapped her nose.

"But I don't think a wedding is for me anyway," I went on. "The whole till death do us part? Bit ridiculous, isn't it?"

"Oh, death schmeath," Barbara tutted. "How about life's too short to be second-guessing yourself the whole way? You can only go with what you feel right now and if you feel like it might make you happy, even for a while, jump in with both feet, girl, and get wet."

I eyed Barb curiously. Was she that good at reading people or did she spout off wisdom all the time and this just happened to be exceptionally relevant to my interests?

Just then Beth emerged from the changing booth and we stopped talking. The dress was pure white with a boat neck and lace that draped off her shoulders. It hugged her waist and hips and then flared out at the knee. When she turned around, there were tiny silk-covered buttons about three-quarters of the way up her back. It really was beautiful.

Beth looked in the mirror and caught my eye in the glass.

"This is it," she said, "this is the one."

Barbara nodded approvingly, "See, I told you I'd know exactly what you needed."

We left the shop exclaiming about how weird and wonderful Barb was, so I didn't notice her until it was too late. She didn't notice me because she had stopped dead in the middle of the street to rummage in her bag. That's how I literally walked into Izzy on the path outside a wedding dress shop.

"Oh, Saoirse," she said, after we'd both rebounded and exchanged the *I didn't see you there, stranger* sorrys and realised who we were saying sorry to.

I said hi because even I wasn't cold enough to walk right into someone and then ignore them. If I had been paying attention and spotted her earlier, I would have been suddenly distracted by something and pretended not to see her, like a normal person.

Beth stood beside us, beaming, waiting for an introduction maybe. She'd be waiting a long time, let me tell you. When she realised she had stumbled upon something awkward, she mumbled something about forgetting to tell Barbara about buttons, then scooted back into the shop. At least she wasn't a complete balloon. If I'd been with Dad he probably would have started his own chat with Izzy and said something unforgivable like, *Oh, Izzy, how come we never see you any more*, or *I wish you two girls would make up, we miss you around the house*, or God forbid, *Saoirse is stuck in her room all the time, you should come by and take her off my hands.*

Izzy looked past me into the window of Pronuptuous and I saw it dawn on her face.

"Is that *her*," she whispered, even though Beth was nowhere near being in earshot.

I nodded.

"I never thought I'd see the day you two would be hanging out," she said.

She didn't sound appalled, she sounded like she might be impressed by my personal growth, but I had the sensation of being caught doing something shameful.

"It's not a big deal." I smiled tightly and I rubbed my thumb into my scar.

Izzy noticed and gave me a look like she was trying to tell me something. If we were friends, I'd probably know she was trying to tell me that I couldn't fool her and I should stop pretending. But we weren't friends, so I decided I was totally baffled by whatever mysterious thing she was attempting to communicate.

"We could talk about it," she offered.

"I have to go," I said, and I hurried off, leaving her on the street looking after me. I mean, I assume she was looking after me. I couldn't see that part but I'd been watching a lot of movies lately and it felt like the right thing, dramatically speaking.

A few seconds later Beth caught up with me.

"I got the impression I should give you two some space," she said. "What was that about?"

I rounded on Beth, stopping us both on the footpath.

"We're not friends, Beth, OK?"

"I know," she said, and her face fell. "But I'd like to be. I don't have a lot of friends here. It's hard to get to know anyone when you move to a town where everyone's been best friends since they were four. It's kind of lonely."

Her vulnerability was excruciating. I couldn't bear someone being that needy. It made me want to claw my own skin off. Imagine admitting to anyone that you were lonely. Wouldn't you just die?

"I really don't have that problem," I said.

"If you say so," Beth replied, and I thought I saw a flash of something in her eye. I couldn't tell if it was sadness for herself or pity for me. "You know where to find me if you change your mind."

Given that a shriek of frustration would have been a regression too far, I satisfied myself with storming off in the opposite direction, grinding my teeth. Where did she get off being so fucking understanding all the time?

16

When I was little, Mum would take me to the museum. I hated it. She'd stand staring at the paintings for ages and I'd get bored. I didn't know why it took her so long to move on. So I'd tug on her hand and drag her along. The only bit I liked was the gift shop with the colourful toys and books.

Now I took her at least once a month and I stood there as long as she wanted. It was practically empty early in the morning so it was one of the few places we could go where I didn't feel like everyone was looking, wondering what was wrong with her.

When I'd picked her up that morning, Mum's key worker, Nora, mentioned she'd taken a shine to some young girl who worked there on the night shift and they had watched a video of a concert online. I gave her a stony glare and she scurried off. Some girl making my mum sit through a grainy phone video of whomever was currently top of the charts was not cute to me. Mum was a wonderful, glorious snob who may have smiled indulgently when Dad wanted to rhapsodise about an obscure band but always found somewhere else to be when he played his music through the sound system.

He could never keep up with her either. She was too quick, too well-read; she had facts and figures at her fingertips and their discussions over the dinner table would always end with him laughing and agreeing that she was definitely right and he didn't know why he even argued. She would say she didn't know why he argued either because she always kicked his ass. When I got older I would join in; it was the one time when me and Mum were a team instead of me and Dad. When she started to lose her thread and get confused, I stopped wanting to argue. Especially since she moved out. If he tries to goad me now with a stupid comment that he knows will rile me up, I do my best not to take the bait. It makes me sad. I don't think he understands that.

The people in the home didn't know these things about her. I thought about telling them. I crafted long speeches where I told them what she was really like and gave them a piece of my mind. But I never did. They were just doing their jobs. And there was a part of me that thought if I shared those things with other people they would become diluted. I'd lose the little part of Mum that I owned from knowing who she was before.

When Dad told me Mum had to go into the home, that it wasn't safe, we couldn't provide enough supervision, I couldn't accept it. Sure, she was deteriorating, I could see that. We were in a state of constant alert. There was very little else going on in our lives. But I was OK with that. It was my mum. We could manage. We would try harder, I said.

I cried and yelled and told him it would happen over my dead body. Or his, preferably. But not long after he brought it up, things changed. I was at school, Dad was at work, and the care workers who came in six times a day were between visits. Mum left the house and got lost. She was always trying to leave and it was hard to manage because you couldn't have an eye on her all the time and you couldn't just lock her up in a room. That wasn't fair or safe. But it wasn't safe to let her roam around either. She was too confused.

That day, the care worker got to the house and found the front door open. She couldn't find Mum anywhere. She rang my dad and couldn't get through to him. She called the police. Then she called me at school. I phoned Dad over and over and tried his office but they said he was in a client meeting and had left his phone on his desk.

Hannah was the one who got me home in the end. She called her dad to pick us up and they drove me around the town looking for Mum. Hannah held my hand as we traipsed up and down the promenade, along the beaches, through our entire neighbourhood. We were still looking when Dad finally turned up. I wanted to shout at him and make him feel bad for not being there but the stricken look on his face stopped me.

I always thought I lived in a small place until that day. A little seaside town. When I realised my mother could be anywhere, it felt infinite. I didn't cry all day, though I probably bruised Hannah's hand I was holding it so tight. Eventually, the police got a call. They picked her up at the side of a dual carriageway. Her face was scratched, a drop of blood trailed from her hairline, and her trousers were soaked with urine. We never found out what happened to her, how she got those scratches. Whether she'd fallen or if someone had hurt her. Part of me wanted to padlock her in a room in our house just so she would still be there, where I could see her every day.

I still resented the relief I saw on Dad's face when I told him I wouldn't fight him on the home any more.

Most of all I tried to pretend I hadn't felt it too.

"How are you?" Mum asked later, in the museum café. There was no sign of the meltdown she'd had yesterday. She was in good form and had enjoyed wandering around the exhibitions. It was nice to see her in her element. She put her hand on mine. I closed my eyes for a moment and relished the pressure. Mum would always hug me if I went to hug her, but she didn't always initiate physical contact these days. The waitress put two scones down in front of us and gave Mum a big smile. She was here all the time and I was sure she recognised us by now.

I cut Mum's scone in half and buttered it and slathered

it in jam. She started telling me this story from when she was little, about her dad.

"So every time the season changed I wrote a letter to a new fairy. The spring fairy or the summer fairy. And in the morning I'd go out into the garden and I'd pick up the stone and the note I'd left would be gone and there would be a new note written in fairy language. Dad would tell me what it said because he understood fairy language." She looked as happy remembering as she probably did those mornings when she found her notes.

Mum talked about her dad a lot. Not her biological dad, but her 'real' dad as she called him. He died before I was born, but even when I was little she talked about him so much I felt like I knew him. He sounded like he made magic happen. I was so grateful that the memories she kept revisiting were ones that made her happy. It didn't always work out that way. There was a woman in her home who relived her parents' deaths as though they had just happened. All that grief and trauma over and over again.

I wondered if I got stuck in time, what I would say about my dad.

There'd be swearing, I imagine.

Mum stood up and looked around, biting her lip.

"Where's the bathroom?" she asked.

I told her I'd bring her and I took my bag but left our half-drunk tea and Mum's cardigan to show we were coming back so the waitress wouldn't think we weren't going to pay the bill. I ushered her past the till to the disabled bathroom and loitered outside. Mum didn't usually need help with the toilet, but you still had to wait for her, especially in a place she could get lost or disoriented easily. I couldn't help but think of the day when she would need help inside. It's not that I'd mind, but I knew that she would.

Mum opened the door and looked out at me.

"I . . . the sink doesn't work?" she said. I looked over at it and saw it was one of those fancy ones where you had to hover your hands under exactly the right spot to get soap and water, so I took her over and helped her wash her hands. At the same moment we were exiting the bathroom, a man scooted past me in the narrow hall to get to the men's room. He stopped when he clocked us.

"You shouldn't use the disabled toilet if you're not disabled," he said in the most teacher-y tone of voice.

I gave him the coldest look I could muster, hoping he would jog on and leave us be. Instead, he seemed to wait for a response. Mum's face crumpled and she took a step behind me.

"Sorry. I'm sorry," she said.

I don't think she really understood why he was giving off, but she could sense the tone.

"Feck off," I said, tempering my language because Mum hated swearing. "Mind your own bloody business."

The man tutted angrily and when his back was turned I gave him the finger. On both hands. And there was a little dance too.

We went back to our table to drink our tea and finish the scones. A few minutes later I saw the man talking to the waitress and pointing in the direction of the toilets. He was really racking up the busybody points today. I turned away from him and silently prayed my mother would finish her tea soon so we could leave.

"Hi. I'm sorry I was rude to you there. I didn't know."

The man loomed over us, and though his words were technically remorseful, he seemed so unused to apologising they came out like hard, constipated little words, straining out of the puckered arsehole he called a mouth.

"Didn't know what?" I said in clipped, disdainful tones.

"The waitress said there's something wrong with your mum. I didn't realise. She doesn't look . . ." He trailed off, but he wasn't done yet. "Anyway, she said you care for her, and I think that's really admirable." He looked at me more with pity than with admiration, though, and he didn't look at Mum at all, even though she was the one who deserved the apology.

I wanted to tell him off. Give a moving speech in defence of minding your own business and not judging people. Later in bed I'd think of the words, but I didn't have them right then. The man didn't wait for a response either; he sauntered off, smugly thinking he'd been so humble and nice today. I concentrated very hard on my scone.

"I have to go now," Mum said suddenly, breaking my focus.

I recognised the hint of urgency in her tone. She was getting upset.

"Everything's OK," I said soothingly. I didn't want that guy to ruin her day. "We're having a nice time."

Her forehead creased into a frown and she pulled the kind of face you make when you smell something unpleasant.

"I really do have to go now. I have work." She looked around the café. "Can you take me home?"

"Mum, please." I rubbed the back of my neck. "We're having a nice time. Everything is OK. You don't need to go yet."

"I have to go." She stomped her foot under the table. I hated myself for checking to see if the waitress was watching us now. For a second, I was so angry I wanted to stomp my foot too. Mostly I wanted to scream. I wanted to tell her, your dad is dead and you had to quit your job because you couldn't remember your own last name. You have literally nowhere better to be. I pressed hard into the scar on my palm. I needed to breathe and calm down.

Mum looked so lost. The clouded expression on her face broke my heart. I stared up at the ceiling so I wouldn't cry. It would only make it worse.

"I'll take you home," I said, and I gathered up our things. "Come on, give me your hand."

Her expression cleared and she stood up, happy again, like nothing had happened. She took my hand and I squeezed it.

"I love you, Mum."

"I love you too," she said. And even though I knew she only said it because I had, I savoured hearing those words in my mother's voice.

17

4. Frolicking (as seen in all of them, apparently).

8. Date on a rowboat (as seen in *The Proposal, 10 Things I Hate About You*).

Saoirse
Ruby meet me at beach at 1 a.m.

Ruby
Mysterious

Saoirse
It's time for No. 8

Ruby
I thought that was Saturday?

Saoirse
At 1 a.m. it will be Saturday.

I spotted Ruby before she saw me. I couldn't make out her face in the dark but I could tell it was her by the way she moved. I liked these moments of observing her when she

185

didn't know. It was like seeing a secret. When she got close I could see she was wearing old trainers and a pair of shorts with a trim of multicoloured pom-poms. Her legs were long, and her thighs were thick and muscular.

"It's so quiet," Ruby whispered, even though there was no one around to hear her. It was dark but you could still see black cloud swirling around pinprick stars. "It's eerie."

"I like it."

"Me too." Ruby shivered.

I took her hand and led her down the strand.

"This is beautiful." She sucked in the sea air and lifted her head to gaze at the stars. "I think I can see my star from here." She pointed at the sky. "But how are we going to do number eight?"

"Four and eight, I'll have you know."

"Four was?"

"Frolicking," I reminded her. "I wasn't sure what the hell we were going to do for that but I figured it out. Two birds, one stone."

"How so?"

"Well, Ruby, we're going to steal a boat."

She stopped walking.

"What?"

"A little bit down the way there are pedalos. We're going to steal one."

"You're not serious?"

"When we first met, we stole someone's beloved pet, and now you're balking at borrowing a plastic bird?"

"What do you mean a bird?"

"Stop changing the subject. Are you in or not?"

She looked like she was thinking about it. She tossed her hair from one side to the other and then, with a determined look on her face, she nodded.

"I'm in," she said.

When she saw the pedalos she laughed. They were shaped like swans, about ten feet high, and they were absolutely decrepit. I was certain they hadn't been replaced since I was a kid and there was Sharpie graffiti all over them.

"OK, OK, it's not a rowboat—"

"It definitely is nowhere near as dignified as a rowboat."

"—but she's seaworthy, I swear."

We gazed at the herd of plastic swans.

"Which one do you want to set free?" she asked, pretending to consider them carefully.

"I can't decide between the one with the elaborate goatee or the one that has four stars and *would ride this bird again* written on the arse."

"Four stars, though, we can't argue with that kind of review," Ruby mused.

The mighty bird was trapped in a shallow part of the sea enclosed by a fence of buoys. It was supposed to prevent children from pedalling off into the horizon and perishing at sea, but it was extremely inconvenient.

"We're going to have to wade in and pull it out on the sand," I decided.

Ruby nodded. "OK, well, you do that, and I'll be here waiting."

"Oh, come on, wuss. It's three inches of water. Get your butt in with me, Quinn."

Ruby sighed and kicked off her shoes.

Getting the swan to the shore was easy enough, in spite of the freezing water lapping at our ankles. Getting it across the sand, past the enclosure, and back into the sea was the hard part. There was grunting, sweating, and much profanity.

"Isn't this nice," I panted, once we had finally set sail. We'd squeezed into the swan side by side and we were pedalling off into the distance. Neither of us felt the cold any more.

"Maybe I've overlooked master thief as a career option. What do you think?"

I laughed. Then Ruby laughed. Then we couldn't stop laughing.

"We stole a ten-foot swan," she said between peals of laughter.

"We stole a four-star, ten-foot swan," I corrected her. Then I laughed again. It wasn't that it was that funny.

It was just ridiculous and the giddiness of it was making us silly.

"I don't think this happened in any movie," Ruby said finally when we both calmed down. She let her hand drift along the surface of the water. Like the night at the drive-in when I thought we might have been stranded at the mercy of a back-seat serial killer, I considered pointing out that if this were a horror movie she could lose a hand right now to a water demon or be dragged out of the boat by a serial killer and I'd have to leave her and paddle to shore. But I thought it might spoil the moment.

"I'll include it in my memoir," I said instead. "When they make the biopic, it'll be one of the early scenes."

"Oh, you think you're interesting enough to have your own biopic?" she teased.

"Maybe not right now, but once I've cured cancer or brokered world peace, they'll have to give the public what they want."

"What *do* you want to do, you know, 'when you grow up'?" Ruby asked.

What was I supposed to say to that? I didn't have some big plan or grand passion that I wanted to follow. I wouldn't let myself have something like that. And I couldn't tell Ruby why having a plan seemed kind of pointless under the circumstances.

"Not as many things as you do," I joked.

Ruby smiled but she didn't say anything. She waited

for me to say more. That was normal. This was a totally normal conversation. It's all anyone had talked about for a year at school. What have you applied for, what do you want to do, etc.? They never tired of it because even though everyone had asked everyone, the point was never to find out what someone else was doing, but to talk about what you wanted to do.

I didn't get the feeling that was why Ruby asked. I was going to have to give her something else. I could do that, though. It wasn't breaking the rules. Maybe just nudging them a bit to see if they had any give.

"Honestly, I don't know."

"I feel like that too."

"You feel like that because everything sounds like a good idea to you." Ruby considered every career that came up, even in casual conversation, as a possibility; she saw potential everywhere. I wasn't like that. "Nothing sounds like a good idea to me." I realised as the words were tumbling out of my mouth that it sounded terribly close to a maudlin admission of my true feelings, and *that* was dangerously close to having a deep and meaningful conversation that I was not supposed to have. Not if I wanted to stick to my rules. And I did, of course. Because they were working.

Ruby took my hand and rubbed her thumb along my palm.

"No, I feel like that because—" Then she paused and

turned my hand over to look at it. "You have a scar here," she said, surprised. "How have I not noticed that before?"

It was pretty well hidden, as it followed the crease of my hand. I'd even tried holding my own hand to see if you could feel it that way and you couldn't.

"Well. *There's* a story," I said, clutching at the opportunity to change the subject. "See, I ran into a burning building."

"Uh-huh." Ruby rolled her eyes.

"No, I did. To save some kittens."

"Kittens, you say."

"Yep. Your favourite. And orphans. You like orphans? I'm a goddamn hero."

"And you just got one long scar on your hand in this brave rescue?"

"Yeah, I'm a hero and also super flame resistant. What can I tell you?"

"How about you tell me something real for a change?"

Ruby locked eyes with me. Her blue freckle looked like a drop of nighttime had fallen out of the sky on to her cheek. Her face was soft curves and luminous skin. She might have been the prettiest girl I'd ever seen.

"How about this?" I pinched her chin between my thumb and forefinger, drawing her face close so I could whisper onto her lips. I wanted to tell her how much I liked her, how I felt this tugging feeling in my stomach that drew me close to her, but I couldn't let the words out of my mouth because it felt like unleashing something I couldn't control.

Instead I said, "I want to take you somewhere special."

It was my favourite part of the beach, farther up out of the tourist areas, off a small cove with rough shingle instead of sand. If you climb over the stone inlet there's a natural pool, entirely enclosed and about six feet deep and five feet wide. Somehow the water there is warmer than the rest of the sea. Warmer, not warm. That's important. We lodged the swan into a crevice in the rock and it bobbed absurdly, a giant white getaway bird, as we climbed over the rock.

Ruby breathed out a low sigh. "This really is special."

It was our own private pool lit by stars.

I sat on the edge of the water and dangled my feet in. Ruby stretched her legs and shook them out. Maybe I hadn't really been doing all that much pedalling, if I'm quite honest, but she had those muscly gymnastics legs so I would have only been slowing her down. She reached her arms overhead and I tried not to stare at the places where the hem rode up. Instead, I patted the ground beside me and she sat and dipped her toes into the water.

"That's nice," she said, and she leaned her head on my shoulder, bits of her messy hair tickling my chin.

"Good," I said slowly. "Because I was thinking we should go skinny-dipping."

Ruby's head sprang up.

"You're joking."

I shook my head.

"It's really montage-y, don't you think?"

"It's not on the list."

"Have you done it before?" I asked, trying not to sound jealous of the person who might have swum naked with my . . . with Ruby.

"No."

Suck it, imaginary person.

"It's absolutely freezing." She looked mournfully into the water. Though the pool was too small for waves, it was dark and ominous and it made gulping, gurgling sounds as it flowed from the sea through the rocks.

"A minute ago you said it was nice," I scoffed.

Her eyes searched mine, trying to figure out if I was serious, and I held her gaze.

"Let's do it." She leapt up and growled like she was psyching up for a battle against the elements.

"Are you sure now? It won't be too cold for you?" I teased, standing and tossing my jumper onto a high, jutting part of the rock.

"If I lose a nipple to frostbite, I'm holding you personally responsible," she said, kicking her trainers off.

"I promise, I take full responsibility for your nipples."

I wriggled out of my shorts and felt a pinch of doubt as a wave of cold water splashed over the rocks and the spray hit my legs. Ruby grasped the corners of her T-shirt with both hands and pulled it over her head. I wasn't sure if I was allowed to look or not. A constellation of freckles across her torso looked like someone had blown them onto her skin like sprinkles from their hand. Her waist dipped in and her hips were full and wide. A bulge of soft stomach sat above the waistband of spotty pink underwear that was a size too small. It dug in and squishy hips and belly strained against the fabric. If you don't think that sounds beautiful then you haven't seen her.

She was covered by a striped blue bra, and I didn't want to seem like the boy who's been let into the locker room, eyes pinging straight to the chest, but the swell of her breasts disappearing into the fabric made me want something so bad it was like an untamable creature inside me, clawing its way from my stomach, searching with greedy hands. I thought of closing the space between us, but there's an unspoken quid pro quo of getting to look at someone in their underwear. I peeled my top over my head and held it in my hand, covering most of my body for a moment before I let it drop. I was afraid she wouldn't like what she saw. My cheeks got hot as her eyes scanned my body. I thought I saw the same expression reflected in her eyes that must have radiated from mine and it made me feel beautiful. I unscrunched myself, letting my shoulders drop and my arms relax to my sides.

"Don't look," she said as she reached around her back to unhook her bra, and I squeezed my eyes shut. A few moments later I heard a splash, combined with a scream and followed by quick shallow breaths. I opened my eyes. Ruby was treading water furiously, her face taut with the pain of being plunged into cold water.

"Er, maybe I shouldn't get in after all." I pretended to put my top back on.

"Oh. My. God. Get in. Immediately. Or. I swear. I'll. Kill you," Ruby said, her words struggling to get out between laboured breaths.

She swam in the other direction to warm up, discreetly giving me the privacy to slip out of the little clothing I still had on. It was strange having nothing on outside. I tried to think of any other time in my life where I might have been completely naked outdoors, but unless I'd been a baby it had never happened. The cool air was nice, ticklish in places that aren't often exposed. I imagined the water would feel less pleasant. I hesitated for a second at the edge of the pool, contemplating the jump. Then I decided to lay my clothes on the edge and try to slip myself in, inch by inch.

"Ahhhhh!" I screamed.

"Are you in?" Ruby asked. She was facing away from me, using the edge of the pool as a rest for her arms.

"Not yet."

"Just jump."

I couldn't do it. I inched myself in further.

"Oh God."

The water hit me in parts that don't usually see the great outdoors and I responded with a high-pitched squeal.

"Get you in the fanny, did it?" Ruby said knowingly.

"Don't make me laugh. This is a delicate operation," I said, but I couldn't help giggling and I lost my grip and slid into the water, grazing my leg on craggy bits of rock sticking out. Strike three for my poor knee.

"Owww. Oh, it's cold and it hurts."

Ruby turned, bobbing in the water. I could only see her from the shoulders up. She paddled towards me, trying not to laugh.

"It's OK after a minute. It doesn't feel so cold now."

I pumped my legs and swam in small circles around the rock pool until my heart rate slowed a bit and I stopped feeling like the cold was burrowing into my body.

"This was your idea," Ruby said, laughing, when she saw the expression on my face.

"I have bad ideas."

I didn't mean it, because I was in a rock pool, in the nip, with a girl who was also naked, and that was pretty much the best thing that ever happened to me. I swam closer to her and we trod water, lazily. Her leg slipped against mine, and with imminent death by freezing no longer an issue, the wanting creature returned. It was the strongest urge I'd ever had. I got close enough to Ruby to put my hands on her waist and I pulled her closer to me. Her skin was silky underwater. Though we were prevented from getting too close by our legs kicking to keep us afloat, every bit of skin-to-skin contact burned, like it should glow from beneath the dark water. My hands on her waist, her hands on my hips, our legs brushing up against one another.

She pulled me closer to kiss me and my breath caught. It wasn't just her lips on mine, but her whole body slipped and slid against mine in a way that was gentle but set me on fire. The gulping of the water trapped under the rock and the hushing waves faded. She hooked her legs around my waist. I kissed her back until I couldn't take it any more. I wanted to run my hands all over her, I wanted to find the secret places on her body and I wanted her to do the same to me, but instead, we broke apart.

Wanting more felt good too. Like a good ache.

We climbed out without looking at each other. Somehow even though I'd felt her body wrapped around mine, the idea of being seen was different. I wrung my hair out, twisting it into a rope and squeezing, water splashing onto my feet. Ruby's teeth chattered as she got dressed.

Dressed in damp clothes, Ruby kissed me on the nose.

"You have good ideas," she said.

It was a different kind of kiss to the ones in the water, but it felt really nice too.

18

An International Man of Mystery
Whatcha doin'

Saoirse
When did you get my phone??

An International Man of Mystery
I can't tell you that. I'm stealthy.
Like James Bond. Definitely not when
you were in the toilet, that's for sure.

Saoirse
OK, I am kind of into this one.
The soundtrack is awesome.

00Gobshite.
I'm going to need more than that

Saoirse
Watching 10 things I hate about you.

00Gobshite.
I don't know if I've seen that one.

Saoirse

Turn it on. I only just started it. I'll pause.
Let me know when you get to the bit
where she's reading the bell jar.

00Gobshite.

OK I'm there.

Saoirse

I'm into intense goth friend.

00Gobshite.

Hard same.

Saoirse

Why are there so many bets in teen
rom-coms?

00Gobshite.

More importantly, between all the
betting and romantic antics, when
do these people do their homework?
They're about to finish school? I still
have nightmares about the leaving cert
and it ended weeks ago.

Saoirse

The thing is, either you fancy someone or
you don't. If you have to create an elaborate
serenade to Can't Take My Eyes Off You to
get someone to go out with you, the person
probably doesn't like you very much.

00Gobshite.
Not all of us were blessed with
your raw animal magnetism.
Like a walking Lynx advert.

> **Saoirse.**
> Gross. It's only cute because Heath
> Ledger is cute. If he was a bog standard
> lad, you'd be calling the guards like.

00Gobshite.
Did she seriously just flash the teacher
to get him out of detention?

> **Saoirse**
> Yep. Can you imagine flashing Mr Connolly?

00Gobshite.
I mean I can. But I'm very proud
of my nipples so . . .

> **Saoirse**
> I'm going to ignore the fact that you brought
> up your nipples.
> Wait why is she doing the apology poem
> when he's the one who made the bet?

00Gobshite.
Because she's not a feminist any more
because of love. I'm pretty sure that's the
moral of the story.

Saoirse
That doesn't make any sense.

00Gobshite.
But they're all so good looking
it hardly matters.

Saoirse
Aw he bought her the guitar because he
supports her angry girl music dreams. I
mean, I personally wouldn't forgive him,
but it's kind of sweet I suppose.

00Gobshite.
You're turning into such a sap.
I'm going to tell Ruby.

Saoirse
Oh no. Please don't tell the girl I like that
I secretly enjoy the films she loves. That
would be a disaster.

00Gobshite.
You tricked me. I'm just a pawn in
your mind games aren't I?

Saoirse
You'd have to have a brain for me to
play mind games with you.

00Gobshite.
Critical Hit. Ego -2000pts

19

~~9. Having one of those "No, you hang up" conversations on the phone (as seen in *The Truth About Cats & Dogs*, *Pillow Talk*).~~

On Thursday we scheduled a phone call where neither one of us would hang up. It was the thing on the list I most wanted to avoid because no one likes actually being on the phone. It's torture. And all the rom-coms where people don't want to hang up on each other are from before technology granted us the gift of texting.

But it was on the list so it had to be done. For authenticity, I agreed to call on my dad's home office landline to the landline at Oliver's house. I prayed Ruby would be the one to answer. I even texted her a warning. If this was something old people had to struggle through when they were young, it's a wonder the species survived.

"Hello?" A confused male voice answered the phone. Of course, it was Oliver.

"Is Ruby there?" I said, pitching my voice high and trying to sound super polite and professional so he wouldn't recognise my voice.

"Saoirse?"

Of course.

"Yeah, what?" My voice dropped back down to its normal level soaked in disdain.

"It was weird. I heard this ringing noise and I wondered where it came from. I found this strange machine covered in cobwebs."

I almost laughed but that would only encourage him.

"Can you put Ruby on?"

"Is your phone broken?" he asked, ignoring me. He sounded genuinely curious as to why anyone would utilise such outdated modes of communication.

"No. Yes. Look, it's none of your business."

"Is this part of your romantic game thing?"

All my extremities turned cold. This was the most embarrassing moment of my entire life.

"What?" I squeezed my eyes shut and hoped somehow he would say something, anything, other than—

"Ruby told me about your little list. It's adorable," he drawled. "Who would have guessed you were such an old romantic? Are you making a scrapbook of the experience? Do you write about it in your journal at night? Do you want me to snip off a lock of Ruby's hair for you?"

"Go away," I groaned, and I would have hung up then if I hadn't heard Ruby on the other end.

"Oliver, stop it," she said to him. "Hi," she said to me.

"So. I know this call is supposed to be us not wanting to hang up but actually, I really want to hang up."

Ruby laughed. "Why, what's wrong?"

"You told Oliver?"

"Yeah, so?"

"He's my nemesis. And you showed him my weakness. My soft underbelly."

Ruby laughed again. "Oliver is not your nemesis. And surely your weakness is your pitiful lower body strength and inability to mime pedalling?"

"You knew I was faking?" I really thought I'd made it look like I was working that pedalo too.

"I was doing all the work, of course I knew! My glutes were on fire the next day."

"I see . . ." I trailed off. "Awkward."

"Do you think I should be a professional sailor? I could join the navy."

"Based on your pedalo experience? Probably not."

"I could be the first woman to sail around the world in a swan."

"Saoirse, what are you doing in here?" Dad walked into his office with a coffee in one hand and a tablet in the other. "Are you on the phone? Did you lose your mobile? I'm not buying you a new one."

"I'm on a call. Please leave."

"Is that your dad? Tell him I said hi," Ruby said,

sounding more excited than any teenager ever has about a parent eavesdropping on a conversation.

"Oh, Saoirse, did you see one of the big swans escaped," Dad said, flipping his tablet so the screen faced me. It was on the homepage of the local newspaper. "Peda-Low Life Steals Giant Swan" was the headline, and there was a photograph of our bird, recovered, with the owner.

"No way," I said.

"Why not?" Ruby asked.

"I know, right?" Dad said. "It was quite the scandal. They think it was kids joyriding. It was found wedged into a rock further up the cove."

Joyriding. Honestly.

"I mean no way to Ruby. Dad, give me a sec, would you?"

"Oh, it's Ruuuuby," he said, childishly drawing out her name. He made kissy noises that would put you off locking lips for life.

"Why no? Can't I say hi to your dad?"

"This was a terrible idea," I said, more to myself than Ruby or Dad.

"Why don't you ask Ruby round for dinner on Saturday night?" Dad said, smirking over his coffee.

I shook my head fiercely and mouthed *no way*.

"I heard that. I'D LOVE TO COME FOR DINNER," Ruby shouted in my ear, and I instinctively held the phone out to prevent permanent injury. My heart started pounding. She couldn't come here. Not to meet Dad anyway. Maybe if he was out and we had the place to ourselves . . .

"Ruby, we have that thing," I said, trying to remind her about number three on the montage list. We were going to get a train into the city and go to do karaoke at this bar that I was pretty sure didn't ask for ID. It was the only way I could envision singing. And even singing sounded preferable to this dinner.

Dad shouted back at the phone held aloft in my hand, "ARE YOU ALLERGIC TO ANYTHING?"

I gave Dad a wide-eyed "don't you dare" face. He ignored me. I could expect that from him.

"NO, BUT I REALLY HATE MUSHROOMS."

"Ruby, we have other plans," I said. She didn't catch my annoyance.

"GOT IT, NO MUSHROOMS."

I gave Dad a look that asked, *Are you done now?* He nodded and backed out of the room. "I'll give you some privacy." He winked.

Too little, too bloody late.

20

After the phone call, I tried not to panic. Which I take as a sign of serious personal growth. I went up to my room and started to watch one of the films, *500 Days of Summer*, and ignored the fact that my foot wouldn't stay still but kept tap tap tapping against the bed frame. Unfortunately, the guy in the film wouldn't listen to the girl in the film telling him she didn't want something serious and that did not help distract me from Ruby, so I switched to a proper film with a demon child and a cursed mansion. Dad popped his head in to say he was going out. He had a gift bag in his hand. I grunted instead of saying goodbye and didn't ask what was in the bag. Partly because I was furious with him and partly because I was afraid it was something gross like lingerie for Beth.

When the film ended, I was still agitated and decided I had to get out of the house. I needed to go see Mum. I'd seen her that morning as usual, but the urge was overwhelming. I wanted to hug her and smell her Mum smell and curl up in a ball beside her and be comforted by it even though she wouldn't know what to say. The idea that Ruby was going to be in our house, talking to Dad, was giving me palpitations and no amount of demon children could distract me.

There was no way she could come around here and not violate the rules somehow. So dinner with Dad wasn't exactly on the list per se but it was a very serious couple thing to do. That was "we-ing" on a metaphorical level if not a literal one. And there was no way we'd get through a whole evening without something to do with Mum or the blasted wedding coming up. She'd want to know all about it, and I wouldn't want to talk about it and then there really would be a fight. We'd be in serious relationship territory then. Ruby was sticking her nose in where it didn't belong. Maybe this whole montage thing was a bad idea. She obviously didn't understand boundaries. I mean, OK, those boundaries hadn't exactly been spelled out for her, but she should have waited for me to invite her, not my dad shouting over the phone.

And yet, I didn't really want to end this whole thing over a dinner, did I? Maybe I could get out of it somehow. I needed to talk to Mum. It might not be the same as before but talking to her still always helped give me some perspective.

Nora waved at me from the other end of the hall. She must have wondered why I was visiting a second time in one day. Or maybe she wasn't thinking about me at all because she was a busy person and I was an egomaniac.

When I got to Mum's door it was slightly open and I heard a low voice. Dad's voice. I checked my watch. It wasn't his normal time to visit. I thought about turning around but something made me listen at the door. Habit maybe. It felt like being a kid again and I felt the same rumble in my stomach, as though I could potentially hear some more terrible news. As though the worst hadn't already happened.

The last time Dad and I had visited together was before I found out he was seeing Beth. I wouldn't go with him after that. I couldn't stand to see him sit there and talk to her knowing that he was lying and cheating and she didn't even realise it.

I peeked in the door, thinking that if they did catch me looking, I'd stroll in and pretend I had just turned up. But they were sitting facing the window, their backs half turned away from me, though I could still see their faces in profile.

"What do you think?" Dad asked. "I thought I remembered you saying you wanted one like this years ago. I guess I should have got it for you then, but we had no money and I forgot. Till now anyway."

He was holding out a small box. She didn't pay any attention to it so Dad opened it and showed her what was inside. I couldn't see it exactly but I thought it might be a bracelet. She picked it up and said thank you but she was getting restless, I could see it in the way she was fidgeting. Dad could sense it too. His voice took on that enthusiastic primary school teacher tone I caught myself using sometimes. He picked up another box. A larger one.

"What do we have here?" he said, rattling it.

He pulled on the ribbon and ripped off the paper like a child on his birthday.

It was a black square picture frame, though I couldn't see what was in it.

"I love it," he said in the same kind of voice he used when I'd give him Father's Day mugs or handmade cards, as though it was the best thing he'd ever got. He took Mum's hand and kissed it. "You always know exactly what I want. Happy anniversary, love."

I totally forgot it was their anniversary. It wasn't the kind of thing I'd ever paid much attention to anyway. Mum smiled. I wanted her to do something. To reach out and hold his hand or lean over and kiss his cheek. She didn't do either of those things. She got up and walked away, chattering about something completely unrelated. A sharp pain hit me in the chest and I had the overwhelming urge to try to reach in and dig it out because I couldn't bear it.

Eyes blurry with tears, I walked as quick as I could back down the hall. When I saw Nora again I stopped her and swallowed hard.

"Did someone take my mum out shopping to get my dad a present?" I asked.

She shook her head. "No, dear, that's not really part of our job," she said gently.

"She gave my dad an anniversary present. Where did she get it from?"

Nora smiled. "Well, if I remember this right, your dad got a present on his birthday a few months back too."

When I looked confused, she whispered behind her hand like it was some kind of cute secret she was telling me.

"I think he buys them himself and then gives them to her, to give to him. It's quite sweet."

Dad always signed my birthday cards *Love Mum and Dad*. I thought it was something he did for me, out of habit or pity. I pictured him wandering the shops picking out gifts for himself from Mum, taking care to wrap them up and write cards because she would never want to miss a birthday or anniversary. He did it for her. Some sort of emptiness in me filled up and it hurt.

I couldn't speak, I just nodded at Nora and she left me standing in the reception wiping tears on my sleeve.

21

Unfortunately not ~~3. Karaoke. Where one or both people reveal their hidden singing talent or lack thereof (as seen in *My Best Friend's Wedding, 500 Days of Summer*).~~

I paced the living room, alternating between rubbing the scar on the palm of my hand and rubbing the cold sweat off the back of my neck.

Dad was humming as he set a pair of candlesticks on the dinner table. They were sort of incongruous with the papery disposable tablecloth with holly wreaths around the border.

We were half an hour out from the dinner disaster. I mean, Dad and Ruby in one room. I'd spent the last few days trying more and more desperately to get out of it. I told Dad that Ruby cancelled but he didn't believe me and threatened to call the Quinn house and invite the whole family around. He knew I didn't want this night to happen, but he thought it was only because I was embarrassed. I told Ruby that Dad had to work but she suggested coming round anyway if I had an empty house and I couldn't think of a reason why not, so the next day I said he didn't have to work after all. She seemed suspicious after that. I'd even stood at the top of the stairs contemplating throwing myself down there, wondering if a broken leg would save me, but knowing how determined they both were, I didn't see how they'd accept anything less than fatality as an excuse. The only thing I hadn't given any real consideration to was telling the truth to either of them.

"No talking about anything . . . controversial," I said. I'd been barking orders at him all day. "Don't be trying to start a debate or have a 'serious conversation' or anything."

I tried to convince myself it was totally possible to go the whole night without Dad mentioning Mum. Why would he mention her, after all? He stuck her in a care home so he could forget about her.

"This is a *casual* dinner," I snapped. "Don't be asking lots of questions. You don't need to know her life story, OK? I'm doing you a favour letting her come here and meet you. Don't make me regret it."

Dad rolled his eyes dramatically and I got the impression he thought he was impersonating me.

"Thank you, your highness, for the great gift you have bestowed upon me. I shall finish making all the food for your guest and then I will stand in the corner with my face to the wall."

Dad bowed silently and hobbled off to the kitchen all hunched over like Quasimodo. Mum used to say we had the same sense of humour. She couldn't have been more wrong.

I began fussing with the table settings, straightening forks and moving the salt shaker. My stomach flipped over. And over. Something looked wrong.

"Why are there four place settings?" I said, my voice getting high-pitched. "You didn't invite Beth, did you?"

"Of course," Dad said, shaking his head at me like I was being absentminded.

He really didn't get anything. It wouldn't even occur to him that I might not want her here. I go on one appointment with her for her stupid dress and he thinks everything is grand. Or rather he *wants* to think that and will happily ignore any evidence to the contrary. That was Beth's fault for not ratting me out about my little outburst. She tried way too hard.

"She's so excited to meet Ruby."

Beth and Ruby. Oh God. I hadn't even thought of that. Ruby didn't know who Beth was. I'd never even mentioned her name. She'd wonder who this woman was. Had I actually even said that Mum and Dad were split up? She'd think Beth was my mum. She might call her Mrs Clarke and then there'd be a horrible awkward pause and someone would have to explain. There's no way they wouldn't talk about the wedding. Ruby would absolutely be asking questions about where my mum was after all that.

Nope. This couldn't happen. I had to do something. Anything. Even if it seemed suspicious to Ruby. I was kidding myself if I thought there was any way that we would get through the night without one of my stupid secrets coming out.

OK, I could pretend we would reschedule and then I'd find a way to get out of it later. It wasn't perfect, it wasn't a permanent fix, but it would buy me time. I snatched the candlesticks off the table and hid them behind a cushion.

"Uh, where are those candlesticks?" I asked Dad, like I was deeply concerned that the table was missing a vital ambience-building decoration. "You were holding them a minute ago, weren't you?"

Dad frowned at the table. "I thought I put them out." He wandered off to find his misplaced items and I pulled my phone out and pressed call on Ruby's number. She picked up on the first ring.

"Saoirse?" She sounded confused.

I coughed dramatically into the phone.

"Are you OK?" she asked. She sounded worried. I almost felt guilty, like I was stealing sympathy.

"Maybe you shouldn't come. I feel really sick. I might be contagious. I have, um . . ." I cringed. I couldn't say it. I had to say it. It was for the greater good. I could not have Beth and Ruby meeting. My whole carefully balanced system of rules and boundaries was going to come crashing down if I didn't do something drastic. Even if it meant totally mortifying myself. "I have diarrhea," I squeaked into the phone.

"And it's making you cough?" The sympathy was gone, replaced by a healthy dose of scepticism.

The doorbell rang. I held my breath, hoping Ruby wouldn't hear it.

"Get that door, will you?" Dad yelled like that absolute moron that he was. "I keep meaning to give Beth a key but we're moving so soon."

"Oh . . . yeah, sort of. I have a sore throat too. I'm in bed. I feel terrible," I whispered into the phone.

Distracted, I opened the door with the phone cradled between my shoulder and my jaw. Sure enough, Beth was standing there with a bottle of wine.

Right next to her was Ruby.

She was wearing a paisley knee-length dress, dozens of strings of beads wrapped around her neck, and a look that I hadn't seen before, but was the much angrier cousin of the one I'd seen flash across her face that day at the drive-in when I'd snapped at her.

Dad appeared and spread his arms and his smile wide.

"Ruby! I've been dying to meet you."

She shifted her features into a smile and gave my dad a bunch of poofy pink flowers she was holding. Beth looked nervously between me and Ruby. Dad had no idea what was going on. My heart thumped so hard I thought it would escape. There was a distinct possibility that I would throw up right now. That wouldn't hurt actually. I could actually get away with my lie about being sick then.

"These are from my aunt's garden. I was going to steal one of her bottles of wine, but I didn't know if you'd be mad about that seeing as Saoirse's only seventeen. Didn't want you thinking I was a bad influence." Ruby said all this so jovially I wondered if she might not be too mad.

"Oh, I know Saoirse better than that. Thank you, Ruby," Dad said.

"Let's go find a vase," Beth said, glancing at me before gripping Dad by the elbow and steering him into the kitchen. Beth had obviously heard my phone call. How long had she been out there with Ruby? What might she have said?

"You're early," I said, offering a tentative half smile like it was all a silly misunderstanding.

"How rude of me," she replied. She did not smile back. Nope, definitely mad.

Silence fell like a curtain between us.

"I should go," Ruby said when I didn't say anything. She looked angry but she sounded hurt. And even though I was the one who had panicked and tried to stop her coming, I hadn't meant to hurt her feelings. I didn't like seeing her feel that way and I definitely didn't like knowing it was because of me.

"Please don't go," I said, and I was surprised and embarrassed to hear a break in my voice. I wasn't going to cry. That was stupid.

"You obviously don't want me here."

"No. It's not that. I mean, OK. I tried to stop you coming. But I was nervous. My dad. He's weird and annoying and I'm afraid that if you meet him you definitely won't want to finish the montage."

It was half the truth. He could definitely do or say something that would put an end to this thing. And I realised how much I wanted to keep it going now that she looked like she might walk away.

"Because your dad is weird?"

"Well, it sounds stupid when you say it."

"No, trust me, it sounds stupid when you say it too," she said with a smirk.

I laughed and took Ruby's hand.

"Please. I'm a dick, I know but I promise it was not about you."

Ruby looked at me, appraising my excuse. It was weak.

"Fine. But you better make it up to me."

"Oh yeah?" I waggled my eyebrows suggestively.

"As if. How about next time you're nervous about something, you actually tell me the truth and we talk about it instead of making silly stories up."

"Well now, that wouldn't be very rom-com of me, would it? The guy always gets himself into a stupid situation because he tells some ridiculous lie. If anything, I'm just really committed to our bit."

"You're not the guy," Ruby pointed out. "That's the whole point. Neither of us is the guy. In the lesbian rom-com, we

218

would discuss all of our feelings until our throats dry up and our bodies shrivel."

"I promise. No more lies," I lied.

"I found the candlesticks!" Dad said, appearing with two completely different candlesticks. Why did we have two sets of candlesticks but only one Christmas-themed tablecloth?

"What are you going to study at university, Ruby?" Dad asked around a mouthful of flavourless stir-fry.

"Dad, honestly. Stop grilling her." I grimaced. "You're not a guidance counsellor." I shook my foot nervously, wondering when this would be over and whether or not I'd survive it, relationship intact. Of course I'd told Ruby to stay but that meant I had to be more vigilant than ever. My secrets were bombs that could detonate at any second and the only thing that was making me happy these days would explode.

"Oh, for God's sake. That's the first thing I've asked."

"It's really OK." Ruby put her hand on my arm before replying to Dad. "I'm not going next year. I'm going to take a gap year," Ruby said, giving me a reassuring kind of look. She thought I was trying to protect her from Dad's interrogation.

"Good for you. Do some travelling or something?"

"Well, no. Not quite. I'm going to stay home."

I didn't know that. I'd thought before that Ruby must

be going travelling and I'd kind of decided that was true without thinking about it again. I didn't ask her about it for obvious reasons. You know, because I like to stay in the moment.

Kidding. It was because I selfishly tried to avoid any conversation that might lead back to me.

"Do you live anywhere near Oxford?" he asked, pointing at me. My throat seized up. This was it. Doom. I scanned the table as though a smooth change of conversation would leap out at me and I noticed Beth watching me.

"Not really," Ruby said, a little sadly I thought. "But it's so impressive that Saoirse's going there."

I buried my face in my hands. I couldn't do it. I couldn't keep up the pretense. Lying to Dad and Ruby (OK, and Beth), acting as though I was excited, because who wouldn't be excited about Oxford? I felt as though the world was coming down around me and I was supposed to paste on a smile. Dad would see through me finally. He'd turn white and demand to know why I didn't want to go. I wouldn't be able to speak. I'd be backed into a corner with both of them bearing down on me. He would say *Is this about your mum?* Ruby would say *What about your mum?* Dad would tell her all about it and then Ruby would look at me with that pity face and tell me how awful it all was. Meanwhile, Dad would clutch his chest and stop breathing, a heart attack caused by the sheer audacity of someone turning down a place at Oxford. He'd collapse onto the table and die facedown in a plate of egg fried noodles. I'd basically be an orphan and Ruby would be furious I'd lied to her and never speak to me again.

No, I'm not being dramatic.

Shut up.

Just then Beth leapt out of her chair and yelped.

"Oh no!" she squealed. "Rob, get a fire extinguisher."

Across the table, the candles had tipped over and a small flame was slowly (comically slowly) eating through the crappy paper tablecloth.

Dad looked at Beth, who appeared stricken, and laughed.

"I don't think we need a fire extinguisher, love." He patted the flame with a tea towel that was still slung over his shoulder from making dinner.

Beth put her hand to her chest and breathed in a few deep breaths.

"Oh my goodness," she said, fanning herself, "that was scary. Oh, Rob, weren't you saying you think you know Ruby's dad?"

"Yes, my brother Vincey was friends with your dad – Mike, isn't it?"

I looked at Beth, who was now happily munching on a soggy green bean like nothing had happened. I looked at the candlesticks. I looked at Beth again. She gave me a small smile.

"That's my dad! I didn't realise you knew him." Ruby

seemed delighted. If I met someone who said they knew my dad I'd probably apologise or run away.

"He's a good man, Mike. What's he up to these days?"

"Well, he works for the civil service, but I get the feeling he'd rather be a professional football commentator. He's practising really hard."

Dad laughed. "That's the dream."

In a very mature fashion, I declined to point out that Dad often called soccer Gaelic football for wimps.

"What about your mum?" Beth chimed in.

"Oh, she isn't working." Ruby cleared her throat. She looked like she wanted to add something but she didn't.

"That's lovely," Dad said encouragingly, "always having your mum at home when you get back from school."

Ruby nodded but I noticed her smile was tight and she filled her mouth with wilted broccoli spears.

"Saoirse's mum started working from home when she was wee so she could be around too. It's nice for kids, I think, to have their mum at home."

Oh God, this was it. My face got hot and I cut across Dad.

"Remember what we said, Dad," I warned, but tried to keep my voice light.

"What's controversial about that?" Dad said bewildered.

I faltered for a brief moment before it came to me.

"You're being sexist!" I announced. He *was* being sexist

but I wouldn't have bothered bringing it up; I only wanted to steer him away from talking about Mum.

"Am I?" he asked, looking to Beth for reassurance. Surprisingly she nodded and took my side.

"I mean, why did you say it's nice for kids to have their mum at home and not, for example, 'a parent'? If we had a kid do you think I'd stay home with it while you swan off to work?"

"Er . . ." Dad blustered. "No, I didn't say that. It's not like I think women should give up work and be chained to the dishwasher. I'm not a dinosaur."

"Good, because I make more money than you."

I snorted a laugh before I could stop myself. I felt weirdly proud of Beth for a second.

"That's good with me. I'll stay at home and eat bonbons and mind our imaginary baby," Dad joked. He received stony glares in response.

"Because that's what mums do?" Beth raised an eyebrow. Why could everyone do that one-eyebrow thing but me?

The ghost of a thousand other dinner conversations lingered. Dad saying something stupid he didn't really believe and Mum snapping back and setting him right. A spectre of Mum could be sitting where Beth was sitting right now.

"It's a joke," Dad said.

"Jokes can be sexist too," she said, simply like Dad's comment was too stupid to be worth any more of a response. Which it was.

Dad waved his napkin in surrender.

"OK, OK. I only said it was nice. I didn't say it was mandatory. I can see I'm outnumbered here. Don't burn me at the stake, all right?"

"That's sexist too," Beth said lightly, like she was pointing out he had spinach in his teeth. "Implying you're at some kind of physical risk because women are disagreeing with you, not to mention invoking a type of capital punishment historically used against women who didn't conform to patriarchal standards."

Ruby mouthed at me, *She's great.*

A thought occurred to me, unwanted, but I knew it was true: in a parallel universe, Mum and Beth would be best friends. It felt like something was stuck in my throat.

"You're right, I'm an arse," Dad said, though I caught the glint in his eye that told me he enjoyed all of this. "I shall go prepare a peace offering. It comes with ice cream." He kissed Beth on the forehead before he left and winked at me. She shook her head at his back.

"Men!" she said, exasperated. "It's all a joke because there are no consequences for them."

I got the impression that the consequences would be a serious talking-to from Beth later and it made me feel better.

"Yep. He's basically a knob. But you're the one choosing to go out with him. I'm stuck on account of the whole 'being my dad' card he keeps playing."

She laughed and for a moment it felt like Beth was on my side. Or I was on hers.

"He isn't perfect," Beth said fairly. "But he cares and he's open to changing his mind; that's a great quality to have."

I was going to argue that it would be better to not be an arse to begin with but Ruby spoke first.

"What's your job, then?" she asked.

"I'm an ethical advertising consultant," she said. "Firms hire me to collaborate with them on creating ethical campaigns and to root out stereotyping in their work. There's a whole team of us. We look at different issues according to our specialities."

"That sounds so interesting. How did you get to do that?" Ruby was staring at Beth like she was some kind of rock star now. It did sound interesting. I hadn't realised that's what Beth did. Advertising blah blah was the gist I had caught up to now.

"Well, I did Women's Studies at university. Eons ago. In the States at an all-women's college. I was particularly interested in how advertising can both create and drive patriarchal narratives. I wondered if there was a way to counteract that or to even harness that power for something positive."

"Do you think I could do a job like that?" Ruby asked, wide-eyed.

Beth laughed. "I don't see why not. But I have to warn

you, I don't know how successful an endeavour it really is. Sometimes I feel like I'm only changing the parts of the machine when I should be dismantling it, but other days we do something really amazing and put it out in the world and I feel like maybe it does do some good."

Ruby nodded seriously. "Every little helps, doesn't it? Like those tampon ads where the boys have periods and they all talk about them like it's some kind of badge of honour and then they showed the facts about period shame and poverty around the world . . ."

"That was us!" Beth said excitedly.

"Seriously? Everyone I knew was talking about that. The same week it came out we had to decide our health class project that term. I started a campaign about period poverty and raised all this money for a charity that distributes free sanitary products to low-income women."

I watched Ruby's face as she spoke, animated and glowing. How did someone so lovely and thoughtful want to be with me with all my sarcasm and selfishness? She was incredible. Beth was so happy she looked like she was going to cry. Dad walked in on the words *sanitary products* and walked out again, muttering about forgetting the chocolate sauce.

22

Ruby and I escaped to my room after dessert to watch *Pillow Talk*, even though it was positively ancient and kind of homophobic. Dad jokingly called up after us to leave the door open.

"I don't want to be a grandfather this young," he wailed.

"That's pretty amazing what you did at school," I said, shutting the door behind us. "With your campaign."

I thought if I started the conversation, directed it, I might distract her from any of the weirdness that had happened downstairs. In my mind I thanked Beth for having an interesting job.

Ruby blushed. "It was important to me."

This girl was too good for me. This girl was also going through all the open boxes of my things.

"Er, what are you doing?" I asked, settling myself cross-legged on the bed.

"Being nosy," she said.

"Oh, OK, so long as you know."

"I like your room," Ruby said, inspecting a ceramic giraffe I'd had as long as I could remember.

"It's a box graveyard now and not exactly like your

227

room," I said, thinking of the high ceilings and expensive furniture in Ruby's room.

"That's not my room," Ruby said. "It's nothing like Oliver's house."

"What's it like?"

She thought about it. "Claustrophobic. Not because it's small though. Although it *is* small."

That didn't make sense. I had a picture of Ruby's room in my head and while it probably had the decorative sensibilities of Aladdin's cave, I assumed it also had the expansive square footage.

I had to stop making things up in my head and then believing them as if they were true.

"Why, then?"

"Do you actually want to know?" Ruby stopped rummaging and rounded on me, hands on her hips.

"Of course I do," I said. I could feel a hot flush on my chest. I had obviously avoided asking Ruby anything about her life back in England and she clearly noticed because she's not stupid. But if I avoided it now, it would look really odd.

"It's not *fun*," she said, and I heard a note of bitterness.

"That's OK," I said. Perhaps I had to be a bit more flexible or it would only highlight how cagey I was being. I hadn't thought about it like that before.

"Is it, though? I mean, you didn't tell me your dad was getting remarried in a few weeks, which is really weird. You never even mentioned Beth."

I didn't like where this was going. We were meant to be having a conversation about *her* family. I felt tricked.

"It's pretty recent news to me too. I was going to tell you." I tried to force my tone into something resembling patience. "I thought we could go to the wedding together before you leave," I offered. "Check off the slow dance there."

Of course I'd never intended to tell her about the wedding, but she knew now so I might as well try to use it.

She didn't respond to my invitation. Rude.

"What else don't you talk about? Do you ever tell me anything real? You're really weird whenever Oxford comes up."

I suppose it was too much to hope that she hadn't picked up on that, in spite of Beth's diversionary tactics.

Ruby wouldn't look at me; she looked at her hands instead, her fingers twisting into knots like she wasn't used to confrontation and she didn't much care for it. I felt my heart open up and let in something I'd been trying to keep out. I could tell her this. She deserved to know something and maybe we could talk about it. Maybe she'd get it. It didn't mean I had to talk about Mum. But I could let this one thing out and maybe it wouldn't feel like I was keeping so much trapped inside me.

I took a deep breath.

"I applied to Oxford last year. I passed the interview. I'm probably going to get the grades I need, but I don't think I want to go any more and I haven't told my dad. He'll go ballistic." It was stupid but I felt nervous saying it and my voice wobbled over the words. When had I become so incapable of being honest?

"OK . . . ?" She drew the word out like a question. "But why couldn't you tell me that? Why is it such a big secret?"

I laughed, feeling lighter already. "I suppose it isn't."

It never occurred to me that I could tell Ruby I didn't want to go to Oxford and she wouldn't find that so suspicious that she'd ask loads of follow-up questions.

Later I'd wonder if there was a part of me that wanted her to ask, that wanted her to drag the truth out of me when I couldn't make myself say it.

She sat down beside me on the bed and played with the loose tendrils of hair around my neck. "You can tell me anything," she said. "And your dad is going to get over it. It's obvious he loves you so much. If you want, I'll help you figure out a way to tell him. I'll even be there with you if you need me." She kissed me on the nose.

Tight bands of pressure around my chest released a little. I felt like I'd gotten away with something huge and even got some of the worries I'd been hanging on to off my chest.

"Tell me your thing," I said, and I meant it. Not just because I'd been burning with curiosity for weeks but because I finally thought that maybe we could share *some* things without the world cracking open and swallowing me whole. Bend the rules without breaking them. For the good of the montage.

"Really?" she asked softly, looking at me finally.

"Yes. Please tell me." I reached to hold her hand. "If you want to, of course."

"It's not a secret, although it's been feeling like one lately," she started. "The only reason I didn't tell you is because I thought you might not want to hear it. You never asked why I was here or why Mum was in America even though I mentioned those things and it made me think you didn't want to know anything about my life back home."

I'd been ignoring it for my own selfish reasons. More guilt to stow deep down and never examine.

"I'm so sorry. I didn't want to pry," I said, hoping that was a good enough explanation for me being totally rude.

"The reason I'm here staying with Oliver's family in the first place is my parents are in America. My little brother needed surgery. A kind you can't always get on the NHS. We don't have any money so Uncle Harry paid for everything and they went to the States because the best surgeon is there. Uncle Harry insisted on the best. I agreed to stay here until they get back so they wouldn't have to worry about me or spend any more of his money bringing me with them."

She said all this in one breath like she'd been holding it in since I met her.

My mind flooded with questions I didn't know if it was OK to even ask. What was wrong with her brother? Could he die? Had he always been like this or did he get sick suddenly? Had he had the surgery yet? Did it work?

"What's his name?"

"Noah."

"Tell me about him."

Ruby told me all about Noah. How he had a specific type of cerebral palsy and the surgery was meant to improve his walking and balance and reduce muscle spasticity (which Ruby had to explain to me). It had to be followed up with a lot of physical therapy. She also told me that Noah was Ariana Grande's biggest fan and that he wore a Spider-Man outfit six days a week. Her family had gone out early to have a bit of a holiday and then they'd be staying awhile for recovery and aftercare. She said complications were rare but she still panicked every time her mum phoned just in case. When they got back Noah would be spending a long time getting intensive physical therapies in a treatment centre in London. Thankfully it was a short commute from their home. Ruby was putting off uni until next year because she wanted to be around to help and get a job to help pay for some of the cost of all the travelling and extra things they needed. It surprised me that they didn't have money. Somehow I'd assumed that because Oliver's family were rich, Ruby's family were too. But it didn't surprise me that Ruby would do that for her family. I thought about her story about the gymnastics classes, the way she rescued (stole) kittens, her period campaign, and how even after I messed up and lied to her she still wanted to be there for me and help me with Dad. She would do anything to care for the people she loved.

Unlike me.

She was so cheerful and positive and though she was obviously sad that her little brother had to deal with such big things, I couldn't see in her the horrible things I saw in myself. The frustration and tiredness and self-pity. The shame or anger or hopelessness.

"I think next year when things are a bit more settled I'm going to try and do something like what Beth was talking about at uni. I did psychology A level – do you think that would be relevant? It sounds so cool. Do you think she'd let me tag along to a meeting or something?" Ruby chattered, and she seemed lighter and happier than ever. And it was the first career option she'd considered that had lasted more than fifteen seconds.

"Probably," I said, swallowing the horrible thoughts.

Now that Ruby had finally been able to tell me something that was so important to her, she was giddy and free like she might float away on a strong breeze. But the lightness I'd felt earlier vanished. A ton weight of guilt kept me firmly grounded.

"You should ask," I said, swallowing it down. "Maybe you could get a job there after university. You could branch out to films and TV and work on improving lesbian representation in the media."

"No more suicides or turning into hawks at the end."

"And a thousand percent more kissing."

In a spontaneous burst, Ruby threw her arms around me and hugged me tightly. "I'm really glad I told you, Saoirse. It doesn't feel right keeping something so big from you."

"I'm glad you told me too."

She pressed her lips to mine and when she pulled back, her flecked hazel eyes locked on to mine, able to make my skin tingle without a single touch.

"If you ever want to talk about anything else, I want to hear it too. Even if it isn't 'fun'." She air quoted the word, like the silly game we'd been playing was over now.

But it was one thing for to Ruby show me something that only made her seem more beautiful, show how strong she was when her family was under pressure. If I told her about Mum, she would see all the ugliest parts of me and I didn't want her to see that. She was staying home to help her family, and I had applied to leave the country without thinking about my own mother. I couldn't tell her any more than I had already. There was no point sharing my flaws and failures and ruining everything when it would all be over soon.

"I don't really have anything else." I grinned.

Move along now, nothing to see here.

Ruby hesitated. "Where's your mum?" she asked, forcing lightness into her voice as though the question had come from nowhere in particular.

My jaw clenched involuntarily and I forced it to relax. "She's around. Her and my dad are divorced, that's all."

True.

"Do you still see her?" Ruby asked.

"All the time."

True.

Ruby's forehead crinkled. "Oh, OK. Will I get to meet her before I go?"

"Yes, of course."

Lie.

23

Saoirse
Do you think people who have been friends for years can suddenly fall in love?

Saoirse
PS honestly. How did you do it this time? I haven't seen you in ages?

My Lord and Saviour, Oliver Quinn
Saoirse, I'm very flattered but I'm just not that into you.

My Lord and Saviour, Oliver Quinn
And I had a helper.

Saoirse
I'm watching When Harry Met Sally. He's confessed his love to her by listing a bunch of things she does. Oh and tell Ruby she's a filthy traitor.

Lord of the Flies, Oliver Quinn
Keep your dirty talk between you two, thank you very much.

Saoirse

Do you though? Think best friends can suddenly
start fancying each other? I mean surely if you
weren't interested in them in the beginning then
after years and years of being friends, are you
not just settling?

Lord of the Flies, Oliver Quinn

People change though. Maybe when
they first met they weren't right for each
other but after experience and time,
they grew together. I mean some people
get married, divorce, and then years later
get married again. Anything is possible.

Saoirse

Didn't know you were such a romantic.

Lord of the Flies, Oliver Quinn

I'm a man of hidden depths.

Saoirse

So why don't you have a girlfriend
then?

Lord of the Flies, Oliver Quinn

I don't know. No one has ever really
seen me that way I think. I'm the
party guy, not the boyfriend guy.

Saoirse

I think you'll make a good boyfriend
someday.

Lord of the Flies, Oliver Quinn
Because of my dashing good looks
and honed lovemaking skills?

Saoirse
No, because of your cool car and vault
full of gold coins.

24

2. ~~One person teaches the other a skill (as seen in~~
~~*Say Anything ...*, *Imagine Me & You*).~~

One of the unchecked boxes on our list was for one of us
to teach the other a skill. You know, like how the sporty
character (the man usually) gets behind the adorably clumsy
character (the woman, obvs) and helps her swing a golf
club. Or the rich cultured one brings the average Joe one
to the theatre and teaches them to appreciate the beauty of
the opera. We discovered that neither of us was the sporty
one, unless you counted Ruby's gymnast past, and I was
not going to attempt headstands. Neither of us was rich
or cultured either. In fact, we were two distinctly unskilled
people with no great talents in life. No penchant for oil
painting or the violin or singing or even computer games
or podcasting or making zombie-themed zines, basically
anything that makes a character quirky and interesting.

"Do you think we're just two really boring people?"
I lamented over the tub of melting vanilla ice cream I held
limply in my hand. We were on a picnic blanket on the
sand, in the fading evening light, me on my stomach, Ruby

on her bum with her knees pulled into her chest. The thrum of people packing up their beach bags and kids for the day played in the background.

"Of course we're not," Ruby said, shaking her head. "You always jump to the worst possible conclusion."

"Are you sure? We're both eating *vanilla* ice cream," I pointed out. "I've never even tried most of the other flavours."

"Well, technically *I'm* eating the ice cream."

I looked across at her and then down at my hands. She'd stolen my ice cream without me noticing.

"Thief," I said, reaching for my tub back.

"No way. You were letting it melt."

"Fine." I gave up. "I must have some kind of skill or hobby. I . . . I can . . . um . . . nope. I've got nothing."

"Same," Ruby agreed, cheerfully licking the spoon.

"But we're not boring?"

"No. We're normal."

"In rom-coms, the girls always have a special skill."

"Yeah, well, it's usually always women's magazine journalism or personal assistant. What is it with rom-coms and journalists?"

"That's true. Maybe I should be a women's magazine journalist?" I sounded like Ruby.

"Do you even read any women's magazines?"

"No. I already know all ninety-nine tips for driving my man wild." I turned and sat up, pulling a cardigan over my shoulders, the warmth of day leaching out with the cool breeze over the waves.

"Maybe we should find you another passion, babe."

"Babe," I repeated, mocking her English accent. She flicked me with her forefinger.

"What do we do, then? We don't have anything to teach each other. Unless you want to hear about what I learned about Prussia for Leaving Cert history? To be honest, it feels like the exam was ages ago now, so I don't actually remember much any more," I said.

"Why don't we both learn something new?" Ruby suggested. She stretched her feet out, digging her toes into the sand, and the last rays of sun lit her up like the light was coming from the inside.

"Ukulele?" I offered.

"No, something practical that we can actually use in real life."

"Budgeting?"

"All right, something a bit less practical. Like . . . cooking? We could take a cooking class." She brightened. "That's a great idea. It's something we can both use, it'll be fun, and every time you make fresh fettuccine you'll think of me."

I pictured future me in the kitchen of a cosy flat. There'd be music and candles and Ruby would be playing with our dog while I flambéed stuff.

Our dog? What a ridiculous thought.

Ruby was very much a cat person.

Cooking was a good idea, though. I hadn't considered how I would feed myself if I went to uni or moved out. I hadn't got any of those jobs yet but surely somewhere would soon find themselves in need of a totally unqualified teenager? Even if I stayed living at home, cooking something that was not frozen pizza would probably come in handy. I should have done it years ago and saved myself the torture of trying to force down whatever Dad had boiled to death.

"You're brilliant," I said, and sat up to kiss Ruby's freckled nose, more freckled now than when we'd met.

"I know." She reciprocated by nibbling on my bottom lip, "You should be celebrating the day you ever met me."

"I do," I said seriously. "I got a free bottle of vodka that night."

"You're such a romantic." Ruby fluttered her eyelashes at me. "That's why I l—"

We both froze to almost comic effect.

"Why *we*," she started again, the frozen moment vanishing unacknowledged, a glitch in the matrix, "are so good at this montage thing."

A few days later we stood in my old school's home economics kitchen with four straight couples in their thirties gazing adoringly at each other, sparkling rings blinding us from the left hand of each of the women, and one seriously old man on his own. Ruby nudged me when she saw him and made a sad face, so we took the bench behind the old man. It was us and him on one side of the room and the loving couples on the other.

Being in school was weird. It had the eerie abandoned feeling of summer, but it struck me that it was probably the last time I'd ever be in this building properly, unless you counted when I picked up my results. I hadn't thought about it on the last day of school, maybe because I knew we'd be back in the exam hall in a couple of weeks or maybe because I was concentrating on how much I wanted the bell to ring so I could leave.

Everyone had been running around the halls spraying silly string and getting their shirts signed in permanent marker. I just wanted to get out of there, finish my studying, and avoid the friends I'd already left behind. As I was walking down the steps to the front gates, I spied Izzy from the corner of my eye. She was holding a Sharpie and I had a feeling she was going to ask me to sign her shirt even though we hadn't spoken in months. That's the kind of person she was. The sentimentality of the day would make her think we could somehow make it up. But I spotted Dad in the car park and practically sprinted to the door. I wasn't mad at her any more. I had been angry with my friend who'd known I was going to get my heart broken and didn't tell me. But Izzy wasn't my friend any more and I simply didn't care. I didn't want to be rude and refuse to sign, but I also didn't want to sign and pretend that I would look back fondly on memories of us, as if the last eight months had never happened.

Relationships change and the past isn't some static thing you could keep forever like a photograph. No one else seems to understand that. Just because something happened, it doesn't mean it will mean the same thing to you forever. It changes with you. The friendship you cherished, the wife you adored, the child you raised. It can all become meaningless so easily, which means it was always meaningless from the beginning and you just didn't realise it.

But if everything is meaningless, you might as well have as good a time as you possibly can.

I squeezed Ruby's hand and she kissed me on the cheek. I couldn't help but wonder if the other couples noticed. Sometimes I forget that I'm a lesbian. As in I forget that it's statistically unusual and that some people have strong feelings about it. Even though I've encountered a few thoughtless comments or downright cruel ones, especially at school when I first came out, for the most part, the people in my life don't care. But people still looked. I saw it when Hannah and I walked down the street. People would glance at our clasped hands. Briefly. Sometimes they smiled, occasionally they frowned, mostly they just moved on to noticing the next thing, but it always made me feel watched. Sometimes it's the little things. Being noticed doing something that would be invisible if I were with a boy.

"Good morning, everyone. I'm Janet, your instructor today." A small but round woman with an enthusiastic smile bounded into the room, rubbing her hands together. The couple opposite us dropped what they were doing immediately and paid rapt attention. The old man in front of us turned up the level on his hearing aid.

"You're all beginners here, is that right?" the woman asked. She had the fervour of one of those American preachers and I got the impression she really fucking loved cooking. She also didn't wait for an answer.

"By the end of the morning, you will be beginners no longer. You are going to learn basic skills you can take home and practise, and if at the end of the day you feel like *By God I love this cooking malarkey*, you can sign up to my six-week course starting in September, where you will learn the answers to all those burning questions like, What the hell is a scallop? Can I make it at home instead of paying twenty euros for a starter in a restaurant? And why does everyone act like making risotto is so hard when it's just mushy rice?"

I chanced a glance at Ruby, who was hiding her mouth behind her fist.

"But today . . ." The woman dropped her voice dramatically and the old man rattled his hearing aid pack like it was broken.

"We're going to learn how to make . . ." She paused for dramatic effect and I bit down on my lip so I wouldn't laugh out loud.

"CHICKEN PIE!" She yelled the last word and the old man jumped. The kiss-ass couple opposite us started to clap but trailed off when no one else joined in.

"There is no need to be that excited about chicken pie," I said to Ruby.

"Maybe it will be the best chicken pie of our lives." Ruby jazz hands'd and all three kiss-ass couples shushed us simultaneously. It was kind of spooky.

Janet set us about the steps of making pastry and peeling potatoes. The main steps were actually written on a handout, but she still stood in front of the class explaining why you cook potatoes from cold water instead of pouring boiling water into the pot. The kiss-asses were making notes. Ruby and I inspected the paper instructions.

"You want to peel and I'll make this into bread crumbs somehow?" I said, surveying the pastry ingredients with suspicion.

"OK, but what about him?" Ruby nodded in the direction of the old man, who was holding a potato peeler in one hand and the sheet of paper right up to his nose in the other.

Ruby looked at me with puppy-dog eyes and I sighed and nodded.

Half an hour later Ruby and I were in stitches.

Morris, our new old man friend, was mostly lovely but seemed deeply suspicious of anyone as cheerful as Janet.

246

When she cheered because the Kiss-Asses made an edible sauce, he said, in what he thought was a conspiratorial whisper, but was actually a roar over the clattering din of the kitchen, "I think she's on one of those legal highs you hear about on the news."

I half expected her to respond that she was high on life but she politely pretended that she hadn't heard. You can get away with a lot when you're old.

"How come you girls are here on your summer holidays helping an old man learn how to cook?" Morris asked as we waited for our pie to cool enough to take a slice. It looked golden and flaky and I had perfected a scalloped edge that made the teacher almost wet herself with glee. I had high hopes. Perhaps Dad's cooking curse had not been handed down to me.

"Saoirse wanted to learn a life skill and I want to help out at home," Ruby answered.

"Aren't you a good girl. None of my kids ever cooked a day in their life when they were at home. Spoiled rotten. Well, that was my Anna's fault. She doted too much."

Ruby and I exchanged looks. I'd already assumed Morris was recently bereaved given he was here learning to cook by himself, but I hadn't wanted to bring it up.

"What was she like?" I asked gently.

"Anna? She was a grumpy old sod. But she made me laugh. Always f'ing and blinding about one thing or another. It was just her way. But she was a devoted mother."

"How did you two meet?" Ruby asked, poking the pie crust to see if it was still too hot.

"We met at a party. 1962, I think. A friend of mine. I can't remember his name now. I was nineteen, she was seventeen. She was the prettiest girl there. I was no slouch myself, you know."

That was not what I expected. Somehow I couldn't imagine Morris at a house party knocking back beers. Maybe he meant like a dinner party?

"Did you ask her to dance?" Ruby asked dreamily. I could tell she was picturing some black-and-white movie scene.

"What? No. I'm a terrible dancer. I couldn't let her see that. No, no. She got drunk and kissed me and I had to carry her home. The next day I brought her a seltzer and some aspirin and we were married a year later."

"That's . . . er . . . so romantic." Ruby faltered. She would not look me in the eye.

"How many kids did you have?"

"We had twin boys about six months after that. And now you know why we got married so quick." Morris tapped his nose.

I couldn't help it. I snorted.

"I didn't believe in soul mates before I met her. But you know, we didn't spend a night apart from the wedding until the day she passed. Sometimes life knows what you need better than you do." Morris fell silent then. Ruby coughed and busied herself with clearing up and I thought she was trying not to cry. A second later the moment was broken by Janet's giddy voice.

"All right, class. Your pies should be cool enough. Let's find out how you did. I for one simply cannot wait another second." She rubbed her hands together and made a beeline for one of the kiss-ass couples. I noticed the couple in front of them rolling their eyes at each other.

"Moment of truth," I said, and hovered a sharp knife above our glistening, glazed pie. Then I cracked. The pressure was too much.

"I can't do it, you do it."

Ruby ignored the knife and stuck a fork into the centre of the pie. She swallowed a mouthful. She chewed. I waited. She swallowed.

"Um ... it's ... Did you forget anything?"

"What, no? What's wrong with it?" I took the fork from her hand and took a piece of the pie for myself.

It wasn't horrible. It wasn't really very nice either. It was nothing. It tasted like nothing.

"The curse. The curse got me. I am genetically incapable of making food that tastes of anything," I lamented.

Ruby rubbed me consolingly on the back. "It wasn't just you. I made it too."

"My powers are so great they even cancelled out your input."

"It's OK. We'll try something easier next time," she

continued, patting me on the back as I slumped onto a stool. "Like soup. From a can."

I laughed a sad little hiccup laugh and peered over Morris's shoulder at his pie.

"How did yours turn out, then?"

"Do you think your presence ruined his too?" Ruby nudged me, grimacing.

"You can't try mine," he said, shielding it protectively, "I need it for tonight."

I forgot about my terrible pie skills and my heart ached for Morris, thinking about him alone at home with his pie.

"My date is going to love this," he said.

"What?" I said, lifting my head. "You have a date?"

"Morris, you old dog." Ruby laughed.

"My Anna's been gone five years, girls. Do you really think I would stay on the market long?"

"You said she was your soul mate," I said.

I didn't mean it to sound like an accusation but it did, and Ruby hit me on the arm to tell me to stop making the old man feel guilty for not spending the rest of his life in mourning.

"She was," Morris said, surprised. "I think there's another one out there and I'm going to find her. And the searching is good fun."

"You don't get more than one soul mate," I said, annoyed. Morris was clearly just a dirty old man.

"Says who?" He didn't seem angry with me for berating

him. He just laughed a gentle wheezing laugh. "Girls, I don't often go around giving advice to wains because I think you have to make your own mistakes in life, but I'll tell you one thing. I don't believe there's one right person for everyone, and I spent fifty-one years with the same woman. But I do believe there's a right person for you at different times in your life. Whether that relationship lasts a week or fifty years is not what makes it special."

25

The last night before the move, Ruby and I set up camp in my old room one last time to watch the only half-decent romantic comedy with lesbian characters, *Imagine Me & You*, surrounded by junk food and twinkly lights. It was a little weird knowing Dad was in the house, and he made his customary contraception jokes. But after the dinner, having her over didn't seem like such a big deal. They'd both had their chance to be nosy about one another and I'd asked her to come over late enough that they wouldn't really have time to interact. Besides, she had insisted on helping us move the next day because she is an angel. An intrusive kind of angel who doesn't take *no, seriously you don't have to do that* for an answer.

If I was being honest, I kind of liked the idea of spending my last night here with her. Dad suggested we spend the last night watching a horror film and eating our weight in Jaffa Cakes, but that picture in my head came with Mum somewhere in the background tutting about our terrible taste in cinema and food. Memories of my childhood haunted this house and I did not want to spend my evening with ghosts.

In my head, this evening with Ruby would look like something from Pinterest, where I would get loads of fairy lights and make a makeshift fort out of bohemian blankets. In reality, I could not figure out how on earth you were meant to make the blankets stay up. I tried using the boxes but I didn't have any big enough throws; the whole structure kept sagging in the middle. I didn't have any fairy lights either so I got some from the pound shop, but then when I went to put batteries in them I remembered I'd packed the batteries with other junk drawer stuff, and I was not going back out to the shop. Instead, I put all the pillows I could find on my bed, pushed the stacks of boxes and bin liners full of crap to one side, and set my laptop on a chair.

"There's like no kissing in this movie, you know," Ruby pointed out. "What kind of romantic comedy has barely any kissing?"

We were squished together on my bed and she was curled under my arm. She had a little pile of Maltesers resting on my stomach, which was periodically depleting.

"A gay one. The bit at the football match where she teaches her to scream at number nine? That should have been a kiss moment. At least in this she doesn't go back to men in the end."

Hard side-eye to *Kissing Jessica Stein*.

"Sure, but there had to be a man in there somewhere.

Even though Matthew Goode is adorable, I want one where the character isn't realising she's gay because of the cute girl she met. I mean, she's thirty – are you telling me she's never met a girl before? Never even thought about it? She seems so shocked by the whole thing."

"That happens in real life, though," I pointed out.

"Yeah, I know, but I wish there was a big Hollywood movie about girls who already know they like girls. There are no blokes in the way and preferably it stars Kristen Stewart. Yes, she has sexual tension with every woman in every film, but I want it to be there in the script, you know?"

"You feel very strongly about this," I said. "Maybe that's your future career."

"What?"

"Write scripts. You don't even have to wait for university to start doing that. You could be the gay Nora Ephron."

Ruby raised her eyebrow. "Nora Ephron?"

"I know stuff now," I said defensively. At least I was capable of googling.

"That does sound really cool. Everyone thinks I should be a nurse because I have a disabled brother. Like that means I want to be a nurse or a doctor or a medical researcher." Ruby rolled her eyes. "People always want to limit him and tell him what he can't do. He doesn't listen to that and I won't either. If there's more to my brother than his disability then there's more to me too."

"Is that why you're still trying to figure it out?" I asked, thinking of the many career options Ruby had pounced on.

"That's why I'll consider anything. I don't want to be pigeonholed into something. Don't get me wrong, I love that I've been able to be there for him. I want to do everything possible to help with his rehab too. But I want to see what else I might be good at if I just get the chance to try it."

I could understand that. Teachers who knew about my mum would sometimes suggest the same thing to me, social work or nursing. *You could help more people like your mum.* Even Dad had mentioned it when I was picking my A levels. I looked after Mum because she was my mum, not because I'm some kind of Patron Saint of Dementia. I wanted to tell Ruby this, to let her know I understood her.

"How is Noah?" I asked instead.

"He's doing really well. Mum called me this morning at like half two. She doesn't seem to grasp time differences, or more likely she doesn't even think about it, but I got to talk to him too. He sounded really happy. He said he missed me. I really miss him. I'm used to spending most of my free time with him."

I squeezed her closer.

"He'll be back soon. It'll fly by."

It occurred to me that if Noah would be back soon, that also meant our time would be over soon. Our eyes met and I wondered if she was thinking the same thing. Then she grinned at me and sucked a handful of Maltesers into her mouth.

"What about you?" she said with a mouth full of chocolate.

"What do you mean? You know how I feel about Oxford."

"Right, but you'll still do *something*. What were you planning to study at Oxford?" She did a fake posh voice when she said Oxford.

"You realise you don't have to fake an English accent? You have one," I joked. But really I was thinking that I hadn't considered anything other than Oxford for university. Sure, I'd filled in forms for Irish colleges and universities, but only because the career guidance teacher wouldn't let it go. Oxford to me represented the whole university experience. When I said I didn't want to go there, I meant I didn't want to go anywhere. Yes, it was in England, which was an added disadvantage now that I wasn't trying to run away from Hannah. But what would be the point of any degree? I was still likely to end up in a home at fifty. Maybe earlier because I wouldn't have a family to take care of me.

"Yeah, but it's not posh. And don't change the subject."

"Law, I think." I vaguely recalled my reasoning being that maybe I'd make a ton of money and I could spend it on one of the really good care homes for Mum.

"What made you pick law?"

"Nothing in particular," I said, getting testy. "I don't

want to talk about it. What bloody difference does it make anyway? One course is the same as the next. You go study, you get a job, and you die."

Ruby looked taken aback at my sudden detour into nihilism.

"I didn't mean to upset you," she said quietly.

I rubbed my face. I was being an asshole. It wasn't her fault she didn't know how much I wanted to never think about this topic. That for me it really didn't make any difference what I learned because I'd forget it all anyway. She didn't know that the only reason I'd worked so hard to get into Oxford was because I was under some misguided idea that it would make my mum proud. Except the day I told her I got my conditional offer she said, *That's great*, and then a few minutes later she forgot. It wasn't some kind of bond we had, some connection over a shared future. The real bond we shared was shitty genetics. What good had all her degrees done her?

"No, I'm sorry. It's just stressful not knowing what to do. I shouldn't snap at you, though, it's not your fault."

"I get it. I probably sound like your parents. What are you going to do with your life, etc." She made a face.

I did not deserve so much understanding.

"You don't have to know right now," she continued. "I bet anyone who's sure what they're going to do now, for the rest of their lives, is probably wrong anyway. I have no idea either."

257

She was right. But it wasn't comforting because it wasn't the same for me as it was for Ruby. I wasn't going with the flow and falling in love with a hundred different options. Ruby needed somewhere to funnel her energy and enthusiasm. I didn't have any. I was lost. I'd spent most of the last few years taking care of Mum or centering my life around visiting her. Before she got really bad, my life was centered around Hannah. Look how that worked out.

Sometimes it occurred to me that I might not end up like Mum, that I could spend decades waiting for the disease to take hold and it never would. I wouldn't know if I'd wasted half my life until it was too late. Which was worse?

"I know. It'll be fine. I'm sure when I get my results I'll know what to do," I lied, trying to sound breezy. "I'm just glad I escaped school alive. Now I just have to escape Dad and Beth and their constant mauling the face off each other."

I'd walked in on them playing a game of "how to traumatise your teenager" yesterday when they were supposed to be making a seating chart. Thankfully they'd only got to level one: kissing with slobbering sound effects, but I was still going to have to wash my brain in acid.

"You must miss some things about school? I was so sad on my last day because I knew I wouldn't get to see my friends as much."

"Trust me, I'm not going to miss anyone," I joked.

"I stopped talking to my old friends long before school ended. I'm glad to escape them too."

"Sounds like you have a lot of things you want to run away from," Ruby said seriously. "What do you mean you stopped talking to your friends?"

Oops. I hadn't meant to say that. Or rather I hadn't remembered not to say something like that.

"Oh, nothing. I fell out with some friends a while back. And then I was stuck in school with them for another eight months. Awkward."

"Why did you fall out?" Ruby said, undeterred by my attempt to make light of it.

An itch at the back of my neck started to bother me.

"It's stupid. Seriously. Girl drama, that's all."

"So tell me," she said. It felt like a test. I'd already messed up once that night.

"A relationship broke up. Sides were taken. It was all very dramatic."

"A relationship? Whose?"

"Mine," I said, my throat feeling tight.

"OK . . . with who?"

"No one."

Ruby huffed. I could imagine smoke coming out of her nose if I didn't come forth with a few more details.

"I don't mean no one. I mean it's not important any more. Her name was Hannah."

"And what? Your friends picked her side?"

"Yeah, well, our best friend. Izzy. They were friends first, I guess. She really got the jump on me those first two years of primary school." I tried to laugh but it came out bitter.

"You were all friends from year three? And she dumped you as a friend because you and Hannah broke up?"

"Yeah. Sort of," I lied again.

I could feel the pity about to pour out of her but I chose that over telling her the truth. The words rattled around in my brain. *I dumped Izzy because she didn't tell me Hannah was going to break my heart. I dumped her because I was embarrassed that I'd gushed about how Hannah and I were going to spend the rest of our lives together, that we were soul mates, and she'd known that Hannah didn't feel the same way. I dumped her because she chose Hannah and I felt like I didn't matter.* I couldn't say those things out loud. She wouldn't get it.

"Don't worry, I got over it. It's not that big a deal."

Ruby seemed to struggle with what to say next.

"Do you want me to kill them?" she said finally.

Relief flooded my body.

"Let's watch the rest of the film and decide after. It's so hard to do homicide when you're stuffed full of Maltesers."

She arched her neck to kiss me and soon we'd left the film behind in favour of a haze of heavy breathing, soft skin, and eyelashes that fluttered against my cheek when we kissed.

*

Ruby spent the night and if you really must know, we didn't do anything that involved taking your pants off. After she fell asleep I tossed and turned and it took me ages to get to sleep. I kept thinking about her saying that there were a lot of things I wanted to run away from. It sounded like something Mum would have said. I thought of all the things I'd wanted to run away from this summer. Thinking about what I'd do with the rest of my life, thinking about what the rest of my life might look like if I inherit Mum's dementia, Dad and Beth's wedding, thinking about leaving Mum behind. I'd filled up all that space with Ruby. What was I going to do in a few weeks when she was gone and I had to face all of those things by myself?

26

The next morning, bleary-eyed and groggy, I made Ruby and myself a cup of tea. The kettle, a box of tea bags, and a few mugs were the only things in the kitchen not wrapped in newspaper and stuffed into a box. We had a few large items Dad had decided to replace rather than move that were being picked up by a disposal service tomorrow for recycling – the worn-out sofa, the oven with the wobbly door, our old mattresses – but the rest was up to us.

"You don't have to help today, you know." I kissed Ruby's cheek and tried to sound like I only wanted to spare her the hassle. "It's really not your job."

Truthfully, I was struggling with the guilt of skipping out on Mum. I couldn't exactly disappear for an hour this morning without Ruby noticing. If she left now, I could still go.

"I want to. I get to be with you." She smiled and flipped her hair from one side to the other and I felt an ache. She really was the prettiest girl I'd ever seen in real life. Over the last few weeks I'd grown used to her in a way and she just looked like Ruby, but sometimes, like in that moment, I saw her as if she was a stranger again. I noticed her blue

262

freckle and the way her hair always looked like she had been running her fingers through it; I saw her hazel eyes, wide and wondering; I saw the curve where her waist met her hips in a way that made me want to grab her close, and I could barely believe that she let me kiss her and touch her and do all the things we did that made the air between us sticky and hot.

I supposed I could skip seeing Mum this one time. My two lives were getting uncomfortably close in a way that was giving me palpitations and anxiety sweat on the back of my neck. I reminded myself that Ruby would be gone in four weeks and everything would be back to normal. Somehow that didn't comfort me the way it should have.

Even though it felt like I'd been packing for approximately six months, there was still stuff all over the house. Things had to be cleaned and fixed before we left for good, like scrubbing the insides of the kitchen cupboards and tightening the loose hinge on the bathroom door.

Beth had already moved into the flat three days ago, so she was helping too. She was giddy all day and a little part of me begrudgingly thought it was kind of sweet. She was obviously really excited about the move. She was also intent on making sure that my desire never to see her and Dad snogging again remained unfulfilled. I caught them in the bathroom, leaning against the shower, Beth with an arm wrapped around my dad's neck and a bag in her hand that she'd thrown toothbrushes and shampoos into.

"I need to change my tampon," I said loudly and grumpily. It wasn't true but I liked to embarrass Dad. They broke apart. Surprised but utterly unembarrassed. By the kissing anyway. Dad scarpered, muttering about feminism ruining his life. I wondered if he ever thought about how lucky he was that Mum had had the talks with me before she got really bad.

"Oh, here, I packed the toilet roll," Beth said, rummaging in the bag and producing a loo roll like she was presenting me with a great gift.

"You know, I think it's OK if we actually leave one of these behind us. We can get more toilet roll for the new flat."

"Thanks for the advice, smart-arse," Beth replied.

"You know, if you two can't keep it in your pants, maybe we should do this zone by zone. You and Ruby take apart the bed frames upstairs and Dad and I will take downstairs."

"Yes, ma'am." Beth saluted and playfully shoved me on the shoulder before she skipped out of the bathroom.

Weird. She was usually so thirsty for my approval and mortally wounded by the slightest sarcastic remark from me. If she was getting used to me I was really going to miss that sad frowny face she did when I was being a total wagon.

*

264

"Wi ooh dismahah e dsk," Dad said to me as he lumbered past the kitchen, stooped under the weight of a crate of books, a screwdriver between his teeth. I was making another cup of tea. I needed a caffeine top-up to get me through the rest of the afternoon.

"Want to try that again?" I said, taking the screwdriver and wiping the saliva on his shirt. "Gross."

"Will you dismantle the desk? The one in my office?"

"Seriously, I told you to do that yesterday," I groaned.

"I needed it," he said.

"So you do it now," I pouted.

"I'm busy." He shifted his weight, readjusting the crate of books to make his point. "And you're out here slacking and making tea. Again."

He was such a child. If he could get out of doing something he would, and we'd both had enough of deconstructing flat-pack furniture over the last few days. I'd already dismantled a bathroom cabinet, a rusted kitchen trolley, and a chest of drawers I'd ruined about ten years ago by gluing stickers of the Irish Olympic women's swimming team all over the doors during a swimming phase I had. Come to think of it, that might have been the first clue I was a lesbian.

The desk was in Dad's office, which used to be Mum's office, and it used to be her desk too. It was lopsided, the drawers stuck all the time, and there simply wasn't space for a home office in the new flat, so we'd agreed to get rid

265

of it. I started by pulling the drawers out of their sockets and unscrewing the handles. This required a lot of elbow grease and one screw in particular was so tight it took a bottle of WD-40 to get it unstuck. I wiped a sheen of sweat on my forehead and pulled out the last drawer. It jammed on the metal track and I sighed. If in that moment, the world saw fit to drop a giant comedy anvil on my Dad's head as karma, I would have been OK with it.

I reached, shoulder deep, into the drawer space and felt around for anything that was preventing the drawer from coming out. I couldn't see anything but I poked the screwdriver into the space behind the drawer a couple of times and felt something release. It came out easily then, and onto the floor fell a blue card file. I recognised it immediately. Those were the files Mum kept her client notes in.

When she stopped working, out of necessity and less than willing, we'd forgotten about the files. After she moved into the home, we realised we couldn't really hold on to them. Most of the clients she'd been seeing up until she finished working requested to have their notes sent to new therapists, but there were a lot from former clients who were off on their merry way and had no idea what was going on with Mum. We asked one of Mum's old colleagues what we should do and she thought for confidentiality we should destroy them. This one had evidently escaped the cull.

A few months ago when Dad shredded those files I hadn't really thought about what was in them. They didn't interest me. It was a bunch of mouldy old work papers. But sitting on the floor of my dad's office, I was suddenly mad with curiosity about what was inside.

The angel on my shoulder told me that this was private and I shouldn't look. Mum would kill me if she knew I read a client's file. It wasn't like she never talked about them. She sometimes told me a joke she'd heard from one or I'd hear her talking to Dad about people she was particularly worried about, but she never mentioned their names and there was a separate entrance to her office, so the closest I ever got to identifying someone was when they walked around the house to the side door. A blur through the blinds that revealed a blonde or brunette, maybe the colour of top they had on, that was it.

A name was written in Sharpie in the corner. Dominik Mazur. Heart beating slightly faster, as though she might walk in and catch me, I flipped open the file. The first pages looked like standardised forms so I skipped forward a bit.

Dominik began session saying his week was good. Talked about his mother's new job. She is enjoying it. Dominik is relieved his younger brother is happy at school. When prompted to talk about his own week he was initially reserved. Later he admitted he was locked in bathroom by peers and got in trouble for missing class. Did not tell mother about incident as he did not want to worry her. We role-played conversation with Mum. It's clear D does not want to discuss his difficulties out of fear of upsetting her. I asked what would be so wrong with her being upset.

I flipped back to the beginning of the file to see what age Dominik was. Fifteen. It said he came to her after an overdose. But that was ten years ago. He'd be in his twenties now. I skipped ahead to the middle of the file.

Dominik expressed anxiety about sitting Junior Cert in second language. He said he was afraid to make mistakes in grammar and punctuation. Then discussed anxiety about forgetting Polish. Woke up in the middle of the night unable to remember obscure vocabulary. He laughed but appeared distressed by this. Said he talked to his mother about speaking Polish more at home and she agreed. Previously she insisted on English to encourage learning second language but feels they are sufficiently fluent now. I expressed how incredible it was for D to be fluent in English when it is his second language. He appeared embarrassed. Discussed his inclination towards perfection and whether other students were also likely to make mistakes in punctuation and grammar.

For half an hour I sat with Dominik's file and tracked a year in his life through my mother's notes. He was bullied and anxious and felt alone. I thought about him coming to my house every week and talking to my mum. I wondered if it helped.

Discharge session. D brought Junior Cert results. Appeared proud and pleased. Spoke animatedly about transition year. Decided to move school for a fresh start. Visited St C's last week and discussed his past experience with principal and parents. Expressed some concern that bullying would reoccur in new school but said that if it did he would be more comfortable raising it with new principal who he likes. Sad to end sessions (both of us!) but D happy to move on and demonstrates increased confidence and greater openness in discussing his difficulties with family.

I searched for Dominik online. Many came up but only one in the same county as me. I clicked into his social media profile. His wall was private but some personal information was open. Dominik Mazur. Twenty-four. Works at TEFL Singapore International School. In a relationship with Chloe Durand. His photo was him, tan and handsome, with his arm around a short girl with curly hair. They looked like they were in a pub.

I'm not stupid. I know that social media doesn't tell

the full story about anyone's life. He was hardly going to post a picture of himself looking depressed. But he *was* alive. He was teaching English in Singapore and he had a girlfriend. So at least some things were good and maybe part of that was down to Mum. I blinked back a few tears rudely trying to escape.

"How is this not done yet – Saoirse, is that one of your mum's files?" Dad's tone shifted from exasperated to sharp in the same sentence. He marched towards me with stern knitted brows. He'd left a mirror propped up against the wall in the hallway.

"Uh . . ."

"Saoirse! Those are private." He took the file out of my lap. "Your mum would go ballistic."

I hung my head. I knew it was *technically* wrong but I didn't feel like I was spying on this stranger, this fifteen-year-old boy, so much as I was spying on a version of my mum that I sometimes forgot existed. I didn't really regret it and judging by Dad's sceptical expression, my acting was over the top.

"Wise up and get back to work, it's getting late," he said gruffly. But he didn't really seem mad. Before I could stop myself I blurted out a question.

"Do you think she *really* helped people?"

Dad stopped in the door. His expression softened.

"Of course she did. Not everyone. Liz would be the

first to say she wasn't the right therapist for everyone. But she was the perfect therapist for some people."

"That's nice, I suppose."

"Why do you ask?"

I shrugged. "I don't know. I guess it's nice to know that there are people out there who remember her. Who are living better lives because they knew her."

Dad crossed the room in a beat and put his arm around my neck, pulling me in. He kissed the top of my head. When he pulled away I thought his eyes were watery but he blinked and it was gone.

He stepped back into the hall and jumped.

"Sorry, Ruby. I didn't see you there."

I heard Ruby tell him it was OK and did he know where she could find a dustpan. Something about the high pitch of her voice made me wonder what she'd overheard. My heart started that uncomfortable palpitating. It was like I was in a room that kept getting smaller and smaller. That nightmare from childhood that you're going to be crushed by the walls.

For the rest of the day I tried to tell if she knew something from the way she looked at me or the things she said, but she acted normal, kissing me on the cheek as she walked past with a box of mugs, interrupting me sweeping the almost empty kitchen to show me a picture of Noah and her parents eating cheeseburgers the size of your face.

The room eased up. A little more oxygen circulated around me. She must not have heard anything.

By the time Dad and Beth got into the van to take the last trip over to the flat, it was around nine p.m. and it was starting to get dark. My muscles already ached in anticipation of tomorrow and the thought of unpacking everything again made me want to cry.

Dad called me over to the van and rolled down the window. He dangled a set of keys at me.

"Can you lock up and follow us over?"

I looked at the keys and looked at Ruby. The last time we'd taken the car we had nearly driven into someone and then stranded ourselves. Although the bit in between had been good.

We watched Dad and Beth drive off and Ruby put her arm around my waist and leaned her head on my shoulder.

"Let's not go straight over."

"Where do you want to go?"

"Let's not go anywhere just yet," she said, and she pulled me back into the house, her hand in mine as she led me to the couch.

27

An intense longing coursed through my body, my breath tightened, and all the things I wanted rushed into my head like a wave. I lay on top of Ruby, propped up on my elbows, and looked into her eyes for a moment. I saw that look. The one where something passed between us without words. Then I leaned in and kissed her, soft at first, but it was like tiny fires were catching all over my body and she was the cool, dark water that would save me. Her mouth found my neck and shivers rippled through me. My hands found the hem of her shirt and I peeled it off, tossing my own on the floor. She reached around and unclipped my bra and took her own off too. Somehow I felt almost embarrassed to look, like she'd see how much I wanted her and she'd laugh. She touched me first and the sensation rippled all through my body. We melted into each other, her body pressed against me, her skin sticking to mine in the humid summer.

Twenty minutes later we surfaced. Rumpled, out of breath, and unable to keep the smiles from our faces.

"I don't want to do it for the first time on a manky,

old sofa," Ruby said, clambering back to sitting, out of breath and rumpled in a way that made my stomach flutter. "I'd still rather something more traditional."

"Like after prom?" I suggested, thinking of the montage.

"Like in a bedroom," she said.

"Right."

My mattress was still upstairs to be picked up by the recycling people tomorrow, but the bed frame had been moved and the sheets and pillows were packed. I didn't think Ruby was going to be any more enamoured of a bare mattress in an empty room somehow and I wasn't either. I pictured soft bedding, soft lighting, and soft music.

But don't tell anyone I said that. It's embarrassing.

We caught our breath in silence for a second, holding hands even though our palms were sweaty.

"So," I said very casually and not at all in a higher pitch than normal. "When you say first time, do you mean first-first or like *our* first together?"

Ruby flipped her hair from one side to another, a few slick strands stuck to her forehead.

"First, first."

"First with a girl first or . . ."

"First ever. I've had a few girlfriends but nothing serious. I've never even kissed a boy."

"Oh my God, maybe you're secretly straight but the lesbian agenda got to you before you had time to figure it out," I joked. Mostly I was trying not to think about those other girls. We all know being jealous of someone in the past is stupid, but it doesn't mean you don't still feel it.

"I'm not," she said, her voice hoarse, and she kissed me again so I could feel the heat coming from her mouth, her skin. "Or they've done an excellent job of implanting some really super gay thoughts into my head right now."

It seemed redundant to blush after everything but my cheeks didn't get the message.

"What about you?"

"Well, you already know I kissed Oliver once. I mean, it's something I'd dearly like to erase from my memory but sadly the technology does not yet exist."

Instantly I flinched, realising what I'd said. Ruby didn't seem to notice.

"I forgot you told me that before. So weird."

"We were about eleven. It was not one of the erotic highlights of my adolescence."

"Did you and Hannah . . . ?"

"No." I felt myself turn colder at her name and tried to remind myself that it wasn't Ruby's fault. She didn't know what talking about Hannah did to me.

"I haven't had sex with anyone."

I hadn't had sex with Hannah and I'd obviously never had sex with any of the straight girls I'd kissed between Hannah and Ruby. Would having sex with Ruby be a step too far? Would having sex with Ruby break the rules?

It wasn't one of the harbingers of doom specifically but it was pretty serious, wasn't it? Would it mean something because it was the first time? If literally everything I'd ever heard was right, the first was one you remembered forever. It was important. Whether it was good or bad or weird, you wouldn't forget it. Then again, I knew it was perfectly possible to forget extremely important things. Husbands, children, thirty years of your life.

Ruby smiled and kissed me. "We should probably go. Your dad will be wondering where you got to."

I didn't want to go but I pulled my T-shirt over my head anyway and I watched Ruby put hers on too. There was something more intimate about seeing her putting her clothes on than taking them off. For a second, I saw us in our imaginary flat in our imaginary future again. Waking up beside her and getting dressed before going downstairs. It was the kind of moment you only shared with one person and most people probably didn't think about it much at all.

When I drove Ruby back to Oliver's, the car only stalled four times. I parked in the driveway and we kissed until the sensor light turned off. Then we agreed it was definitely time for me to go home before Dad started calling to see if I'd been in some kind of serious accident.

"Hey, so why are your mum's files at your house?" Ruby said as she twisted in her seat to retrieve the purse she'd tossed in the back. She sounded deliberately casual, as if she was always interested in mundane details about filing.

"Got stuck down the back of the desk, that's all," I said. But all my sleepy happiness vanished, like it was sucked out, leaving me cold.

"Why did your dad say your mum would be mad?"

"Because they're private." I wouldn't look at her. I made a production of checking my mirrors instead. My chest tightened.

"No, I mean he said your mum *would go ballistic* instead of *will go ballistic*. And you asked if she helped people. Like it was past tense. But she isn't . . ."

"Dead?" I finished coldly, trying to cover for the nauseating sense that the thing I'd been trying to stay one step ahead of was about to reach out and grab me. "You'd be being pretty insensitive if she was. Why were you listening to our conversation anyway? And memorising the exact phrasing to catch me out like you're bloody Jessica Fletcher or something."

I crossed my arms in front of my chest. I wished she'd just get out of the car. Why was she ruining everything? She kept doing this.

Ruby huffed and threw her hands up.

"Get over yourself," she snapped. "No one's listening to your secret conversations. I didn't mean to overhear."

"Get over myself?" I blinked, disbelieving. I heard my voice rise. "Get over myself? What are you, twelve?"

"I'm twelve? You are so immature. It's not interesting and mysterious to keep secrets, you know. Fine. I *do* know there's something going on with your mum. I don't get why you won't tell me. I told you about Noah."

My heart stopped for a second and when it started beating it did so at double time. Bubbling anger churned in my stomach and my head was loud with buzzing.

"How do you know there's something going on with my mum?" I said through gritted teeth.

I suddenly remembered the dinner, Beth and Ruby arriving together. Had they spoken about it on the doorstep? Had she known all this time?

"It's obvious." Ruby said it as though I was stupid for not realising. "You never talk about her and I knew you were lying when you said I could meet her, so I asked Oliver—"

Oliver.

After our talk about how it was my business and ethics and everything, he'd told anyway. I felt betrayed by both of them.

"You went behind my back?"

"I wanted to ask *you*." She pointed her finger at me, her face contorted. "But God forbid we have a serious conversation about anything to do with you."

"So instead of respecting my privacy, you found a way around it? Nice." I spat the words out.

Ruby paused and then she sighed. It was the second

when I gained the advantage. Later I'd wonder why our fight was a game I was trying to win.

"OK, you're right." She took a deep breath, then took my hand. "That was crappy. But I don't get what the big secret is."

I snatched my hand away. "It's not a secret! I just don't want to talk about it with *you*."

Ruby looked like I'd slapped her. A point for me.

"Because I'm just some girl you want to have a little fun with over the summer and then forget," she said quietly.

I shrugged. "What do you want me to say? You knew that going in." A body blow.

"You don't mean that," she whispered. "But it is totally fucked up that you'd pretend you do."

"How do you know what I mean? You don't know me," I shouted, and she recoiled. "That was the whole fucking point." My voice cracked and I felt furious tears falling down my cheeks. And then I couldn't stop. I cried until I couldn't get enough breath.

"Saoirse, take a deep breath," Ruby said firmly. "In through your nose. One, two, three, out through your mouth. Come on."

I did what she said. She counted breaths out to me until I was able to do it for myself. I saw her hand twitch and I knew she wanted to reach out and stroke my back or my arm, some comforting gesture, but she was afraid I'd push it away again. I wanted to tell her I wouldn't but the words got stuck in my throat.

"I'm sorry," I said, wiping tears away, "I didn't mean that. But that wasn't what this was about. We were supposed to be having fun. I don't want to come and cry to you about my mother having dementia. I wanted to have a good time with one person who doesn't feel sorry for me."

"Dementia?" Ruby said, her mouth falling open slightly.

"Oliver told you that," I said.

"No, he didn't. I asked him but he told me I should talk to you. But why didn't you tell me? It's nothing to be ashamed of."

I closed my eyes. Even though it wasn't a secret I felt somehow that I'd lost by telling her. Oliver's integrity was something I'd have to think about later. I swallowed the hard lump in my throat. She knew now and it was my fault. But really, how else could this argument have ended?

"I'm not ashamed," I said. "But I don't want to talk to you about how my mother lives in an old people's home and she doesn't know who I am."

Ruby's eyes were wide and sad and she bit her lip.

"I don't want to talk about how it was my fault she's in the home to begin with because I wasn't able to keep track of her and she got hurt."

She opened her mouth to speak and I kept talking so I didn't have to hear her say the words that everyone said. *It's not your fault.* Because lies didn't make me feel better.

"And I definitely don't want to tell you about how it's only going to get worse. How someday soon she'll forget how to eat or clean herself and she'll have to wear a nappy and be bathed by nurses even though she's only fifty-five."

I couldn't look at Ruby any more because truthfully I *was* ashamed of those things, whether it was the right thing to feel or not, and I knew she'd be disgusted with me if I admitted it.

Out of the corner of my eye I saw her mouth open and close like she was trying to find words, but she didn't say anything.

"Tell me you don't feel sorry for me now," I said bitterly, and I kept my eyes trained on a point straight ahead because I didn't want to look her in the eye. She started to cry silent tears.

"OK." She sniffed and shook her head as if to clear her mind. "OK. I admit it. I feel sorry for you. Anyone would. But what is wrong with that? I care about you. Fuck the montage. I don't care."

"*I* care." I hit the steering wheel with the heel of my hand. Stinging pain shot up my arm as the horn beeped and Ruby flinched, whether at the noise or me, I didn't know. She felt sorry for me now; how would she react if she knew that I might end up like Mum? She could never know that.

"I *told* you I didn't want something serious." My anger

flared up again. "I agreed to this montage thing because we were going to have fun."

My head felt like it was bursting. I didn't like it. With great effort, I shut all the anger behind a door and locked it.

I was good at that when I had to be.

"I still want that," I said finally. "We only have four weeks left. Can't we make the most of it?" I turned in my seat to face Ruby and I took her hands. "Let's do the rest of the things on the list and forget about this. Can we keep things as they were? We can pretend this never happened." I was ashamed of the pleading note in my voice but I said it anyway.

Ruby looked past me, staring into space for what felt like forever.

"No," she said eventually.

My heart fell like a stone into my stomach. I barely noticed when she pulled her hands away from mine.

"I can't do that. I agreed to the terms, I know that. But it's different for me now. I want it all. The good stuff and the bad stuff." Ruby ran her fingers through her hair, tossing it to one side, and her voice quivered as she continued talking. "If you don't want that too, then it has to end now." Her bottom lip trembled but her shoulders were stiff and braced and I knew she'd made up her mind.

I nodded. I was numb.

I told her that I wished it didn't have to be this way.

She said she had to be honest with me and with herself.

The words sounded like a script. I let them wash over me.

She opened the car door. I looked at her. There was one last plea not to do this in my eyes and she hesitated. For a second, I thought she might change her mind. But then she wiped her eyes with the back of her hand and smiled sadly.

"See, the thing about the falling in love montage," she said, her voice hoarse, "is that when it's over, the characters have fallen in love."

28

Dad and Beth were cuddled up on the sofa when I finally arrived at the flat. They were watching some American late-night talk show. The boxes were everywhere. I was really sick of seeing boxes everywhere.

"I was just about to call the police, missy," Dad said.

I grunted and went into the kitchen for some water. There were no glasses. The glasses were in a bloody box somewhere.

"For the love of God, did you unpack *anything*?" I snapped. I got grim satisfaction from their bemused expressions.

"I'll have you know I unpacked your duvet and pillows and put sheets on your new bed while you were off gallivanting so you didn't have to do it when you came home."

"Class, well, I'm going to bed then. And turn the TV down, would you? The walls are paper thin in this shithole."

I stomped down the hall like a stroppy teenager, which I was allowed to do because I *was* a stroppy teenager. I had a year and a bit of legitimate stropping left and I was going to wring every last drop out.

Dad stared after me but I knew he wouldn't say anything. I dove under the duvet without changing. Except for wriggling out of my bra because I am not a masochist. That would have been a bitch to sleep in. I wanted to fall asleep. I was exhausted. Moving house and breaking up in one day really takes it out of you.

My brain did not cooperate.

Instead, it decided to replay the argument over and over again until details started to blur. I couldn't quite remember exactly what Ruby said and what things I really said versus what I wished I'd said.

I wondered if that was a sign that my memory was already going.

The next morning the sun beat down on me and I woke up sweaty and unrested. There were no curtains or blinds yet and I lay uncomfortably for a few minutes until the smell from my own armpits insisted I shower. At some point around the fourteenth rehash of the argument and the millionth time I considered texting Ruby, I decided I was not going to fall apart. This wasn't like with Hannah. There was no investment. We were only having fun. It did not hurt. I was not going to be a pathetic mess. I remembered pathetic-mess Saoirse. She was the reason I didn't do relationships to begin with.

After Hannah, I cried in bed. I cried in the toilets at school. I cried at the dinner table and on the walk home from school. I sent texts to her that made my cringe glands almost explode, things like *I still love you*, *What can I do to fix this* and *Did you ever love me?* At first, she would answer immediately with some guff about wanting to be friends, and then it took longer and longer and I began to imagine what she was doing in the time it took her to reply. I stalked her Instagram and Facebook. For a while I tried to be her friend and show her that she could still love me. I'd end up saying something needy or bring up in-jokes from our relationship to try to remind her of how good we were together. She would smile sadly and change the subject. I cried to Izzy over and over, and bored her to tears, asking questions like *Did she say anything about me? Do you think we'll get back together? Is she seeing someone else?* All before I found out she'd known all along that Hannah was planning to break up with me, of course. That's when I cut them both off. I only wished I'd done it immediately and spared myself the humiliation.

That girl broke me, and I wasn't going to go through it again.

What if I did get the dementia and my stupid brain decided to pick this year to be stuck in, the way Mum thought she was young? If I moped around about Ruby I could be stuck in post-breakup depression forever.

Had the montage experiment worked out? Not exactly. We technically had four weeks left, but what did it matter? We'd have broken up then anyway. I had more time to prepare for whatever was coming next. I wasn't going to dwell on the past. Even if the past was yesterday.

I let the shower wash off the night before and thought through the upcoming weeks. Exam results, the wedding . . . and whatever came after that. I was keenly aware I still hadn't mentioned to Dad that I wasn't totally on board with Oxford. Every time he brought it up I reminded him I might not be going but I knew he thought I was being cautious about my grades. There'd be a party too, of course, on results night. I could get drunk and kiss girls. It would probably be at Oliver's, though, and maybe I shouldn't show up there. I didn't want to look like I was following Ruby around. Although if I *didn't* go I was purposefully avoiding her and that would look like I was not totally over it.

I know what you're thinking. *Why do you care so much what other people think, Saoirse?* But at the time it did not occur to me that I was only considering what it *looked* like and not what my actual feelings were. At the time they seemed like the same thing. Like if Ruby thought I was over it, then I would be. Appearances were reality. And what did people who were definitely not depressed about their ex-not-girlfriend do? They got on with life, and I would too.

In the kitchen, I clicked Beth's fancy espresso machine on. I was wrecked from a bad night's sleep, but I was going to visit Mum the same as I did every day. I'd missed her yesterday for the first time in a long time because of Ruby so I wouldn't do it again. After Mum? Well, that was a problem for future Saoirse. One step at a time.

I found glasses and mugs in the cupboard. Beth and Dad must have stayed up late and put away some of the kitchen things. I felt a pang of guilt for snapping at them but it wasn't a feeling I was comfortable with so I ignored it. I didn't actually drink coffee so I don't know what I was expecting but it tasted terrible and I ended up downing an espresso like a tequila shot as Beth padded into the kitchen in an ugly nightie and fluffy socks. It was weird seeing her in the morning. I didn't know how to feel. It was like I thought I should feel mad at her or mad at Dad maybe, but the feeling wouldn't come. Maybe that was the exhaustion, though.

"You're up early," she yawned, filling the kettle.

"Didn't sleep well," I said.

"Oh yeah," Beth said like she had forgotten something in her sleep haze. "I wanted to go and talk to you but your dad said it was better to leave you alone. Did something happen? Did you and Ruby fight? You were gone a long time."

Dad had said to leave me alone. Classic. *If I don't ask you how you feel I can pretend everything is fine.*

"We broke up," I said brightly. "But it's fine. It was for the best."

"Really? That's sad, Saoirse, you two seemed really sweet together. What happened?"

"We weren't serious," I said. "Nothing *happened*. It ran its course."

Beth's head started to tilt, her eyes softening.

"Don't look at me like that, Beth. Seriously, I'm fine. It's not a big deal."

"If you say so," she said, eyeing me as though I might break down.

"I do."

"OK, say no more." She shrugged but I had the feeling she wasn't really going to let it go. "Do you want a cup of tea?" she asked, pulling mugs out of the cupboard.

"No. I'm going to go to see . . . Mum." I stumbled over the word *mum*, like mentioning her might offend Beth somehow, but she didn't notice.

"Do you have plans after that?"

"No, I guess not."

"Great. Want to come look for a bridesmaid dress? It's getting so close and we haven't even looked yet." She rubbed her right temple, strain showing on her face. "I know you've been busy so I didn't want to bother you but I've seen a couple of things. You need to try them on, of course."

"What do you mean bridesmaid dress?"

Beth's face fell. "Your dad said he asked you."

"Er, no," I said. I tried to work out quickly how I felt about being a bridesmaid. I wasn't thrilled exactly but I didn't feel the intense revulsion I thought I would. Exhaustion again? "Did he actually say I said yes?"

"Yes, he did," she said emphatically. "He *specifically* said you said you'd love to do it. If you don't want to . . ." She trailed off, looking like a wounded puppy.

"No," I said, rubbing the back of my neck. Patience. "Of course I will. Don't ever trust Dad to do things, though. He's kind of a tell-you-what-you-want-to-hear person."

Beth grimaced. "Noted. I'll deal with him later – but listen, I saw this amazing lavender number in Debenhams that I think would look brilliant on you."

I mentally made a note to murder Dad. At least it would be a good distraction.

Mum was still her in her jammies when I got there with my bag of supplies. I'd noticed a couple of days ago that she was fussing with her hair. She opened the door and I could see her bed was unmade and her TV was on.

"What are you watching?" I asked, thinking it was probably something terrible, but it was a broadcast of a classical music festival. Something my mother would actually have liked a lot, once upon a time.

"Looks dead boring," I said approvingly, but I turned it off because it's harder for her to concentrate on conversation with background noise like that.

"That fringe is so long I don't know how you see out of it," I said. "Come on, let's give you a trim." I fetched a towel from her bathroom and wrapped it around her neck, tucking it in at the collar. She relaxed and closed her eyes.

"Ruby and I broke up," I said. "It's OK, though. I mean, we were going to break up soon anyway," I said, snipping at the ends of her hair.

Mum said that was terrible and asked me if I was OK but I realised I didn't want to talk about it, even with her. I changed the subject quickly, asking about her day. I couldn't follow her train of thought all the time but I made the appropriate noises and responses when I could.

Afterwards, Mum's hair looked bouncy and neat again. Maybe I should be a hairstylist. I winced at my own thought. I squeezed my eyes shut, blocking out the words that made me think of Ruby.

Mum brought me her memory book. It had been sitting on the coffee table like someone had used it recently. I knew it wasn't Dad because although he'd never admit it, I knew he hated going through the old pictures. It must have been one of the staff. That was kind of nice, I thought, that someone was taking time with her like that.

"I want to show you something," she said.

"OK then," I said reluctantly, rubbing my palm scar absently. If it made her happy.

Mum showed me a photo of her and Claire and told me a story I'd heard seven thousand times. I didn't mind, though, because I didn't concentrate on the words. I looked at her face, which was shining and happy, and a horrible hot, aching feeling in my throat threatened tears. In a few weeks I was supposed to leave the country and I hadn't told

Dad I didn't want to. I was afraid I'd end up going by default, swept along by the momentum of his expectations, following a plan I'd made when I was heartbroken and looking to escape. And now I felt that itch to escape my life again. But if I did that I wouldn't be able to come here every day, or even every week or month. When I arrived that morning Mum wasn't surprised or distressed by me turning up at her door. She let me in and she was relaxed as we talked. What if all that went away when I couldn't keep up the routine? I knew she didn't really remember she had a daughter but most of the time she knew I was someone she was familiar with. That was something. It was a pathetic scrap of something but it meant everything to me. If I didn't turn up every morning, would I become a complete stranger? How come abandoning my mother still felt like she was abandoning me?

The thought made me feel achingly lonely. Then I thought of Dad wrapping presents for himself and I wondered if he felt the same thing. If we were two people feeling lonely in the exact same way. Was it so hard to see him leave her because I knew that if I was ever going to be free to make my own life, I might have to do the same thing?

"Who's this?" I asked Mum, pointing at a picture of her with Claire. They were sitting in front of a mirror, putting make-up on. Mum looked like she was trying to refuse having her picture taken, Claire was preening for the camera.

"That's me," Mum said, pointing at herself and laughing.

"Who's that?" I asked, indicating Claire.

Mum inspected the photograph. She held the book closer to her face and her forehead wrinkled in concentration. She looked at me, a bit lost.

"That's you?" she asked.

The picture was from about 1985. It was a party. Claire wore a horrible shiny dress and had little lace gloves on. Not exactly my style.

I put my arm around her and pulled her into a hug. "That's you and Claire," I said, and I kissed her on the head, which smelled of apple shampoo.

She tried to turn the page but I closed it over. Dad wasn't the only person who didn't exactly love poring over old photos. I knew this album by heart. I'd helped make it.

"That's enough for today."

29

For two weeks I didn't think about Ruby. I didn't think about Ruby when I got spam email from that karaoke place we never actually went to. I didn't think about Ruby when I walked past the Ferris wheel or the cove or the pedalos. I didn't think about Ruby when I ate dinner or washed my hair or clipped my toenails either. I stopped watching stupid romantic comedies, not because the happily ever afters made my heart ache, but because I don't like romantic comedies. They're stupid and sexist and perpetuate the idea that we only matter as people if someone is in love with us. I ignored Oliver's texts, not because I was afraid he would mention Ruby but because he was a pain in my ass and he always had been.

So what did I do if I wasn't doing those things? I watched a lot of horror movies. I watched people die in a variety of gruesome ways. Impaled on spikes, decapitated and defenestrated, driven to madness by ghosts and changelings and creepy forest demons. Some died slowly, others by surprise. They all soothed my soul. I even helped with the wedding. Yes, hell truly had frozen over, but Beth kept piling on menial tasks for me to do and I wasn't exactly busy with anything else. It's not like I was starting to think she was OK or anything.

All right, all right. Shut up.

On exam results day, I woke nauseated and numb. The lavender bridesmaid monstrosity was the only thing in my wardrobe because I hadn't unpacked yet. I couldn't bring myself to put everything in the wardrobe if I had to move again in six weeks. That might sound like a long time but the pain of packing was very fresh in my mind. But I hadn't put anything in my suitcase either. I picked a pair of jeans and T-shirt out of a box.

I refused to go to school to pick up my results at the crack of dawn because everyone else would be there like puppies panting outside the exam hall, waiting for their slips of paper. If I could hold off for an hour I would miss seeing everyone. I didn't even go to see Mum that morning; I was too anxious and she picks up on that kind of thing. I figured I'd go after lunch. So I spent an uncomfortable morning pottering around the house with Dad asking me if I was quite sure I didn't want to go yet. He was more invested in the results than I was. He and Beth even took the morning off work so we could all have a celebratory lunch after.

In spite of my ambivalent feelings about Oxford, I couldn't help but worry about what I would get. I had studied so much and I worked so hard, but what if my memory wasn't as good as I thought? What if it had failed already and I couldn't actually remember that I'd done badly, or I thought I'd answered the questions fully but it was only because I couldn't remember that there was all this other stuff I was supposed to include? Getting the results I wanted seemed like it was more a test of whether or not I'd succumb to the dementia. As if getting all As would somehow prevent it.

At ten, Dad and I pulled up to the school gate and sure enough, I couldn't see anyone around. With a swaying seasick feeling in my stomach, I left Dad in the car, drumming his fingers on the steering wheel, trying to act cool.

When I was halfway up the stairs that led to the front door, he shouted frantically out his car window.

"I love you no matter what."

I looked around, pretending to see who he was shouting to, because I obviously did not know this weirdo, just in case anyone was passing by.

"Saoirse!" Louise, the school secretary, had a big smile for me when I walked through the doors. "Don't tell me you slept in?"

I did my best impression of "sheepish," as if I was so embarrassed I'd slept in on exam results day. Oh shucks.

"Hold on – I took the rest of the results into the office for you stragglers."

She had a stack of about ten envelopes on her desk.

She sorted through them and handed me one from the middle of the pack. A grin on her face told me she definitely wanted me to open it in front of her. I smiled politely and put it in my bag. Her face dropped.

"Nice to see you," I said, waving on my way out the office door.

"Ooof," I grunted as the door hit me. Someone had tried to come in just as I was trying to get out.

"Oh my God, I'm so sorry," the person said. Then, "Saoirse."

"Izzy." I was surprised to see her but I recovered, rearranging my open mouth into a polite but empty smile. "We have to stop nearly concussing each other like this."

Rom-com, tragedy, slapstick. All I needed now was to meet a guy with knives for hands in the abandoned quarry and I could really round out my life-as-a-movie metaphor.

Izzy returned a small smile. I let a whole second of uncomfortable silence pass and then I tried to scurry out the door. She turned and put her hand on my shoulder.

"Wait a minute, will you?"

"Um . . . my dad is . . ." I gestured towards the car park.

"Please?" she said, a pleading note in her voice. "Just a second."

It would be beyond rude to refuse. I eyed the door, considering a quick getaway anyway. My head said that was childish but my legs were getting ready to spring into action.

But damnit, I was just too nice to do that, so I waited while Izzy went into the office to collect her envelope. I took a seat on the bottom of the stairs that led to the art room and thought about how polite I was.

Then Izzy emerged from the office. She smiled shyly at me and took a seat on the stair next to me. Neither of us said anything for a second. She had new highlights in her hair from the last time we collided on the street. It looked really pretty. She also had a deep tan and I wondered if she'd gotten the lifeguard job she'd been applying for, unsuccessfully, for the last two years.

"I'm so mad at you," she said finally.

"Wait, what? You're mad at me?"

She nodded. She didn't *seem* mad. She seemed really calm and collected.

"I'm really mad."

"What do you have to be mad about?" I said, indignant.

"You ditched me, Saoirse," she said.

"You—" I started to remind her of her gross betrayal of trust.

"Yes, I know I didn't tell you that Hannah was thinking of breaking up with you. I know. You told me that. I heard you. I apologised a bunch of times. And I thought about it a lot and I get it. I know why you were mad, I do."

I tried to interrupt again but she held her hand up.

"Let me finish. I know why you were angry, but I *don't* know why you couldn't forgive me and I'm mad at you for that. We were friends for *ten* years and you decided I was nothing to you because I hurt you *once*."

My mouth opened and closed like a goldfish as I scrambled for a defence.

"It wasn't like that. You picked Hannah over me. The ten years we were friends obviously didn't mean as much to you as the twelve years you were friends with Hannah."

"That is such bullshit. I was stuck in between my two best friends. If I told you what Hannah told me in confidence, I'd have betrayed her. Not telling you, I betrayed you. She put me in a crappy position."

"Tell that to Hannah, then."

"I did. I was cross with her too. I told her I was pissed she put me in position where I had to lie to you or tell on her."

I didn't know what to say. I didn't have to, though. Izzy wasn't done yet.

"You know, maybe I should have told you. At least I think Hannah would have forgiven me. At least I mattered to her enough for that."

In Izzy's version of events, I sounded selfish and petty. Maybe she was right.

"I didn't really think of it like that." I struggled to get the next words out. They would expose me and leave me vulnerable. I was starting to think I hated emotional conversations as much as my dad. Maybe that's what made me say it, finally.

"I thought I didn't matter to you. All I saw was you putting her first when she broke my heart and it felt like you didn't care about me," I said. "I was protecting myself."

Izzy looked like she wanted to argue, but she paused before speaking.

"I can see why it looked that way," she said.

"I can see why it looked like I didn't care about you too."

We fell silent. My feet begged to run out the door.

"Do you remember when you met me?" Izzy asked after a moment.

"First day of first class?" I guessed.

"No." She shook her head. "I thought you'd say that. But all that summer we'd been friends. You lived up the street and you hadn't started school yet."

I'd forgotten. Mum and Dad and I lived in a rented place before they bought our old house. Mum dragged me up the street to a neighbour's house because she'd met another mother and they arranged for us to play.

"I remember now. I didn't want to go to your house but then when I met you, you took me into that old tree house, the one that wasn't—"

"Actually in a tree, I know."

"You gave me an ice lolly and then we were friends."

"Simpler times," Izzy laughed. "Then when we started school, you met Hannah. She was my best friend at school and you were my best friend at home, and then as soon as you met each other you became best friends and I was the odd one out."

"It wasn't like that," I said automatically.

"It was. But that's OK. We were all still friends. Until you started going out and I was the third wheel."

There was too much truth in that to deny. Hannah and I spent a lot more time together without Izzy after that. We were a couple, that was normal. But then every time Izzy was with us it felt a bit like she was crashing a date, even if it wasn't actually a date. I got kind of annoyed with her sometimes even though I knew it wasn't her fault. I'd thought I'd hidden it better because she'd never mentioned it.

"We both loved you, though," I offered, and I immediately wondered if *love* or *loved* was the right tense.

Izzy bit her lip. "What if part of me was happy, then, when Hannah told me she wanted to end it? I didn't think I was but what if I was?"

"You weren't." I shook my head.

"How do you know?" she said.

"Well, what if you were? So you had a selfish feeling. I know you, you have a lot fewer of them than most people."

We sat for a couple of seconds in silence and I thought about how I really did know the person next to me. I knew the contours of her face more than I knew my own. I knew her so well I could pick her out of a crowd at the funfair, in a sea of people. And I knew what kind of person she was. Even if things changed, if she took up knitting or deep-sea diving or she got married or she adopted fourteen cats and lived in a lighthouse, some things would never change. The years of petty squabbles and sleepovers, first loves dissected, notes passed and secrets shared. It hadn't disappeared because they were over, and it couldn't be undone.

"What now?" Izzy asked.

I didn't know if we could be friends again after one conversation. Had too much time passed or did a few months mean nothing in the grand scheme of things?

"Now we open these envelopes," I said, unsticking the seal and pulling out a sheet of paper.

30

"Beth, we have a genius in our midst," Dad boomed as soon as he got in the door. He waved my exam results like they were a trophy he'd won.

Beth was holding a bottle of bleach and the house smelled like she had disinfected it entirely. In the last couple of weeks of living together, I'd discovered Beth's nervous habit was cleaning. It was also what she did when she was angry or upset about anything ranging from not being able to find her late father's watch to running out of tea bags after the shops were closed.

"Let me see it." She tossed aside a pair of rubber gloves, and reached for the certificate. "Eight H1s, what does that mean?" Beth said, reminding us she was English.

"As," I said. "Only six really count. But you know, some people are gifted with good looks *and* brains. Sometimes it's more of a burden than anything else."

Beth hugged me tight, pulling me in without thinking. She smelled of Dettol and citrus perfume. We'd never hugged before. She started to pull back, uncertainty on her face, in case she'd done the wrong thing. I hugged her tight. It was a special occasion, after all.

She'd better not get used to it, though.

"Will you have got your firm offer yet then?" she asked.

I shook my head. I'd checked the application tracking on the way home. "It'll probably take a couple of hours to show up."

"But you met the requirements of your conditional offer, right?"

"Yeah . . . ," I said, feeling uncomfortable. I had to say something soon. I thought maybe when I got my results I'd change my mind. Maybe I'd want to go. Everyone was so sure it was an offer you don't refuse.

"Your mum would be so proud," Dad said, smothering me with another hug.

Maybe my mature conversation with Izzy had gone to my head. It's the only reason I could think that I chose that moment of parental elation to voice my doubts.

"What if I didn't go to university?"

Dad pushed me away and gaped at me. Beth shifted uncomfortably.

"What are you talking about? You got eight H1s," Dad said, like good grades meant you absolutely must go to uni and of course pick the degree with the highest entry requirements you can possibly meet. I felt my phone vibrate in my back pocket but I thought this would be bad time to answer it.

"Rob, hold on." Beth held up her hand in a stop sign. "Maybe she wants to take a gap year. That's OK. Or do a different kind of course. Not everyone has to go to university." She put her hand on Dad's arm.

"Over my dead body," he muttered.

I ignored them both and made a scene of pouring myself some orange juice. This conversation needed taking down a notch or two, so doing normal things seemed like the best solution. Act casual. I took a sip while Dad waited. Apparently, he wanted a response to Beth's statement even though he obviously disagreed.

Drinking had never felt so unnatural in my life.

"It's not that. I just don't think it's for me, that's all."

Dad blinked exaggerated blinks.

"I mean, let's be honest," I went on, "it's likely going to be a bit of a waste."

"What on earth do you mean *a waste*. How can a world-class education be *a waste*?" Dad shouted the words. Beth winced and with great effort, he reeled it in. "Is this about Ruby? Just because she's not going to university doesn't mean you can sit around here and do nothing. I swear, Saoirse, if you don't go you are not staying here. End of story," Dad said.

"Believe me, I don't want to live with you one second longer than I have to." I spat the words out, hoping for maximum hurt. He was incapable of listening to reason. I should have known better. "I want to be close to Mum."

"Hold on now, Rob." Beth cut across Dad before he could speak. "Of course you can stay here, Saoirse, this is your home. We can talk about this."

Dad opened his mouth and I thought he was going to give off to Beth but she gave him a look that would silence an angry mob. "Don't even think about it," she said. "This is my home too."

"So you want to enable her to waste her life?" Then he turned on me. "Go see what it's like to try and get a decent job without a degree."

"You don't have a degree," Beth snapped at him.

"It's different now. You want to throw all your hard work away because your girlfriend is a slacker? I'm not going to finance that."

Beth looked like she was going to argue but I got there first.

"No one asked you to finance anything. I can get a job." I doubted that would be easy in this economy actually. I hadn't been able to get a job over the summer. Not one of the jobs I applied for called me for interview. Our little seaside economy wasn't exactly busting with well-paying, no-qualification jobs, and commuters to the city had pushed rents up so much I didn't think I'd actually ever be able to live in the town I grew up in. Unless I bumped off Dad and Beth and inherited the flat. Tempting but messy. But I would work it out, right? If I had to.

"Ruby isn't going to university yet because she's staying home to help her family. I know *you* can't imagine sacrificing anything to care for someone but she's not like that."

Dad closed his eyes and his lips thinned but he didn't say anything.

"And anyway, it's got nothing to do with her. We broke up, remember?" I added, knowing Beth had told him, even though he hadn't had the guts to broach the subject with me.

"Well, what the hell is it about, then?" Dad said, his fury and bluster deflated.

"You know exactly what it's about. There's no point in learning a bunch of useless stuff when I'm only going to forget it all later."

Dad took a deep breath and I watched the muscles in his face soften. Beth's fingers covered her lips. She looked sad.

Finally, Dad spoke, his voice quiet but firm. As though he thought if he spoke reasonably enough I would have to agree with him. "Saoirse, you don't know what will happen. You have to keep living a normal life. Your mother did."

Where did it get her? Locked up in an old people's home and she doesn't know her own last name. My phone vibrated again. I only half registered it. "She didn't know this was going to happen. I *know* what the odds are. It changes things."

Dad exchanged the most infinitesimally quick glance with Beth.

"Dad?" I suddenly knew what that glance meant. I knew

it with my whole body because my legs started to feel weak. "Did she know?"

I asked because I wanted him to deny it.

"We should sit down. I'll make a cup of tea," Beth said.

I ignored her.

"Not early," Dad said. "Not as young as you."

Maybe he thought half the truth would satisfy me.

"When?" The word fell out like a stone.

Dad appeared to wrestle with himself and then finally one side won.

"Your mum was adopted, you know that," he said. "But around the time we met, she was searching for her birth parents."

I didn't know that part. She'd never spoken much about them. Her adoptive parents were my grandparents and I never thought to ask her if she'd met her birth family. They never seemed very important to my mum, so they weren't very important to me either.

"She found her mother, Joan. Or rather, she found a relative. A cousin. Joan had passed away already. The cousin, I don't remember her name any more, she told us Joan died young. Early-onset dementia. It progressed rapidly. We did some research and we knew then that there was a chance your mother would get it too."

When Mum had told me I had a chance of getting it too, I had thought, doesn't everyone have a chance? It was a while before I really understood what it meant. Mum and Dad had argued about it. A couple of years after they'd told me about her diagnosis, when I was about fifteen, I overheard them fighting. Mum thought I deserved to know. Dad thought it could wait. Mum said he'd wait forever if he could. Dad said maybe that wasn't a bad idea. Mum said it wasn't right for them to make that decision. Mum won.

"She knew before she had me that this would happen to her?"

I couldn't believe she would do something so selfish.

"No," Dad said quickly. "We didn't *know*. We knew there was a chance. Just as you know there's a chance for you. But the point is, it never stopped her from living any part of her life fully and it shouldn't stop you. I sometimes think we should never have told you. I was afraid you would live your whole life in the shadow of something that might never happen and I was right."

"How could you have a kid when you knew what could happen?" I said, voice shaking. I pressed my fingertips tight against my thumb. Don't cry.

"Honestly," Dad said, rubbing his face, his words coming out from between his hands, "when we found out she was pregnant I asked her if she was sure this was a good idea. Your mother insisted it was her life, her choice to make." Dad's voice cracked. "Then when you came along, I felt so ashamed that I'd ever thought you could be a bad idea." He said it like an apology.

It wasn't the apology I wanted.

"Well, you were wrong," I said through gritted teeth, and I pushed past Beth as she wiped her eyes with her sleeve. "It wasn't just her life."

31

My mother knew before I was born that she might lose her mind. That I'd lose her. That she could abandon me. It was like stepping off the waltzer when your body thinks it's still spinning but the ground beneath you is still. Like the moment of finding out for the first time that Mum had dementia, of Hannah breaking up with me, of realising that Mum had to move out, of being told Dad was getting remarried. Over and over again I kept settling into a new way of living. I'd reel and then adapt and just when I thought I knew what life was going to be now, it threw something else at me. I thought I was living on a roller coaster like everyone else, ups and downs, but my life was more like emotional dodgeball and I kept getting hit. And yet again, like at all the worst moments of my life, I had nowhere to turn.

My phone buzzed again and I checked it this time, more out of habit than any real interest in what the message was. Downstairs, when I felt it go, I had hoped against my will that it was Ruby. But the texts were from people from school asking about my results. Shane and Georgia, who I'd hung about with a bit but hadn't spoken to since the last exam, and a couple of others who I barely spoke to at all, the kind of people who needed to compare their results to everyone else to figure out if they were happy about their own or not. I ignored them all. Another text came in while I was deleting those.

Oliver
Don't you want to know what I got? ☺

Saoirse
No.

Oliver
6 H1s TWINSIES

Saoirse
No.

Oliver
Party tonight?

On the one hand, I really wanted to get drunk, and getting drunk in a group is socially acceptable. Doing it alone is considered "a problem." On the other hand, in spite of what I'd told myself before, I still didn't know if I could handle running into Ruby, even if that's not something totally-over-it people worry about. I wanted to ask about her, but I wouldn't give Oliver the satisfaction. I didn't know what he knew about the breakup. He and Ruby seemed pretty close and he might tell her I was asking after her.

Oliver
Ruby won't be there. She went home
for a couple of days so she could pick
up her results with her friends. Not back
here until the weekend.

Saoirse
Fine. I'll be there but it has nothing to
do with her. We're cool.

Oliver
Whatever you say. There'll be plenty
of tipsy straight girls for you to crack
onto instead.

Saoirse
I don't crack onto anyone. I merely
welcome advances.

My reply felt hollow, though. Kissing girls who don't really fancy you, who just want to see what it's like (hello, my lips are not actually that different from teenage boy lips. I even have a light moustache when I'm not keeping up with personal grooming) feels very different to kissing someone who touches you like they want more. I pushed those thoughts out of my head. They weren't helpful. Thinking of Ruby and the feeling of her skin, of her hands on my body, of the way she pulled me close like she wanted to melt together, wasn't going to get me anywhere good.

Though I'd planned to go and see Mum after getting the results, I didn't have it in me any more and I was too raging to even look at her. I was even more angry knowing that I couldn't go and tell her off, scream and stomp my feet like I did with Dad. So I lay down and tried to ignore the guilt. It wasn't like she'd notice anyway. She wasn't exactly always putting my interests first even when she was well.

I forced it out of my head. I put Ruby out of my head too. I put my fight with Dad out of my head and exam results and the future out of my head. I let it all go blank. Feelings are overrated.

Arriving at the party gave me déjà vu. Same people, same music, same house. The main difference was that as I wandered through the house, being stopped every few minutes, instead of how did I think the exams went, I was asked what results I got. After a few minutes, people began coming up and congratulating me on my results without me saying anything. As I always do at these kinds of things, I kept one eye out for Hannah, my lizard brain on the alert so I didn't accidentally bump into her.

Part of my brain was also on the alert for Ruby, even though it felt a little different. When I thought I might run into Hannah, I panicked. I genuinely didn't want to see her. And yet tonight, even though I knew she wasn't here, a part of me was hoping in spite of myself to see Ruby. Maybe that's what a relationship means, carrying a part of someone around for the rest of your life. I pictured myself elderly and skittish, the ghosts of so many girlfriends past following me around. Lifelong voluntary celibacy seemed like a good option. Unless I didn't get that far. Perhaps whoever they were to me would all crumble away, bit by bit, until I didn't even know I'd forgotten them.

The jostling party organism swilled me around in its mouth and spat me out in the kitchen, where I poured myself a large drink from the bottle at the back of the freezer even though it was cheap Tesco Value vodka tonight.

"Ahhh!" a girl from my English class, Laura, screamed in my direction, though the sound was mostly swallowed up by the music. She embraced me, sloshing half her drink on the floor. We never really spoke much aside from usual class chitchat. She was tipsy but not completely wasted. Her words tumbled out, slippery on her tongue, but her eyes were focused.

"How are you?" she sang. "I heard you got, like . . . all the points? That's wild!"

I didn't tell her that I had a lot of time to study when I had no real friends and nothing else to do.

"What about you?" I asked.

"Average. I did good at maths but it was ordinary level. I got what I needed."

I wanted to tell her she didn't have to make excuses.

That my grades didn't mean I thought she was stupid because she didn't get them too. I thought it would come out patronising so I asked her what she was going to study instead.

"Animation. I had to submit a portfolio. That mattered more than my grades."

I didn't even know she liked to draw. Of course, there was no reason why I would.

"What about you?" she said.

"I don't know."

The final confirmation had come that afternoon, but seeing it in black and white only filled me with dread. I watched as she reached for comforting words she could give me. I could practically see her scanning her brain for the right ones, a child choosing a toy carefully from the shelf to share.

"You'll figure it out," she said. "You can do anything you want with your points."

I smiled and agreed that I would work it out, because what was the use of telling her that I didn't want to go to university anyway?

I heard a dozen different career options from my classmates that night, shouted into my ear with beer breath and crisp crumbs. Biomedical science, hospitality and events, philosophy, graphic design, pharmacology, and the oddly specific town and country planning and landscape design.

I nodded politely and told everyone *that sounds really*

interesting. They asked me what I was doing and I stopped telling them I didn't know. I told everyone something different instead, borrowing from other classmates. When Jennifer Loughran told me she was going to do occupational therapy, I told Shane Nelson I was doing occupational therapy, and so on. I told Aisling Cheung I was going to study forensic science in Glasgow and when she started talking to me about *CSI*, I pretended I had to pee.

Oliver was in the piano room again. He wasn't at the piano this time; he was sitting on the floor against the wall, reading a book. There was an empty glass and a bottle of vodka beside him.

"I knew the good stuff would be in here with you," I said. "You're very predictable, you know." I slouched down beside him.

"This is for you," he said, handing me the empty glass and the bottle. "I'm teetotal tonight. I have to drive in the morning."

I pursed my lips but I took the glass anyway and poured myself a drink. "If being predictable means I get bottle service then I guess I can live with it."

I sipped it. It didn't burn like the cheap stuff. "Where do you have to drive in the morning?"

Oliver blushed. "Summer camp," he mumbled. "I'm volunteering at a summer camp, OK? Ruby saw a flyer about it and my parents wouldn't leave me alone."

I didn't laugh like I normally would have, picturing Oliver rounding up kids and teaching them archery and canoeing. Ruby's name hung in the silence between us. Ruby Ruby Ruby.

"What happened?" Oliver asked eventually.

I swished the memory of the fight around in my mouth like I was trying to extract flavours from a nice wine, but it all tasted bitter.

"I think I fucked up," I said.

"That sounds about right." Oliver nodded. "She didn't say anything. I don't know if I should tell you but she's really upset."

My heart was torn, half aching for causing her pain, half trilling that she cared enough to feel it.

"What kind of fucking it up did you do? Did you pluck some poor girl from your harem and have your way with her?"

I shoved him gently. "No. She wanted something I can't give her."

"Not an STD, then?" he said, grinning.

"Oh fuck off."

"No, come on," he said, putting a serious face on, "I genuinely want to know. I care about her."

I sighed but reluctantly gave him one more chance to act like a human being.

"She wanted something more . . . I dunno . . . real? That's not what I wanted. We had an agreement. I told her that the first night." I realised I sounded like I was defending myself on trial and maybe I needed to tell the truth. "I made all these rules for myself about what I shouldn't do so I wouldn't get hurt. Don't have serious conversations. Don't picture a future together. Don't fight and don't make up. Basically don't have feelings, don't fall in love. I knew it wouldn't work. I shouldn't have let myself get talked into it."

"Maybe you wanted someone to talk you into it," he said, knocking his knee against mine. "Maybe you want something real too. Why are you fighting it?"

I resisted the urge to make fun of his Oprah psychobabble and really thought about it. In the beginning, it felt so important that I didn't tell her about Mum or about anything to do with me, and that was OK because it was a fling. But after a while, it started to feel like a lie and I clung on to my rule of not talking about it even when it no longer did what it was supposed to do, which was give me space *not* to think about it. It was meant to stop me from getting hurt. Instead, I thought about it and it festered and I stomped it down so it wouldn't slip out.

But the thing was, as much as I could have these realisations, they didn't change anything. They only made me more certain that it was not good for me to be in a relationship. If I'd let her in all along, let myself be honest, it still would have ended, and we'd have lost something even bigger. We'd have both been even more hurt. What use would all that pain be? I'd tried to have a relationship where it was only the fun stuff, the kissing and dates and holding hands, but you couldn't have a romantic montage and skip the rest of the movie. As much as I'd tried to avoid feeling it, if I was being honest with myself, the last couple of weeks had been torture. If I wanted to stop feeling pain, and causing pain, I needed to go back to a strict no-relationships policy.

"I think it's for the best. It was going to end soon anyway, so what difference does a couple of weeks make?" I said, not really answering Oliver's question.

"That's the stupidest thing I've ever heard." He shook his head. "You need to get over yourself."

Those words flung me back into the car with Ruby and it got my back up.

"Oh really? If we're analysing people tonight, tell me this, Mr Quinn. Why do you have parties at your house – sorry, mansion – and then hide in the music room and avoid everyone? What's the point?"

He didn't seem hurt. Instead, he rubbed his chin with his hand.

"Funny you should ask. I've been wondering the same thing."

He seemed genuinely thoughtful, maybe even a little deflated, and I felt bad for snapping.

"Any deep insights into your psyche that you want to share?" I teased, trying to bring us back to more lighthearted territory, where I was comfortable. I expected some kind of joke in response but Oliver was serious when he spoke.

"I think I started having these parties so people would like me. I know that's the most cliché thing in the world. But I thought if I had parties, people would come to me, and they'd associate me with having a good time."

Oliver had always been that guy, the guy with the parties, the guy *everyone* talked to and chatted with at school.

"Well, it worked," I said. "You can hardly walk down the hall at school without someone talking to you."

"Yeah," he agreed. "People do talk to me. People say things like *Lad, I was so battered at your party* or *Crackin' night, lad.*" He said these things in a deep bro voice. I tried not to laugh; Oliver trying to impersonate "the lads" sounded ridiculous. "They tell me about the things they did at my house. What a great time they had. And when they stop talking about it, I have another party."

"OK . . ." I didn't see where he was going with this.

"When you and Hannah and Izzy fell out, everyone noticed because everyone knew you were best friends. And you're not popular or anything."

"Aw, shucks, thanks." I scowled at him.

"Who is Amanda Roberts friends with?" he asked.

"Eh, Christina Kelly and Rani Sullivan?"

"Right. And Chloe Foster?"

"Daniel Campbell. Although I think they're definitely boning."

"No, he's gay."

"What?! *More* gays? The top secret gay conversion plot is really working."

"Who are my friends, Saoirse?" he said, and he didn't sound maudlin, more like he was simply curious what I'd say.

I shrugged. "I dunno. Everyone?"

"Right, sure, but who would I go to if I had a problem?"

I couldn't think of anyone. Oliver hung around with everyone; he never had one group of people or one best friend that I could tell.

"Exactly," he said to my silence. "And now we're all going on our separate ways and there isn't anyone I can say I'll stay in touch with."

"No one will really stay friends. We'll all have forgotten each other by Halloween."

"Maybe that's true," he said, although it didn't seem to make him feel any better.

I wasn't used to this Oliver.

"Will you have another party before we all leave?" I asked.

"I don't think so." He rolled his shoulders and stretched his neck. "I think I'm tired of pretending. I don't enjoy these parties. I always end up in here, and no one ever wonders where I am."

I could tell he was done talking about it now. I sat beside him and I didn't talk either. I reached my hand a few inches to the left and touched his hand. Our fingers interlaced. I sipped on my vodka and we didn't talk until I reached the bottom of my glass.

I held our intertwined hands up in front of our faces.

"I'm still gay, though," I said. "We're not getting back together."

"That's good," he replied thoughtfully. "You were cute when we were eleven but I do not fancy you now."

"Sure you do. I'm very fanciable. I wouldn't blame you or anything."

"Ugh, no. You're like riddled with crabs and you're way too butch for me."

"Dude, I don't think you know what butch means. Check out the hair. I'm a tomboy femme. I did a quiz."

"Did the quiz makers see those boots?"

"No."

"I demand a recount."

My phone rang in my pocket but I didn't recognise the number on the screen.

"If this is another person asking me if I've been in an accident that wasn't my fault I'm going off the grid," I grumbled, but answered anyway.

"Saoirse Clarke?"

"Yes?"

"This is Karen, I'm a night nurse from Seaview. Your mother is extremely distressed. She's in an agitated state. I can't get in contact with your father. I thought you would want to come down."

32

Oliver lingered in reception as Karen ushered me down the hall to Mum's room, telling me matter-of-factly that Mum was being aggressive and violent. It happened sometimes. It was when she seemed least like the Mum I knew.

A month or so before she went missing, Dad was in Dublin at a meeting with clients and he'd promised to be back by five. I was home with Mum, making dinner. I mean I'd put frozen burgers under the grill but that counted as cooking to me. Mum was getting in my way, though, fussing around the kitchen, trying to help. I had to leave to meet Hannah in half an hour and Dad wasn't back yet even though he was the one who was meant to make dinner.

"No, Mum, give me that." I tried to take a chopping knife out of her hand but she had a tight grip on it.

"NO," she shouted. "I can help, you know."

"Yeah, I know," I sighed, frustrated. This was why Dad was meant to be back already. It was getting harder and harder to be with Mum and do anything else at the same time. If you left her alone you risked her trying to wander out of the house.

"I don't need anything right now, Mum. Why don't you go sit down?"

She stamped her foot and didn't budge.

I took several deep breaths and reminded myself that she was more frustrated by the situation than I was.

"Look." I tried a more soothing tone. "Why don't we have a cup of tea? If you give me two minutes we can go into the living room together and I'll put on music."

I wondered if I should take out the baby doll. She would hold it and feed it and pace up and down winding it. But it was one of my least favourite "therapeutic tools." It creeped me out to see Mum thinking a lump of plastic was a baby when she couldn't even tell the person next to her was her daughter. So I put on some of her favourite music and when I got her settled on the sofa and distracted her with her photo album, she let the knife drop. I picked it up and returned to the kitchen to flip the burgers over. They were a bit burned on one side.

I called Dad, my third call so far, but there was no answer. I was pouring boiling water into a pot with some broccoli when Mum returned to the kitchen.

"I need something," she said.

My phone dinged with a text from Dad.

Dad
Sorry, love. Left late and now stuck in gridlock trying to get out of the city. Will make it up to you. How does a Ferrari sound?

I swore under my breath. I was not softened by his attempt at humour either. I started typing a furious reply. I could hear Mum in the background but I wasn't concentrating on what she was saying.

"I need something. I need . . ."

I texted Hannah to let her know Dad was not home yet. She would know that meant I couldn't leave. The broccoli started to boil over and I lifted the pot, scaling myself with a splash of water. It wasn't much but the shock made me drop my phone. Tears of frustration stung my eyes.

"Hello?" Mum shouted, banging her fists on the counter.

I snapped.

"SHUT UP," I screamed back at her.

She froze, startled for a second, and a wave of guilt crashed over me.

I rushed towards her, to comfort her, but I'd scared her. She grabbed the salad bowl from the counter and smashed it to the ground.

Salad littered the floor, limp bits of lettuce scattered on the tile and tomatoes dotted here and there like an abstract painting. The glass bowl was split in two pieces. I didn't want Mum to pick it up in case she got hurt so I shooed her away from the mess.

"It's OK, Mum, I'll get it," I said, forcing myself to sound calm. I grabbed for the dustpan and squeezed carefully through the small space between the kitchen island and the oven door, which was open for the grill. Mum didn't move and her eyes flashed at me when I came close. She was upset about the mess and noise and me shouting.

"Come on, why don't you go sit in the living room for a bit."

I thought it was time to get out the doll no matter how I felt about it. She'd fuss with it and it would give me enough time to clean up and finish dinner. I could smell the other side of the burgers burning now, and little tendrils of smoke were curling out from the grill. I put my arm around Mum's back to guide her into the living room but as I did she jerked out of my grip.

"Get away from me," she yelled, and twisted away from me. Like slow motion I saw her foot slide on the floor; the oil of the salad dressing had made the floor slippery. I thought she was going to fall. In an instant, I could see her smashing her head against the tile floor. I reached out to catch her, grabbing her around the waist. But she didn't slip. She screamed at me and wrenched out of my grasp.

"Get *away* from me," she screamed again, and pushed me full force. I slipped on the greasy tiles and fell backwards. Instinctively I reached out for something to grab on to to pull myself up or to save myself. At the same time I felt a burst of pain as I landed on my back on the open oven door and my hand found the hot grill rack. I let go of it in less than a second but it was still too long. A guttural scream ripped out of me. When I looked, I saw a bright pink, raw line of burned flesh across the palm.

I managed to get myself upright, my hand feeling like fire, and called out to Mum, who had fled at the commotion. I was afraid that she'd try to leave the house if she was upset. I couldn't remember if I'd locked the front door.

Hannah arrived ten minutes later. She must have already been on her way to meet me when I texted her. She found me in my parents' room, stroking Mum's hair with my unburned hand, curled up on the bed like I was the mum and she was the child. My skin felt like it was still burning, a terrible sensation penetrating deep into my hand.

"Let me see," Hannah said brusquely. She didn't flinch when I held out my hand, which was shiny and raw. It looked wet almost and a layer of skin had peeled away.

"That's going to need some attention. Antibiotics maybe. Have you run it under cold water? Taken anything for the pain?"

I shook my head. I looked down at Mum, who was clinging on to me. Hannah understood. I couldn't leave her when she was like this. Even if it was to take care of myself. It wasn't her fault.

Hannah left me with Mum and returned a couple of minutes later with a bowl of cold water, a glass of juice, and a packet of ibuprofen. She sat on the other side of Mum and we stayed quiet. I let my hand rest in the water until Mum let me go.

"Running water is better," Hannah said, her voice barely a whisper. The way parents speak when they're trying to make sure not to wake a child. "We might need to take you to the hospital, though."

Hannah distracted Mum, her voice, cheerful and comforting, drifting down the hall into the bathroom as I stood with my hand under the tap, the cool water soothing the fire burrowing into my skin.

I hated myself for feeling fearful as I approached Mum's door. I wasn't afraid of being hurt. I was afraid of how I felt when I saw her that way. Like I just couldn't deal with her any more. I was afraid I couldn't be the calm, soothing person she needed. I was afraid I made it worse. When I entered her room she was shouting at a girl in a care worker's uniform, screaming so loud I couldn't make out what she was saying. Her pillows and duvet had been wrenched from the bed and tossed in a corner. I spied her memory book overturned in the middle of the floor, and clothes and other bits and pieces were liberally strewn around the room.

As if transported straight from my memory into the present day, I saw Hannah standing in front of my mum in that uniform. At first, I thought I was imagining it and then I realised she really was the girl in the uniform. After everything, in the middle of everything, my stomach still flipped over when I recognised her. She didn't look scared by Mum screaming in her face. She didn't look surprised to see me.

"Liz, I want to help you. Let's find it together, OK?" Hannah said, her firm, clipped tones authoritative and still somehow warm.

"Mum." I spoke as softly as I could given she was shouting over me.

She hesitated when she noticed me.

"Mum, are you OK?" I asked.

"She stole my purse." Mum pointed at Hannah.

Mum didn't have a purse. She didn't need one. She had no cash. She had a handbag, though, that she carried when we went out, and sometimes I gave her my purse to put in it.

"I'm going to look for it now, is that OK?"

"She stole it." Mum pointed at Hannah again and kicked her bedside cupboard. I winced, thinking she was going to break a toe, and quickly I went to her handbag, discarded on the floor near the bed. On my hands and knees, I slipped my own purse out of my bag and stood up with it in my hand.

"Is this your purse, Mum?"

Mum looked at it for a minute and I held my breath.

"That's my purse. Give it to me," she said. I held it out and she snatched it from me.

"It must have fallen on the floor," I said.

Mum stuffed it under her pillow. I'd be waiting a long time to get that purse back.

"Why don't we play some music, Liz?" Hannah suggested. I nodded more to myself than to anyone else and went to turn on Mum's speakers. They were missing, though. I scanned the floor for them, but Hannah was already taking her phone out of her pocket. Her fingers slid across the screen and in a moment a song started playing, a bit thin and tinny but loud enough. Mum's face crumpled up like she might cry, the fight dissipated but the energy still swirling around inside her. I picked the photo album off the floor and sat with it on the couch.

"Who's this, Mum?"

"That's my dad," she said. And she snuggled in next to me, though she cast an evil eye at Hannah as she slipped out the door. "That's the day my sister was born. She's ten years younger than me. Mum and Dad didn't think they could have a baby."

We turned the pages and I let Mum tell me stories. Some more coherent than others, every one I'd heard before. We got to the picture of Claire and Mum, the one at Claire's wedding. I normally closed the book there, but I hesitated and Mum turned the page. I reached out to stop her but then for some reason I didn't.

"There's you and Rob," I said. She touched his face in the photo.

"That's me and you, on my first birthday." I pointed to the picture on the opposite page. I was wearing a pair of cotton stretchy dungarees and I didn't have much hair yet.

331

On the next page was my first school picture. Then a photo of Mum and Dad kissing. I still didn't know who'd taken it. They looked happy, though.

When it was time to go, Mum asked me if I'd be back tomorrow.

"I'll see you in the morning," I said, "I promise."

I stretched my arms overhead. I was tired and so sober I'd forgotten I'd been drinking earlier. In reception I was surprised to see Hannah talking to Oliver, their heads close together, serious looks on their faces. They stopped talking when they saw me.

"Hi," I said, suddenly shy.

"Hi," Hannah answered.

"Uh, I really need to go . . . somewhere else for a minute." Oliver stood abruptly and walked around the corner. I had a feeling he would just stand there waiting.

My hands dangled at my sides. Without saying anything I sat down next to Hannah in a moulded plastic chair. My shoes were suddenly fascinating.

"Mum's OK now."

"Good. She's been upset all night. The purse was only one of the things. When Karen called you it was something else entirely. She was shouting for ages. Throwing things. The minute she saw you I think it calmed her down."

I waved this absurd suggestion away.

"She doesn't even know who I am."

Hannah shook her head.

"You're wrong," she said simply. "She might forget your name or exactly how she knows you, but she loves you. You being there made her feel safer."

"You can't love someone if you don't even remember their name," I said. In my head, it had sounded like a simple statement of fact. Out loud, I was embarrassed when my voice wavered over the words.

"I really don't think that's true at all. If you truly love someone, if they were ever important to you, it doesn't disappear. What it looks like might change, but that's only the surface."

I looked at her. Her face was so familiar but it didn't sound like her at all. When had she changed? I felt the twinge of something, like a nudge against a tender bruise, at the reminder that Hannah would continue to change in little ways and I wouldn't be there to see it. It still hurt somehow, even after all this time.

"I see it all the time working here. Your mum, she looks at your pictures. She points to your photograph. She asks me about you. She knows somewhere in the core of her that you're important."

I ignored the ache in my chest and focused on the hum of the fluorescent lighting.

"Why are you here?" I asked after a few moments. I had to squeeze the words out of my throat and they sounded thick and tight.

"I work here," she said blankly, as if it was a stupid question. *That* was the Hannah I knew. Literal to a fault.

"No, I mean, how come you work here and how have I not seen you here before?"

"I do the night shift. I'm going to take a gap year. I needed a job and Mum knows one of the managers. The money is terrible but I like the work."

"*You're* taking a gap year?"

Hannah was always so sure she wanted to be a lawyer that I was surprised she would put that on hold.

"I wanted to figure some things out. Dad let me shadow him at work for a bit so I could see what it was like."

I nodded. I remembered her pestering her dad to let her do that for ages. He always said no.

"Saoirse." She looked at me with wide eyes. "It was the most boring week of my life. Being a solicitor is so *dull*."

I laughed and remembered how Ruby said people who were certain they knew what they wanted to do were probably wrong.

"I thought about it and decided I'd like to work with dementia but I wasn't sure in what capacity. I got a job here to see if the people side would interest me or if I should pursue research."

"You want to work with people with dementia?"

"Yes."

I almost rolled my eyes. It wouldn't occur to her to elaborate.

"Why, though?"

"Because of you," she said like it was obvious. "I saw what it did to you, to your family. I practically lived at your house, Saoirse. Remember? Your mum was always good to me. I wanted to do something for people like her."

I tried to process this. Why would she care so much about me, or my family, when she left me?

"When you truly love someone, it doesn't go away," she said, surprising me again by reading my lack of response.

"What it looks like just changes," I said, and she nodded.

"Don't you still love me?" she asked.

I let my breath whoosh out of me to give myself time to think.

"Yes," I said honestly. "But I don't want to." Brutal honesty. Hannah didn't look offended or hurt by it, though.

"I do," she said. "I don't want to forget what we had. Ever. In the past, we're perfectly preserved, best friends, in love forever. I like that." She looked at the ceiling. "Everything is moving so fast. Before long everyone we know will be scattered across the country, the world even. Our lives will look completely different to what they've always been so far." She put her hand on mine. "I like having something that can't ever change. It's already happened."

Hannah squeezed my hand and stood up to leave. I stood with her and hugged her. I didn't talk much as Oliver drove me home.

33

I was woken by a soft rap on my bedroom door. I opened my eyes and adjusted to the new bedroom. My sleeping brain still expected to wake up in the old house. I shuffled upright and told Dad he could come in. I could tell it was him by his knock.

"Hey, love." He sat himself on the end of my bed, a position that had "serious conversation" connotations. I grunted in response. The last time he had serious talk vibes, we were moving. I had a right to be suspicious.

"I'm really sorry about yesterday."

"Which part?"

His eyes darted away for a second. He meant me going to the home instead of him. He didn't want to talk about our fight, of course, but I knew that when I asked.

"I left my phone down the side of the sofa when I went to bed. I didn't hear it ring. I feel terrible. I've been on the phone to them this morning and told them they shouldn't call you if they can't get me."

"What? Why?"

"You shouldn't have to deal with that stuff. That's my job."

"It wasn't that bad. And besides, what are they meant to do if someone has to go down there and they can't get you?"

"Well, no one *has* to go down there, love."

"What do you mean? They call you every time Mum has a wobbler."

"Because I asked them to. They're professionals. They're perfectly capable of dealing with it themselves, but I don't like the idea of Liz being upset without me being there." He sighed. "I don't know if it matters that much, though. Half the time she's settled by the time I get there."

"So why go?" I said. I didn't know what I wanted the answer to be.

"I love her," he said.

"Try guilt," I said. "If it were *love* she wouldn't be there."

"Do you really think that your mum is in a home because I didn't *love* her enough?" He seemed to squeeze the words out through a constricted windpipe.

I heard a plea for absolution in those words. I saw it on his face. *Tell me I'm not a terrible person.*

But the real question for me was, do I think my mother is in a home because *I* didn't love her enough? Would someone love me enough to stay with me when I couldn't take care of myself? Would I want them to?

I didn't say anything and he closed his eyes for a second. When he opened them he handed me a CD case he was carrying.

"Here, I found this when we were packing up. I thought you might want to have a look. I don't think we ever showed it to you. You don't have to watch it, of course. But don't lose it."

When he was gone I opened the case and on the CD inside, written in black Sharpie, was one word. *Wedding.*

When Dad and Beth had left for work I got out of bed. I knew where our old DVD player was, in a box I'd labelled "ancient artifacts" sitting in the hallway. I pulled it out from beneath a tangle of cables, leaving an actual cassette player, the landline I'd called Ruby on, and half a dozen old mobile phones on the tiles.

Once it was hooked up I sat close to the TV, my thumbnail in my mouth and a tumbling feeling in my stomach. I wanted to watch it from behind a cushion, the way I watched horror films when I was little.

The scene opened on a house, one of those country manor type of houses with sprawling green lawns and a pebbled driveway. A soft violin played something familiar and the camera panned to guests milling in dated, sherbet-coloured dresses with spaghetti straps, and suits that looked the same as every suit I've ever seen. I didn't recognise many of the people there. Aunt Claire and her ex-husband; Mum's parents, I recognised them from photos. Dad's parents were there and I felt a twinge of sadness for my granny who died when I was eight or nine. I didn't think of her often any more. A woman in a silvery slip dress with chunky highlights was kind of familiar. She might have stayed with us a few times when I was younger. A fuzzy memory came back to me, her and my mother laughing in the living room late at night while I begged to stay up so I could be included. The memory smelled like grown-up perfume and red wine kisses on my forehead.

I fast-forwarded through the next few minutes, a squiggly, blurry mixture of people milling around and wide landscape shots of the house. I pressed play when the location shifted to inside. Everyone was seated, the camera only catching the backs of their heads as they turned to face the door. Then Mum appeared, a grandfather I didn't know on her arm. A dress so familiar from photographs it was like I'd seen her in it in real life. She wasn't wearing a veil. A memory came back: being at Izzy's house when we were really little. She put on her mother's veil and flounced around the house, declaring herself a fairy princess. I ran home and asked my mother for her veil and she told me she didn't have one. I was so jealous. Watching the video, I was glad I could see her face.

She was thirty-six, thirty-seven in the video, but she seemed younger. There was a giddy energy radiating from her. I couldn't help but smile as she tried with little success to force her features into solemn repose. The camera cut to my dad. He was only twenty-six or so and he looked far too young to get married. He wasn't trying to look serious;

he was smiling in a way that lit up not just his face, but his whole body. Like he might burst with it. I paused the screen on his face. He must have known in that moment that there was a good chance my mother would end up as she had, and I searched for the slightest hint of doubt in his expression. All I saw was a glimmer when his eye caught hers. They looked like they were sharing a wonderful secret.

When it ended, there was an ache in my throat from trying not to cry.

Then I heard the scraping of a key in the door and I scrambled up. I fanned my face frantically. I don't know why I thought that would do anything.

"Hello?" Beth called out. I heard her drop her keys onto the side table. "I forgot my bloody phone," she said, coming into the living room. "It's boiling out there today. Put some sunscreen on—Oh, honey, what's wrong?"

I was standing in the middle of the room, feeling like I'd been caught doing something bad and unsure how to hide it. When Beth looked at me I couldn't help it. My face crumbled and fat wet tears fell down my face. I buried my face in my hands as though that could hide me. A second later, her arms wrapped around me. My face mushed against her shoulder. I cried a wet snotty patch on her clothes. I made that pathetic sobbing noise people make when they can't catch their breath. She didn't let go. She stroked the back of my head over and over until the tears slowed down and my shallow breathing turned to hiccups.

34

Saoirse
I think I made a mistake.

Oliver
I can't believe you got the highest
possible points in the leaving cert and
it took you two weeks to figure that out.
It's sad really.

Saoirse
Are you going to be a dick or
are you going to help me?

Oliver
Yes.

35

The Grand Gesture

I gave the nod and Oliver pressed play on the background music, then the video call button on his phone. I started running before she answered. Oliver followed beside me on a skateboard. He looked too posh to be on a skateboard but it was necessary for smooth filming.

"What is going on?" I heard Ruby's voice but I couldn't see her face, as Oliver had the camera side pointed at me. All she would be able to see was me running.

"Just watch," he said.

I really hoped I wouldn't throw up. Either from my body rejecting exercise as something foreign or from the sick nerves that had started yesterday when I texted Oliver.

I ran from two streets over, the heat making my hair stick to the back of my neck. This is why running across town or running through the airport is such a big part of rom-coms: running is terrible and you must be really committed to your grand gesture to do it.

Finally, I turned into Oliver's drive, my cheeks pink and shiny, and I used all the energy I had left to clamber up on top of the hood of his Jeep, strategically parked below Ruby's bedroom window.

"Gentle," he screeched, and covered his heart with his hand. I ignored him and took a deep breath, not easy after the aforementioned marathon.

"YOU'RE A WANKER, NUMBER NINE!" I yelled the famous line from *Imagine Me & You*, with as much volume as I could muster in my exerted state. My stomach turned over and I mentally crossed everything I could, hoping that Ruby would open the window. Maybe it didn't take long but it felt like forever before she did and her head appeared in the open space. Her phone was in her hand but I knew Oliver had already ended the call. He had another job to attend to.

"What are you doing?" She swatted a wasp away from her face.

"I'm just a girl," I panted. Then I doubled over with a stitch and held my hand up, a finger held up in a "just a minute" gesture. I retched a little. Was this working out? I stood upright after a few seconds and forced the words out through laboured breaths.

"I'm just. A girl. Standing in front. Of another girl, asking her. To please accept. This grand. Gesture. As an apology for being an absolute gobshite." My breathing eased back to normal(ish) and I pushed away the hairs escaping from my ponytail out of my face. Ruby raised both her eyebrows sceptically.

"The thing is," I continued, all my nerves jangling. My

voice was shaking, but I attempted my best posh English accent. "Sorry, I just, um, eh, this is a really stupid question, and par-particularly in view of our recent argument, but, uh, I just wondered if by any chance, um, uh, I mean obviously not because I am just some git who's only slept with no people, but I – I just wondered uh, I – I really feel, um, in short, uh, to recap in a slightly clearer version, uh, in the words of Heath Ledger—" At this point music blared abruptly from Oliver's iPhone speakers as a backing track and I finished my sentence with a warbled *I LOVE YOU BAAAABY* and the entire chorus of "Can't Take My Eyes Off You." When I got to the end, I looked down, and right on time, Oliver handed me the old cassette player from our box of junk and a set of white A3-size cards. He scooted away and I braced myself. A couple of seconds later the water hit. Just out of Ruby's eyeline he stood with a hose, sprinkling me as though it was raining. I pressed play on the cassette, and though I couldn't hold it aloft, it played "In Your Eyes." I flipped over my cards.

I realise this is taking a long
time now. So I have to do some
combination grand gesturing here.

I love the way you wear the kind of
weird outfits you only see
on Pinterest.

I love the way you flip your hair
back and forth when you're
nervous.

I love the way you have no idea
what you want to do with your life
but everything that comes along
is an option.

I can't think of any more but that's
because I love the way you're
not just a random collection
of quirky traits.

I will stand on the front step for
five minutes. If you accept my
invitation to talk, please
come downstairs.

(No kiss required.)

And then the last one.

But if I'm being creepier than Lloyd
Dobler then just say the word
and I'll leave.

I held my breath and, soaking wet, I carefully slid down the bonnet of the car and hurried to stand on the front step of the house. Oliver pressed start on his phone's stopwatch.

4:59

4:58

4:57

I took a deep breath with my eyes closed.

4:40

I didn't have to wait as long as Drew Barrymore. The door opened. Ruby stood in the hallway with one hand on the door handle and one hand on her hip.

"Did you memorise all of Hugh Grant's *ums* from *Four Weddings*?" she said, her eyes narrowed.

"I wrote a transcript."

She pursed her lips.

"OK, then. We can talk."

Ruby and I sat on a bench in the back garden. A large deliberate gap between us.

"Oliver, you can leave now," I said, shooing him.

"Oh, so you just want to use me for my hose and then kick me to the curb?"

"Gross, no one is interested in your hose."

Oliver pantomimed stomping off like a scolded child.

"So are you two friends now or . . . ?" Ruby smirked.

"Friends. Allies. Enemies who have grown accustomed to one another." I shrugged. "Who can say?"

Then nothing. Or at least no talking. Bees buzzed, birds chirped, the grass became super interesting.

"You asked to talk," Ruby said after a moment. "Don't you have anything to say?"

"I do." I picked paint chips off the weathered bench. "But I'm afraid when I finish talking it won't be enough and I'll have to go. I'm kind of stealing a few extra seconds with you."

I chanced a glance at Ruby but her expression didn't give much away. She wasn't explicitly fuming, though, which I took as a good sign.

"I know I put up all these boundaries between us," I began, and I sat on my hands to stop from fidgeting. "I thought at the time it was healthy. That if I had these strict rules and I followed them then I wouldn't get hurt. But I wasn't very good at following the rules and I'm beginning to think that's a good thing. I had a rule not to get involved with anyone who could potentially like me back and I broke it to hang out with you all summer. And the rule of only having fun with someone, well, I broke that too."

"You didn't have fun with me?" Ruby said dryly.

"Er, no. That's not what I mean. I mean nothing serious, no connection, no crying in bed when you leave. But it doesn't work like that. I found myself thinking about you in a way that made me sad. I thought about how we couldn't last. I thought doing the montage would be some kind of fun blip but I started to think about life without you as something less than what it was with you in it."

"That's how I was feeling too. Except when I started feeling that way it made me want to be closer to you, to share things with you, not to pull away." She sounded angry, which was fair.

"I know. You're definitely smarter than I am. I thought if I didn't do the things that you want to do when you feel close to someone, like tell them about your actual shitty life problems, then I could somehow keep the desire to be close away."

Ruby closed her eyes and looked like she was trying not to shake me because of how stupid I was.

"The thing is that relationships don't last forever," I said. "Love doesn't last forever. I've known that for a long time now."

"This is taking a bleak turn," Ruby remarked.

"I'm gonna pull it all together, I promise," I said. "See, I think love isn't this fixed thing that can beat all the odds. It fades or changes and it can twist into something else. So, I've believed for a while now that there was no point in being in love. Not if it's all going to go away and leave you kind of broken. I thought it wasn't worth my time. Especially if for me, time might be shorter than everyone else's."

"What do you mean? Why would it be shorter?"

I looked up at the sky, to give myself a second to gather

my courage. It still felt unnatural to talk about these things with someone else. I thought about backtracking. Of saying something to get me out of this. But I knew that if I wanted to have something real, I had to say the thing I never wanted anyone to know. Maybe I was wrong to think that it had contributed to Hannah falling out of love with me. Maybe I was right and the pressure of everything ground us down in some way. But either way it was part of my life now and I had to tell Ruby the truth. The whole truth.

"The dementia. It could happen to me too. There's a good chance that it will."

Ruby's face changed from impassive to stricken, for just a second. Then she composed herself.

"Saoirse, that's . . . I'm sorry."

"It's OK. And you don't have to pretend that you're not freaked out."

"I'm a little freaked out."

"Me too," I said. I didn't say anything else. I wanted to give her a second to let it sink in.

After a minute she turned, hitching one leg up onto the bench and facing me.

"If I thought the same thing would happen to me, maybe I wouldn't want to be serious with someone either. Maybe everything *would* seem pointless."

It was soothing to hear the words out loud that had been banging around in my head for so long, even if they didn't tell the full story any more.

"It scares the life out of me. Literally, I'm avoiding having a normal life because I'm afraid of it all being taken away. And I really have to work on that. But I was so wrong about love, about us. Just because something doesn't last forever doesn't mean it isn't meaningful. I got it ass backwards," I said.

Ruby smothered a smile.

"It's the relationships without meaning that aren't worth my time," I said.

"So what are you saying?"

"I'm saying, you're right, I need to get over myself."

Ruby laughed. "I didn't have all the facts when I said that," she protested.

"You were still right. I probably need some kind of therapy. I still have no idea what's going to happen in the future," I said. "I *do* know that right now we have about ten days left before you leave and I want to spend every one with you. I want you to come to my dad's wedding. And I really want to cry and not shower and not sleep and not eat and be miserable when we break up. If that's OK with you?"

Ruby leaned in and kissed me. A big movie kiss that should have had swelling music and soft lighting and a torrential downpour. But it happened in a garden, in broad daylight, and then Oliver turned the hose on us.

"Does that count as kissing in the rain?" Ruby asked.

"Let's debate that after we murder him."

36

"Can you come in here?" Beth's high-pitched voice called out as I passed by the room. I popped my head in and saw her face peeking out from behind a changing screen.

"I found the favours; they were at reception for some reason. I have to put them on the tables and I'm covered in feckin' glitter," I said, surveying the room with as non-judgemental an expression as I could muster.

It had been elegant when we arrived that morning, white with gold accents and French furniture. It still had the gold accents and French furniture but it now looked like the wreckage of a terrible bridal catastrophe. A flower girl's dress was lying on the floor, an obvious chocolate stain rendering it useless; make-up littered every surface; a breakfast tray had toppled over on the bed and there were bright jammy smushes on the white linen. And yet Beth didn't seem perturbed by any of this. Something else was wrong.

"Forget the favours. I need you. Close the door."

Forget the favours? I'd spent an hour looking for those bloody little bags. Nevertheless, I stepped fully into the room and closed the door. Beth emerged from behind the screen. She was wearing sweatpants and a tank top that

351

also had jam on it. Above the neck she was made up like a princess and she had a dozen tiny silver stars dotted through her curls.

"Why aren't you dressed?" I asked, a note of panic finding its way into my voice too. Was she going to make a run for it? I mean, I know I hadn't *really* been fully behind this marriage, nor had I *really* bet on it lasting, but I hadn't even considered the possibility that they wouldn't make it to the ceremony. Dad was going to be devastated.

Beth burst into tears.

"Uh . . . OK." I scrambled over the debris to Beth. "Look, if you want to escape, I mean, I'm not saying it's OK exactly, Dad will be really upset, but you shouldn't marry someone unless you're sure. Should I go find your aunt or do you want me to hoist you out the window?"

Beth's aunt was downstairs in the bar, her tights balled up on the table beside her, and she was telling anyone who'd listen the most embarrassing stories about Beth. She had old-school hippie vibes and I liked her a lot even though I'd only met her a couple of days ago. I didn't really think she'd be much help in this situation, though. Still, wedding panic seemed like a job for family. I couldn't help but think about what it would be like if I got married. Who would talk me down off the ledge, or tie the sheets together so I could climb out the window? I shook myself, realising I'd obviously just go through the door. I'd watched too many romantic comedies. It was affecting my brain.

Beth laughed through her tears.

"Whatever you do, do not get my aunt," she said, one hand clutching her heart, the other stretched out in a firm stop sign, "and I'm not running away!"

"Thank God. I really did not want to have that conversation with Dad." I plopped myself down on the bed. "Whatever it is it can't be that bad."

"I don't fit into the dress."

"Oh." I stood up again.

Beth and I locked eyes and hers began to fill, threatening another tantrum. In that moment I realised I was the only grown-up right now. The stress of planning a wedding in under three months had made sensible Beth turn into some kind of useless woman-baby.

"Right." I clapped my hands together. "We're going to try it on again. Maybe something was just catching. It was made to measure, right?"

"Six *weeks* ago," Beth wailed, flopping into a chair as I picked up the gown.

"Get up," I said, adopting the kind of tone you use to corral children or puppies.

Dragging her heels, Beth shuffled over to me and stepped into the dress, holding her breath. She closed her eyes tight and hitched the straps over her shoulders. I buttoned the tiny buttons at the base of her back and shook my head.

"This fits fine," I said.

"Really?"

"*Yes.* Who was doing it up before? They obviously did something wrong."

"Sarah," she says, her voice quaking slightly less than before.

"The flower girl? Honestly, Beth, you asked an eight—"

I was halfway through the row of buttons and the fabric was getting tighter. I pulled on both sides, stretching them to try to get them to fit together. Beth froze.

"No. Now don't panic, hold on. It's. Not. That. Tight." I tugged on the fabric, determined to get the last six buttons to close.

Beth pulled away and launched herself face-first onto the bed, narrowly avoiding the breakfast tray. Into the pillow she let out a muffled cry of, "Why, God, why me?"

I gingerly extracted the tray and covered the jam stain on the bed with a towel while I made soothing noises about how it was all going to be OK. Although I had no idea what I was going to do to make it OK.

Then it came to me. Obviously.

"I'm going to go and call Barbara," I said brightly. "I bet they delivered the wrong one. Someone else must have got this style too. Don't worry."

I patted myself down, searching for my phone, and my heart dropped into my stomach. I realised my ridiculous lavender dress didn't have pockets. So where on earth had I put my phone?

"Um, Beth? Bad news. I don't know where my phone is."

Beth wailed.

I had a panicked vision of myself searching all over the hotel or accosting some stranger in the hallway to use their phone. *It's an emergency*, I'd scream. *A bridal emergency.*

"I'll be right back, Beth, I promise."

"Saoirse." She lifted her mascara-stained face. I thought she was going to say something like *Hurry back*, or *Get help, please.*

"There's a bloody phone on the desk."

Right.

I mean I'd still lost my phone. Those things are expensive. I didn't say anything, though. I didn't think Beth would really see that as particularly important right in this moment.

I lifted the room phone and asked reception to get me the number for Pronuptuous.

"Would you like me to put you straight through?" the girl on reception asked calmly, like this wasn't a DEFCON 1 situation.

"Pronuptuous. Barbara speaking." Barbara answered the phone after one ring.

"Barbara, it's Saoirse . . . from the Clarke wedding."

"Ah, yes, the little lesbian."

"Er, yeah. Look I'm not saying you did anything wrong but—"

"Let me stop you right there, missy. I don't make mistakes. Not with dresses anyway. My third husband, on the other hand—"

"Yep, don't have time for this, Barb. Beth's dress doesn't fit."

"Did she lose weight? Brides these days. I told her not to lose any weight. Why do you need to be half your normal size because you're getting married. Honestly—"

"No, look, it's too small. In the . . . boob-al area."

"Has she got the jelly tits in? She said she wasn't going to wear them. I told her if she wanted jelly tits she should say so."

"No, she isn't wearing—" I couldn't bring myself to say the words *jelly tits* to an elderly woman even if she'd said them first. "Barbara, it just won't button up."

"I'll be right there," she said seriously. I had a sudden image of Barbara clipping on her emergency sewing-kit belt and getting into some kind of Barbmobile. A VW Beetle with an outsize veil attached to the roof.

"Don't worry, Beth, help is on its way."

Beth lifted her head, her eyes dry but red and make-up smeared all over her face. She looked like less like the damsel in distress and more like a deranged bride-villain that Barbman would have to battle in the final showdown.

"Maybe let's find some face wipes, hmm?"

*

356

Barbara burst through the door, smoke surrounding her and a swell of triumphant music in the background. And by that I mean she had a cigarette dangling out of her mouth and the violin quartet for the wedding were warming up outside. Barb stubbed the cigarette out in an increasingly stale croissant, and swapped it for a needle, which hung between her lips like a cowboy's toothpick. She charged across the room to where Beth was standing, still in her dress, with her make-up restored to its former glory. She inspected the buttons, then whipped Beth around and squeezed her left boob.

"You're pregnant," she said accusingly.

"I don't think so," Beth scoffed, and in response Barb honked on her right boob.

"Three months. You're not showing yet, of course, but there simply isn't any extra room in this dress for pregnancy tits. Not even first-trimester tits."

"I'm forty-four." Beth shook her head vehemently, as though that said it all. "OK, I've missed some periods, but I thought maybe it was premenopause or wedding stress or—"

"You missed your period and you didn't think you could be pregnant?" My voice came out high-pitched and strained as I repressed the urge to grab her by the shoulders and shake her. *Do not think about the possibility of a sibling in six months.*

"Stranger things have happened, love. If you don't wrap

it up, you gotta deal with the consequences." Barb said this with the kind of gravity reserved for meaningful proverbs.

"Oh, gross." I mimed puking into the wastebasket. Though there was a distinct possibility that I would actually puke if we dwelled on this conversation too long. *Do not think about Dad and Beth doing it.*

"OK," I said, my fingers on my temples, "let's put a pin in the baby. Figuratively," I added when Beth winced. "Is there anything we can do about the dress?"

Barb looked witheringly at me over her thick-framed glasses.

"I'm a dressmaker, dear. I always come prepared." She patted a utility belt around her waist. Barbman to the rescue.

I was allowed approximately thirty seconds of relieved slumping against the wall in the hallway after the Beth crisis had been addressed, before Oliver strode down the hallway towards me with the unmistakable air of someone on a mission. He was wearing a pretty snazzy suit that probably cost ten times more than the one Dad had on.

"Your dad is looking for you," he said.

"Seriously? The wedding is supposed to start in ten minutes and I just got the bawling bride sewn into her dress."

"Can I interest you in a refreshing beverage to help you through the afternoon?" He took a flask from inside his jacket pocket and unscrewed it, and a forty-year oak-matured aroma wafted under my nose.

"No, thanks. I think I'm going to need my wits about me today. Don't classes start tomorrow? Also there's a bar in the tent? You don't need a hip flask."

"Well, I don't *need* it, but it makes me look cool. Besides, Trinity has freshers' week the first week so I'm getting a head start."

"I do need a second before I'm ready, though," I sighed.

"Want some motivational music?" he offered.

"What?" I eyed him warily.

"To pump you up. Like when we did the running scene."

"That was for dramatic background music."

"I have the perfect tune," he said, taking his phone out of his pocket. No, wait, it was my phone.

"Hey, where'd you get that?!"

"You left it downstairs. You're welcome."

"You better not have changed your name again."

"Would I violate your privacy like that?" He frowned, feigning hurt.

I narrowed my eyes and snatched my phone away but he'd already pressed play and the opening bars to "Eye of the Tiger" started playing. I couldn't help but laugh. It actually kind of helped. I stopped it halfway through, sufficiently pumped, and then with some trepidation I went to Uncle Vince's room, where Dad was supposed to be getting dressed.

*

He was sitting on a tufted ottoman at the foot of the bed when I walked in.

"Oh God. What's wrong?" I groaned. He lifted his head with a snap and I saw that his expression, although tired, was cheerful.

"No, no, nothing. I have something for you."

"Is that it?" Praise Jesus. That was an easy one. No wardrobe malfunctions or surprise babies. Then I realised that I knew Beth was pregnant and he didn't.

"Yeah, I didn't want to walk around out there looking for you in case I got stuck talking to Beth's aunt again, and no offence, but I didn't trust your friend Oliver with it."

"I could see why you might get that impression. He has a certain *je ne sais quoi* of general iniquity."

He got up and unzipped a sports bag. From my vantage point I saw a pair of fancy shoes, a spare pair of socks, and the best man's gift, a watch, from Dad to Uncle Vince. He rummaged into the corners and pulled out a pink gift bag with a unicorn on it.

"It was the only one they had."

I looked in the bag and saw a mint-green camera. The kind that spits out instant photos. I'd asked him to get one for my birthday.

"It's not my birthday for a couple of weeks," I said, but I was grinning when I took it out of the box.

"It's not for your birthday. It's a thank-you. For . . .

for not making my life as miserable as you could have over this wedding."

"Wow, I really thought I had."

"No, I think you had a lot more in you that you could have pulled out if you wanted to."

After a quiet second of me considering what I could have done better (or worse, depending on your perspective), I agreed and hugged him.

"Why did you want one of these anyway?"

I debated not telling the truth. But I tried to think of what Mum would say in her therapist-y wisdom. It was hard to channel that version of her after so long. But I thought it might be something like, if you hide your feelings from the people you love, then you aren't giving them a chance to really know you. I thought of what Ruby would say. She'd say, be honest, life's too short to pretend.

"I wanted to take more pictures. Not the kind on your phone that you delete or lose or upload to the cloud. I wanted the kind you keep. In case someday I need them."

A silent understanding passed between us, and I wondered if he would acknowledge it. But instead he smiled widely.

"That sounds lovely," he said.

Disappointed, but not surprised, I set my jaw slightly and I turned to leave. As I did I caught the second where his smile faded into something sad. Part of me wanted to walk out the door and get the shoes and pretend I hadn't seen anything. Instead I turned around again.

"Dad, is everything OK?"

He pasted the smile back on his face that I could see now was flimsy and empty.

"Of course." He waved away my concern.

I hesitated.

"Look, I know we aren't really that good about talking about feelings. Unless you count me shouting at you. Do you need to climb out the window?"

"What? No, of course not."

Thank goodness. I didn't think I could really help my Dad climb out the window now that I knew about the baby.

He looked at me, fine lines collecting around his eyes.

"This reminds me of my wedding," he said. I could tell he was having to force out the words because it was exactly how I sounded when I was trying to talk to Ruby about my feelings. "To Liz, I mean."

I wasn't sure I was ready for this conversation.

"I know you think I don't love her—"

"I don't think that. I know you love her still," I said, thinking of the anniversary presents and the way he visited every time she was upset. "In your own way," I added uneasily, thinking of how he was getting remarried less than a year after she moved out.

He closed his eyes in a pained expression.

"Saoirse, you really know how to say the things that hurt the most."

"I don't know what you want me to say. I'm being honest. I know you loved Mum. I watched the video. I could see it."

"But?"

"But you didn't love her *enough*. You let her go." I was afraid to say the next thing but I had to get it out of my head and into a real conversation between us. "Would you do that to me too?"

"Saoirse, you're my daughter, I would never—"

"Well, there you go, then," I interrupted. "You *can* love someone enough, just not her." Though I wasn't sure I believed him when he said that either.

"I had to do it," he pleaded. "Both our lives would have been over if we'd kept her at home."

I didn't know if he meant me and him or him and Mum.

"That might be true. And I don't know what I'd do if I were you. But she's my *mother*. There isn't anything I'd think was too much to give up."

Shoulders stooped, he nodded, not looking at me but at the floor between his feet. Then he looked up at me again.

"Do you hate me for it?"

"I don't hate you, Dad. I love you. But I've been angry with you."

363

"And now?" he asked.

"Now I just wish we could be honest about what is going on and what might happen to me, but you won't even discuss it. I have to live with knowing I might end up just like her and I don't know what I'm supposed to do."

Dad looked up at the ceiling and shook his head.

"You're right. I think if I don't talk about these things, and I hope hard enough, that it won't happen to you. Watching my wife deteriorate and then looking at my daughter and wondering if the same thing is going to happen to her. Saoirse, I *can't* think about it."

"Well, you *have* to, you bloody selfish arsehole," I shouted, startling him. I tried to regain control of my temper. I could say what I had to say without screaming. "You've left me alone in this. Abandoned me to deal with it all on my own and maybe that's even shittier than what you did to Mum. So you know what, if you want me to stop being angry with you, you could start by acting like someone's feelings other than yours matter."

For a minute I thought he would argue back. He seemed to cycle through a lot of emotions at once, all of them jumbled up on his face.

"I'm sorry. I'll try and be better," he said finally.

It wasn't perfect and it didn't fix anything. It would take me a lot longer to forgive him, and myself. But I knew that he still deserved to be happy even if he wasn't the perfect, understanding movie dad I wanted him to be.

"Did the S-word just come out of Robert Clarke's mouth? Someone get me a plaque so I can mark date and time for posterity."

"You have enough cheek for a spare arse, you know that?" Dad laughed. It felt good to break the tension a little. His laugh faded into silence and we looked at each other. This was new territory.

"What now?" Dad asked.

"I suppose now we move on, but differently."

Dad hugged me and wouldn't let me go. He rested his chin on my head.

"Your mum will always be family to me. I hope you know that much."

I was grateful for that. I didn't think our conversation had eased any of the conflict my father was feeling right now but I was glad to see that he was conflicted. At least it meant he cared.

I was about to leave when he stopped me by speaking again.

"I'm glad you and Ruby got back together." He smiled. "I was really worried about you when you two broke up."

I frowned. "Why were you worried? I acted completely normal. Not like with Hannah. I wasn't crying all around the place and not getting out of bed and all that stuff."

"Exactly. It was freaky. I was afraid you were going to end up like me. Burying all your feelings. But I can see now that you're not like that at all."

"What do you mean?"

"You're able to talk about your feelings, even when it's difficult. Even if the talking is sometimes shouting." He smiled at me again. "How'd you grow up with so much emotional intelligence when you have a dad like me?"

"I guess I get that from my mum."

37

The ceremony was mercifully quick, due to the downpour of rain. Dad and Beth had insisted on having it outside. The heat wave through the summer had lured them into thinking they were safe from the changeable Irish weather. We retreated to the shelter of the marquee as quickly as possible. They looked happy, though, and I wanted to be happy for them. I *was* happy for them. Mostly.

When it was all over I found Ruby sitting with Izzy and Hannah. They were laughing when I threw myself into a chair beside them.

Ruby kissed my cheek. She looked incredible in a teal dress with a many-layered skirt, a (fake) ruby necklace, and a string of red beads wrapped around her hair like a headband, and I admit the lavender monstrosity actually looked pretty good on me too. I snapped a photo of the three of them together. How often in my life would my girlfriend and my ex-girlfriend be sitting at the same table? It was worth remembering.

"Where's Oliver?" I asked.

Hannah answered, "I saw him shifting someone in a bush somewhere."

"I was explaining Morris," Ruby said, nodding in the direction of the bar, where he was sipping a glass of champagne.

"Yeah, explain to me why you invited a random old man?" Izzy asked.

"It does seem out of character," Hannah added.

"What can I say, she's made me soft." I patted Ruby on the knee. "Besides, he's fun. I thought he'd appreciate the opportunity to try and crack on with some of the older ladies at a wedding." Personally I was rooting for him and Beth's aunt to get it on.

"I think he already found one," Ruby mused, and we all looked back at the bar. Barbara had sidled up to him and it looked like he was ordering her a drink.

"Not a bad match," I conceded, taking a sip of Ruby's drink. "I give it a couple of weeks before it implodes."

Izzy frowned. "Aw, no, they're so cute."

"Saying old people are cute is infantilising," Hannah said.

We glanced back at Morris and Barb. He had his hand on her butt.

"I hope they use protection," Hannah added seriously. "Chlamydia is on the rise in older populations."

Izzy spluttered into her drink. "Good to know."

By ten the rain had cleared, leaving a cool, crisp night, and the marquee was all twinkly lights and cheesy music.

I started to fade, my energy depleted after a day of putting out fires. The dress issue, and Dad of course, but also searching for a lost flower girl, who I found napping in the hotel under a piano, and putting Beth's aunt to bed around eight when she was too loaded to function. I even reluctantly took part in the Macarena with Ruby because she insisted we had never got to do number five on the montage: a synchronised dance. I had to make a mental note to find Oliver and destroy his phone because I was pretty certain he'd taken video evidence.

Everyone who was still able to stand upright was on the dance floor bopping along to George Michael. I glanced at Hannah when I recognised the opening notes; it still caused me a slight twinge in my chest but I could bear it now. I thought she caught my eye but it might have been a coincidence. She was on the dance floor with Izzy, performing an exuberant dance routine of their own design. It involved a lift and a knee slide and there was a force field of space around them that they didn't seem to notice. I took a photo of them. It was bittersweet, much like this whole day. I was happy that we had found a way to be friends again, but I was sad that it couldn't be exactly the same as before.

I found Ruby on her own, sitting cross-legged on a pillow watching the dancing, her dress hitched up around her thighs and what I thought might be a third dessert sitting in her lap. I held up my camera.

"Do not take a picture of this," she said around a mouthful of cheesecake.

"You look really beautiful," I said in a cajoling tone.

"Oh, all right then, you charmer." She stuck a cream-cheese-covered tongue out at me and I snapped.

I held my hand out to help her up.

"Let's get out of here."

I'd never stayed in a hotel before, so I felt pretty swish with my tiny shampoo and shoehorn. The room was significantly smaller than the bridal suite and the bed took up nearly the entire space, so when we walked in, it might as well have had a neon light over the headboard that said "people have sex here." It groaned obscenely when I sat on it and I suddenly felt really awkward around Ruby.

Not suffering from the same problem, she sprawled across most of the bed, flipping through the channels already.

"*Two Weeks Notice* is on, have you seen that one yet?"

"I think I have actually. I don't really remember it, though."

"Probably for the best. Hugh Grant, Sandra Bullock both at their peak. Should have been amazing but it's one of the only Sandy movies I can't bear to watch. That and *Love Potion No. 9*. Trust me, it does not hold up." She grimaced and changed the channel.

I snuggled in close to her and laid my head on her shoulder.

"How do you feel?" Ruby asked, absently tickling my arm with her hand.

Real feelings.

"Confused." It was the first word that came to mind. "I'm happy. Beth isn't the worst and I like my dad . . . mostly, so I want him to be happy. Sort of."

"But?"

"I think it makes me miss Mum even more. I can't help feeling like it shouldn't have ever had to be like this; this is all only happening because of what happened to her and that sucks." It was futile to feel like that but it was what it was.

"I think that's OK." Ruby kissed my forehead. "It would be strange if you were a hundred percent happy about it. The situation is too complicated for that."

It would have to be OK. I couldn't forgive my father for not making the kind of sacrifice I wanted him to. But I still loved him. He wasn't weak or wrong. He simply wasn't the kind of perfect hero you see in romantic films. There wasn't a cure for the thing that broke our family, but I could try to find something good in the new one. Me, Dad, Mum, Beth, and . . .

"And now . . ." I hesitated. Ruby didn't *need* to know the next part. She wouldn't even be around to see it and it was so embarrassing. The thing was, if I wanted everything I said in my grand gesture to be true, I had to tell her. I had to be honest right up until the very last day. So I took a deep breath.

"Beth's pregnant."

"What?!"

I winced as she shrieked the word directly into my ear. But I was sort of glad she was shocked and I wasn't the only one.

"Yeah. That lace bit at the back of her dress, Barb sewed it in where her buttons wouldn't do up."

"So she hasn't taken a test, then? She might not be?"

"Barb said she was and I trust Barb. She's eccentric but I think she might also be a bit magic."

"Thank you for telling me," Ruby said seriously, and I loved her for knowing when I was making a grand gesture even when it looked really small from the outside. "That's huge," she added.

"If she keeps it."

"Do you think she won't?" Ruby toyed with her lip ring.

"No. I think she will."

"And then you'll have a sibling."

"And everything will change. Again."

"I love having Noah. I know it's not the same but you might end up liking it."

I doubted that. I wondered if it would even feel like my proper sibling when it would be so much younger than me.

"I'm really glad you're here," I said, stretching to kiss her. I only meant to go for a quick smooch but she parted her lips and soon we were kissing properly.

"I'm glad too," she murmured into my neck when we broke apart for air. Her breath left tingling traces on my skin. I wasn't tired any more. I leaned my body into hers so we were pressed together side by side and I kissed gently around her collarbone, leaving a trail of light, sweet kisses up her neck. When I reached her mouth, it became urgent and hot and she tasted like strawberry cheesecake. Our limbs became more entwined, hopelessly knotted, her thigh a cushion in between my legs, and my body felt like it wasn't totally in my control, it was taken over by some need to cling to hers, to explore it, however clumsily. When she exhaled a breathy moan into my ear, the skin all over my body tightened, leaving tiny goose bumps on my arms and legs.

But I pulled away from her anyway. I had to be sure.

"This our last night," I said, almost breathless. Ruby's flight was tomorrow afternoon. Her family had come back to England yesterday and though I knew she wanted to see them, selfishly I wished she wasn't leaving.

"I know," she said.

"Are you sure you want to do this? If we don't have sex it doesn't mean this relationship is any less real or special. It won't change anything."

"I'm sure." She smiled, a different kind of smile than usual, the kind that made feelings spring up in private places. "See, in the words of Heath Ledger, I love you baby."

"Baby?" I teased.

She laughed and then shook her head.

"I love you," she said seriously. "If you want to, I want to."

"I love you," I said, and I thought about how amazing it was that this moment would exist forever. Perfect and unchanged. A moment where I would always be madly in love with Ruby Quinn.

So if you're wondering if we "did it", if we had sex? We did. It was nothing like you see in the movies. And I was wrong; it did change things. Sometimes the best feelings in the world don't last forever. They're explosions in the body or the heart or both at once, and you know that you'll never be the same as before, but it's OK because you can always build something new in the wreckage.

38

"Hi, sorry, can you tell me where the freshers' fair is?" I stop a girl who is walking in the opposite direction. She has a bundle of flyers in her hands and about seven thousand badges stuck to her T-shirt.

"Back that way," she says, pointing in the direction she came from. "Just through the double doors and then turn left, you won't miss it."

Through the doors a village of makeshift stands sag against one another, adorned with bowls of sweets, photographs of collegiate camaraderie, and colourful flyers with club details and Twitter handles.

I promised Dad I'd be a joiner, that I'd get the full university experience, but it's week two and I haven't really bonded with anyone yet. Although all the changes are sometimes a distraction, I'm still pretty sad about Ruby. I miss her, but that's normal. Or so I told myself when I cried the whole first week, face-first into my pillow, and wailed about how I'd never love again.

It would have been so much easier to make friends if I'd been in halls, and it sometimes crosses my mind that it might have been a mistake to decline my place at Oxford.

I just had to put myself out there and meet new people. Of course, Dad will always be a bit confused by how I could give up a place at the mighty Oxford to stay at home and take a course I'd only applied for because the career guidance teacher was bothering me about keeping my options open. But when I got the email about my Irish offers it stuck out; it just felt right. Now I wonder if some part of my subconscious knew better. Besides, UCD is only an hour from home. Most important, I get to see Mum every evening. It's hard because she's not always in a good place, but I like knowing Hannah will be there working through her gap year. Sometimes Dad and I go together.

I wander among the tables but nothing really jumps out at me. Vegan Society – sorry, can't give up ice cream, I grew up on the beach, but like rock on with your plant-based selves. Quidditch Club gives me visions of being winded by some overenthusiastic boy who can't control his broomstick. Trampolining and running are obviously out. I haven't forgotten the last time I tried to run. Cardiac health is overrated. And is origami really a group activity?

My phone buzzes and I pull it out and shuffle into a clear space to stay out of anyone's way.

Oliver Quinn: Untamable Beast of Desire
I know we shouldn't really be hanging
out on account of your lesser intellectual
status but do you want to get a drink
this evening after your visit?

Saoirse
Everyone knows Trinity students are pretentious knob ends. What's it like being returned to the mother ship?

Saoirse
Also yes to a drink. I'll see if Hannah wants to join us after work?

Oliver Quinn: Untamable Beast of Desire
Sure. Can she bring her friend too?
The cute one. Whatshername

Saoirse
Like you don't remember her name. Were you too busy making googly eyes at her to catch it?

Oliver Quinn: Untamable Beast of Desire.
Whatever. Just make it happen, Clarke.

I gravitate to a colourful table decorated with black and red bunting, thinking how weird it is that I'm hanging out with Hannah and it's not weird. OK, I mean, it's a little weird, but it's getting to a not-weird place and I kind of like it. We've even talked about going to visit Izzy in Cork some weekend. I put my hand in a bowl of lollipops, wondering if maybe you have to sign up to get free sweets, and my hand grabs another hand.

"Oh God, sorry," I say.

"It's OK." A girl in a white T-shirt with full red lipsticked lips and dark hair smiles back at me.

"Roller Derby?" a voice barks, and we both jump. Indeed, the sign behind the voice (which belongs to a girl dressed in shorts, ripped tights, and a tank top) says "Roller Derby: No Balls Required."

"Er . . ." I look around me as if a portal will suddenly open up and I can escape through it. Roller Derby Girl has an intensely aggressive stare and I don't think she'll take *Thanks but no thanks* as an answer. "To be honest I don't even know what it is."

"Yeah, me either," the girl in the red lipstick says, and I realise she has a Northern accent. Belfast, maybe?

Roller Derby Girl's eyes light up in a way that makes me think of a witch realising that some small children are eating her gingerbread house. I regret the lollipop.

"Right, so imagine a sprint, in a circle," she says, holding out one hand. She holds out the other hand. "And the brutality of American football and then . . ." She smushes her two hands together.

She looks expectantly from me to Lipstick Girl, waiting for us to exclaim with joy that this is the activities mash-up we'd been waiting for our whole lives.

"Is your ankle broken?" Lipstick Girl peers uncertainly over the table and I see it then too, Roller Derby Girl's foot in one of those space boots.

"Please," she scoffs, "that's nothing. A few pins. I fell

funny on the track but I still finished two more jams on that foot. I'll be back on eight wheels in no time."

"Oh my God! Betty," Lipstick Girl says suddenly, gripping my arm, "we're late for class," and she pulls me away from the booth. I wave a conciliatory goodbye to Roller Derby Girl, who narrows her eyes, and I think I see her mouth form the word *wuss* to herself before she pounces on her next victim.

Around the corner at the Pirate Society, free from the disgust of Roller Derby Girl, we pause to pick up a free Jolly Roger temporary tattoo. It makes me think of Ruby, and I pocket one to send her in the post.

"Should we stay in touch? Instagram or something?" I asked over continental breakfast and secret smiles in our hotel room the morning after the wedding.

Ruby picked at a pastry, flaky bits collecting on her plate though she wasn't really eating any of it. She toyed with her lip ring and flipped her hair over, making my heart hurt a little.

"I don't know if that's a good idea. I don't want to scour your pictures and comments for clues or wonder every time you add some girl if she's your new girlfriend. If I can do that, how am I supposed to move on?"

"We could still text?" I said hopefully, but even as it came out of my mouth I knew that was a bad idea too. It would start off with a daily flow of messages back and forth. Then fewer and fewer until one day they stopped coming. It would be like trying to peel off a plaster millimetre by millimetre so it hurt less. It doesn't really work that way. So I understood when she shook her head.

"We could write letters like ye olden days," I joked, though my laugh was forced.

Ruby didn't say anything for a second. Then she nodded, eyes bright.

"Really?" I said, surprised.

"Maybe not letters. I don't think that's any better than texts. I don't need to know the gory details, but send me things. Send me a picture of something pretty you saw or a poem you read that you liked or, I don't know, it doesn't have to even be meaningful. Send me a free sample of perfume you get in a magazine. Just things from your life."

"Life debris," I said.

"Exactly. What if our story isn't a romantic comedy after all?" she asked. "This bit doesn't feel very funny. Maybe it's an epic romance. Where the heroines separate and years pass but someday when the timing is right they meet again—"

"On top of the Empire State Building?"

"Sure, or, you know, like somewhere a lot cheaper to get to."

"The ticket line of a Ferris wheel?"

She grinned. "That's more like it. Ten years from now?"

"Make it five."

"Deal."

I lifted the breakfast tray, which was set between us on the bed, and put it on the floor.

"There's one last thing we didn't tick off," I said.

"Are you sure? I think we did it all last night," Ruby joked.

"We never got to slow dance."

"You're right." She nodded.

I stood on the bed, my feet unsteady on the springy mattress, and held out my hand. She took it, bouncing up on her feet, the momentum of the mattress propelling her into my arms. With my other hand I took my phone out and then pressed play on the first song that came up on my phone.

We turned in circles, swaying gently to the decidedly unromantic music of Survivor.

"I'm Veronica," Lipstick Girl says.

"Good thinking, Veronica. I really don't think I would have been able to say no to her."

"I think she would have asked us to sign up in blood if we didn't get out of there soon."

"Very likely."

"So do you have a name, then?" Veronica prompts me.

"Right. Yes, I do. Saoirse."

"Like the actress."

"No! She keeps saying Sur-sha and I know it's her name too, and technically she's allowed to say it however she wants, but it's Seer-sha and she needs to fall in line with the rest of the country."

Veronica salutes me. "Yes, ma'am. Will never mention she-who-must-not-be-named again."

"Well in fairness to her she's a national treasure. It's just the name thing."

We come to a stand decked out in rainbow flags and I try not to notice my heart beat a little faster when Veronica marches up and signs her name and email on their clipboard. I add my name and email even though I have no intention of ever going to a meeting. Unless maybe she would be there.

My phone buzzes again.

Dad
Will you pick up some strawberries on the way home for Beth?

Dad
PS internet says sweet cravings are a girl.

He adds a scared-face emoji.

Saoirse
Very scientific. PS I'm telling Beth you used emojis to convey sexism.

"So what are you studying?" I ask Veronica, putting my phone on silent as we amble past more stalls. I'm not paying attention to the names of the clubs any more.

"Drama," she says with jazz hands.

"So you wanna be an actress or something?"

"There's more to drama than acting," she says, and it sounds like it isn't the first time she's had to give this speech. "Drama is stories and ritual and performance and theatre. It's a way of understanding the human experience." Her eyes shine when she speaks and I am almost embarrassed by someone who has so much passion for something and isn't afraid to show it. "And I want to be a director," she adds sheepishly. "I have serious problems with authority. It's either director or dictator."

"Good to know."

She looks me up and down.

"Photography?" She points to the camera slung around my neck.

"This is just for fun. I'm making an album. Memories, you know?" I hold my camera up, my expression asking if I can take one of her. She poses like a fifties pinup with one hand behind her head and one on a popped hip.

"What course are you on, then?" she asks.

"History."

"So you want to read about people who died before you can even remember," she teases, nudging me in the arm.

I take a moment to think about what it means to me so that the words come out right.

"History is who we are," I say finally. "The past shapes us. Even the parts you can't remember."

Saoirse and Ruby's Rom-com Watchlist

Trouble makes the heart grow fonder
50 First Dates
The Big Sick
But I'm a Cheerleader
Crazy Rich Asians
Four Weddings and a Funeral
I Love You Phillip Morris
Love Actually
Say Anything . . .
Serendipity

Mr Right in front of you
Love, Simon
Nick and Norah's Infinite Playlist
Roxanne
Sleepless in Seattle
The Truth About Cats and Dogs
You've Got Mail

The secret lies in love
27 Dresses
Bride and Prejudice
Bringing up Baby
Crazy Stupid Love
Easter Parade
Hitch
Love Potion No. 9
Maid in Manhattan
The Major and the Minor
Some Like it Hot
While You Were Sleeping

Love changes everything
As Good As It Gets
Man Up
Runaway Bride
Sleeping With Other People

Romance on the side
About Time
Bridesmaids
Bride Wars
Bring It On
Miss Congeniality
Practical Magic

A sweet deal
10 Things I Hate About You
Failure to Launch
The Gay Divorcee
How to Lose a Guy in 10 Days
Muriel's Wedding
My Best Friend's Wedding
One Fine Day
The Proposal
She's All That
To All the Boys I Loved Before

A right tangled triangle
Bridget Jones's Diary
The Holiday
Imagine Me & You
Moonstruck
Sweet Home Alabama
What If

Unlikely lovers
Clueless
His Girl Friday
Never Been Kissed
Pillow Talk
Set It Up
Two Weeks Notice
When Harry Met Sally . . .

Not meant to be
500 Days of Summer
The Break-Up
Forgetting Sarah Marshall
Home Again
Legally Blonde
Pretty in Pink
Ruby Sparks

Second chances
13 Going on 30
The Awful Truth (1937)
Always Be My Maybe
Breakfast at Tiffany's
Definitely, Maybe
Hope Floats
Jerry Maguire
Just Married
Notting Hill
Obvious Child
The Wedding Singer

Acknowledgements

Thank you to my family: Mum for listening to me say the same things over and over again, like only a mother could. Dad for telling me to write a book since I was about fourteen (I mean I want to make it clear, I didn't do it because you told me to, but thanks anyway). Thanks to my brothers Rory, Conor and Barry for existing; I bet you'll tell people you have a sister now.

Thank you to Steph for everything, including, but not limited to, endless talksabouts, drying my tears and making fun of me for being so dramatic.

To Darren for tech support, pun supplies and keeping me alive; you're all right, I guess.

To my editors, Stephanie Stein and Chloe Sackur, I have endless gratitude. Youse are wonderful and funny and this book would not be what it is without all your skill, insight and dedication.

Thank you to my agent, Alice Williams, who made my dreams comes true. Thank you to Allison Hellegers for her hard work and Alexandra Devlin for hers. Apologies to each of you for my inability to use the reply-all function.

Thank you to everyone at HarperTeen: Louisa, who answers my embarrassing questions; Nicole Moreno and Jessica White for their general wizardry; Jenna Stempel-Lobell and Spiros Halaris for the beautiful design and cover art; and Meghan Pettit and Shannon Cox in production and marketing.

Thank you to the team at Andersen Press: Kate Grove, Jenny Hastings and Alice Moloney and anyone who Chloe may have asked if they understand the term 'getting the shift'.

Of course thank you to all the people at both teams who I may never meet or hear of, but who also had a hand in this book.

To the coven, thank you for the writing chats and Harry Styles appreciation. Special thanks to Izzy for reading my manuscripts and believing in all of them.

Thank you to my fluffy support team Heidi, Harry and Albus; truly, I don't know how I would have coped without you all begging for food, needing to sit on me immediately, or barking and meowing when I was trying to write.

To the person reading this who thought I should thank them and is now mortally offended, my bad. You're actually my favourite and I will make it up to you.

Finally, with utmost gratitude to anyone who has read this book, writing a book that no one reads kind of feels like talking to yourself. I mean, that's fine and all, but it's not the same as having a conversation with an actual human. So thanks for being an actual human.